UNSUB

Steel and Desire - Book One

KENDRA GREENWOOD

Published by Blushing Books
An Imprint of
ABCD Graphics and Design, Inc.
A Virginia Corporation
977 Seminole Trail #233
Charlottesville, VA 22901

Greenwood, Kendra
Unsub

EBook ISBN: 978-1-61258-244-3
Print ISBN: 978-1-63954-041-9
v1

Chapter 1

Friday

"The dead women found on Gull road out in Hampton Shores weren't prostitutes. They were women involved in the BDSM scene."

The big boss had spoken. And the words coming out of his mouth proved both shocking and somewhat expected. Special Agent Alyx Cameron sighed—part disgust, part lament. Working for the FBI in New York City certainly had its sick twists.

Summoned to a 9:00 a.m. meeting, the eight female agents sat in rigid silence around the conference table. Alyx spoke up, "So, what are we talking, pervs? Bondage? That sado-masochistic shit?"

"Not exactly how I'd put it, but yes," Division Chief Robert Scarborough said. As a supervisor, he rated right up there. Yet he could be intimidating. Tall and strapping, fiery red hair; he reminded her of a Scottish warlord. "We must act quickly, or more women—innocent women—may die."

"So, we're going under in sex clubs?" Marta said, the stocky brunette sitting across from Alyx.

Sipping at her coffee, Alyx contemplated posing covertly as a hooker. She'd done it before and didn't find it particularly difficult. The worst aspect? Dressing the part and then the interminable boredom while she'd waited to lure in a john, and ultimately a pimp. She thought the whole thing a waste of time, actually. If consenting adults wanted to pay for sex, let them. As long as some pimp wasn't holding women against their will, then who cared?

"That's the plan," Agent Scarborough said. "Seven clubs in the metro area have been identified, as well as the one on the east end of Long Island, and we believe a group called the 6X Enterprise—advertised as three X's above a triple X rating, kidnapped these women. The underground population calls it "SEX" for short, you know, six... ex... sex? Myself, I'd call it sick-sex." Rob paused, wondering whether his audience understood his word play. When nobody said anything, he went on, "They sell women as sex slaves. Not your garden variety slave either." He ran his hand over his face, stress lines creasing his brow. "Sorry, I didn't mean that the way it sounded. What I mean is the victims are sold to seriously demented sadists. Men who don't only get off on the sex, they get their jollies beating and mutilating these women, slaughtering them like animals."

"Evil fucks," Alyx murmured, glancing around the table at her fellow agents as a wave of revulsion passed among them, too. She already wanted in.

"So," her boss continued, "we want to place decoys in all the clubs. The local authorities haven't had any luck tracking the perps and asked for our expertise. They've tried to infiltrate with decoy buyers but haven't been successful because buyers need a referral to get invited. And even if they got a referral, they're transported in vans with anti-tracking gear and they constantly move the auction locations.

"I'm not going to blow smoke up your ass, this assignment is a bit unorthodox and purely voluntary. To be convincing, you may have to cross uncomfortable lines. We've fast-tracked some training before you enter the club, which will theoretically make you an attractive target for the slavers. Our most recent intel indicates they're seeking brunettes. There's an auction in two weeks and it's being billed as 'Bitchy Brunettes'."

The glaring fluorescents overhead underscored the foul mood pervading the room. Alyx grabbed her long ponytail of chestnut-colored hair and twirled it around her finger before releasing it. Like her, every woman here was a brunette, except Jenny, who'd probably be heading to the drugstore immediately after the meeting, if she signed on.

"All right," Agent Scarborough said, "we're on a time crunch here. I'll give you until the end of the day to decide, unless anyone is already on board."

Alyx threw her hand in the air. "I'm definitely in." Geez, she looked like a first-grader volunteering to erase the blackboards for her teacher. And seriously, she'd no idea what really went on in a BDSM establishment. Would she actually be required to have intercourse with men she didn't know? It certainly wasn't uncommon, or prohibited, for undercover male agents to become intimately familiar with suspects to crack a case—even though such specifics were kept off-book. Plus, she wasn't hung up on the notion that sex must necessarily be linked with love. It could be for pleasure or playtime. Adult play-dates, possibly.

Agent Scarborough's eyebrows shot up. "I applaud your enthusiasm, Agent Cameron."

"Honestly, Sir, I cannot wait to bring down this perverse

organization," it was the reason Alyx had joined the FBI Division of Covert Operations in the first place.

Then came various responses from her colleagues, "Count me in. Me too. Let's get these bastards."

"I'm pleased to see everyone's a team player." Agent Scarborough distributed a folder to each agent. "Inside, you'll find the name of your assigned club and the agent who will act as your liaison with the club owner. The members of the BDSM community are as anxious to catch these guys as we are and more than willing to help.

"There's also background info on the club and the BDSM lifestyle. We've included online references where you can learn more about protocols for submissives, which will be your role. Do your homework. Each owner has arranged for a trainer in their club to assist."

A roomful of eyes—some wide with astonishment, others unemotional, a few squinting and skeptical—perused the folders' contents.

"On the file tab, you'll find the name of your task force's lead agent. Meet with them immediately. You're expected in your assigned club sometime today. Since the auction is only two weeks from Saturday there isn't much time to get up to speed." He turned toward Alyx, "Agent Cameron, you're working with me."

Minutes later, Alyx settled in at her desk, nursing a fresh cup of coffee with her favorite hazelnut creamer. She studied the folder's sordid contents, then hit the Internet for further research. Her partner, Matt, suddenly appeared at his desk across from her. His blond hair glistened, still wet from a shower. He and his wife had just welcomed a new baby and he'd been late every day this week. His usually bright green eyes were bloodshot and he sank heavily into his chair, landing his elbows on the desk and his head in his hands. He blew out a long breath.

"Goddamn, that kid has no concept of sleep. He's killing me, Alyx. And Jillian is a friggin' crank-pot. I'm not sure I'll survive this."

She loved Matt like a brother and couldn't help but smile while he whined. This had become his new morning greeting. "Poor baby. And I mean you, not the one in the crib."

Matt looked up wearily. "I'm glad somebody has compassion for the father. Everyone is sympathetic to the mother and us dads get ignored."

Alyx smiled compassionately. "Most parents live through this. I'm sure you will too."

"So, I strolled in past roll call. Did I miss anything important?"

"We had a meeting with Rob and actually you weren't included. It was about those murders out in Hampton Shores."

"Same ol', same ol'. Some pimp knocking off ladies-of-the-night?"

"Let's just say you can't make this shit up." Alyx detailed her new assignment, explaining how the girls weren't street-walkers. And, she thought, what if they had been? Every life had value.

Matt frowned. "I don't like it. The Bureau is full of it, actually asking you to undertake something like this."

"I'm not naïve. I'll probably have to get a little dirt on me, but somebody has to help these women. You know that I find sex-trafficking to be about the most heinous crime on the planet, the vics can be as young as fourteen and fifteen. In this case, they're over eighteen but it still makes my blood boil."

"I get it. Just not sure you do. What if the fact you've been sex-starved most of the year is clouding your judgment?"

"Excuse you? It hasn't been a year and this is *not* a joking matter." Yet perhaps Matt had a point. Last night she'd slept in Jason's tee shirt again, which made absolutely no sense. It'd been six months since she kicked Jason-the-Philanderer to the curb and she hadn't missed him for a single minute. This morning, she'd spent nearly five minutes sitting on the side of the tub deciding if she should start another month of birth control. Why bother? Well, her periods were much better on the pill, a check in the plus column. Maybe this would be the month she'd meet somebody new. On the other hand, it might not be a bad idea to give her ovaries a break from hormonal assault.

In the end, she'd swallowed the little yellow pill and chased it with a swig of tepid tap water.

Matt said, "You can't stop me from worrying about you."

She stared at him. "Let's just tie up the loose ends on the MacAvoy case before I have to leave."

They worked right through lunch, the day going by in a hectic flash. When Rob appeared at her desk, Alyx checked her phone: 4:00 p.m.

"Time to go," Rob said. "I hear traffic's already hell."

She bid a quick farewell to her unhappy partner, gathered her purse and followed her boss out of the building.

Climbing into Rob Scarborough's black Escalade, she put on her aviator sunglasses and stared out the open side window. They exited the parking garage and the New York City sun hit her face. The crisp autumn air filled her head with thoughts of pumpkins and apple picking. Fall had always been her favorite season. Maybe she should bake a pie. However, she'd wind up eating the whole goddamn thing herself. Not gonna happen. When you enjoyed cooking, but lived alone, you ate everything you made for an entire month. The last time she'd made a pot of soup she'd had it every day for a week and then finally threw the rest out. She'd tried freezing stuff, but that caused another problem. The contents of her freezer could feed a high school football team for an entire week.

She inhaled deeply and let it out slowly, chewing on a

fingernail. Her plans for visiting some friends in her home-town tomorrow had gotten derailed. The promise of unsea-sonably warm weather for the weekend had teased her with images of walking along the beach and breathing the salty air while the ocean tickled her toes. She'd even hoped to catch a few waves. Life was good in Westhampton Beach and she missed those simple days as a teenager where her biggest worry was whether the surf was up or not. Having inherited her dad's house, she used it as a getaway whenever she could grab some time off. Sadness dampened her sublime mood. Her crazy-ass father, she still missed him.

Sweat clung to her neck, her face suddenly flushed and she leaned closer to the open window. What had she agreed to? Was she out of her ever-loving mind? She twisted her long dark hair into a tight knot and secured it with a tortoise shell clip from her purse. Sometimes the hair falling against the back of her neck gave her a serious case of claustrophobia, especially in the summer. Maybe she should cut it short, it would definitely be easier to maintain.

Daniel parked his black Mercedes in the lot next to the St. Andrew's club. He rubbed his temples and sighed. He really didn't want to be here. The strain of the last few days had taken its toll and he wanted to go home and catch up on some sleep. It'd been a year since he'd played here. Bored with the constant flux of women, he'd abandoned *the lifestyle* and figured he'd try dating the *normal* way for a change. That hadn't gone so well. He couldn't seem to drop the bossy atti-tude in the bedroom and most women resented his need to maintain control. Then he'd met Lacey and well, the fucking wasn't great but he considered it a tradeoff for her other qualities.

Jack, the club owner and one of his former compadres, had lured him here with the pretense of needing some big favor. He and Jack had kind of lost touch, but he remembered Jack's compulsion to play matchmaker and hoped this wasn't another lame attempt to hook him up with some woman.

Zach, the overly muscled security guard at the front door, gave him a huge man-hug as he entered. "Hey, bro, where you been hiding out?"

Nobody in Daniel's circle called him 'bro' and he balked at the unfamiliar greeting. "Zach, good to see you. How's it hanging?" *What was wrong with him? He never talked like that.*

"Good, I'm good. Jack's upstairs in his private quarters. He said to go right up."

"Thanks." Daniel resisted tacking on "buddy" at the end there.

Zach buzzed the door open and the familiar smell of leather, sweat, and sex smacked him in the face. The lingering scent of amyl nitrate perfumed the air as the use of *poppers* frequently compensated for the limited use of alcohol. Jack imposed a strict two-drink limit at the club, and that included staff. Poppers produce an instant rush with few after effects, while at the same time decreasing anxiety and easing pain. Daniel remembered them being particularly popular with the gay community.

Adjusting his eyes to the dark, chaotic atmosphere of the club, he glanced at the bar on the far wall where he knew some of his old partners-in-crime would be slugging down a drink. Although it might still be a little too early for that.

He hoped to sneak by them and, if he'd thought about it, probably should have gone around back to Jack's private entrance. No chance now.

"Holy shit. Daniel? Long time no see." Steve's booming voice penetrated the overly loud music emanating from the dance floor and there was no way Daniel could pretend he hadn't heard him. He weaved his way through the maze of leather clad Doms/Dommes and naked subs engaged in a variety of carnal activities. Moans and screams, mingled with the sounds of slapping flesh, brought him back to a time when he thought this fun. He'd never participated in anything particularly brutal. As a healer, there were certain lines he'd never cross.

Steve leaned on the glass bar spanning the entire length of the room. Daniel reached across, shook the bartender's beefy hand and said, "Steve, good to see you. How've you been?"

"Great, great. How 'bout you? What've you been up to? Too busy saving lives to whip a few asses?"

"It's a long and boring story. But you're right, I've been busy. Too many people abusing their bodies, and I don't mean that in the way you're probably thinking." He gave Steve a wink. *Really, Daniel, a wink?* Who had possessed his body? He regrouped. "Poor diet and no exercise makes for lots of broken hearts to mend." Jesus, that didn't come out right either. He sounded pathetic.

Steve arched an eyebrow. "You sound like Mr. Only-Lonely all of a sudden. Maybe you're in need of some serious playtime."

Daniel had been desperate to make an escape when the onslaught occurred. First, Sam, then Jerry and Colin, followed by Mark and Donna, all established and well-respected Doms/Dommes, and his closest friends at the club, all wanting to visit. He refused the offer of a drink, cutting the reunion short, using the excuse that Jack expected him pronto.

Jack's submissive met him at the door to the upstairs apartment. Her sultry voice and voluptuous body welcomed him. "Hello, Sir, good to see you again."

"Lisa. How've you been? Jack taking good care of you?"

She smiled seductively. "Of course. I wouldn't still be hanging around the old coot if he wasn't."

"Good girl." She offered him a drink, but he refused, saying he had someplace else to be later. These days, he usually only drank at home and when he wasn't on-call. It wouldn't serve a cardiologist to be issued a DUI summons.

Lisa didn't follow him into the stylish living room, not to be seen or heard, like a good little submissive. Jack rose to greet him, pumping Daniel's hand in a generous handshake. A burly, redheaded man occupied half the couch across from Jack and beside him sat a petite young woman. Her inexpensive black suit appeared a bit wrinkled, but her starched, white, button-down blouse was impeccable. They both stood to make his acquaintance.

"Daniel," Jack said, "this is Special Agent Robert Scarborough. We served together in the Marines."

Agent Scarborough held out his hand to make his greeting and introduced his companion as Special Agent Alyx Cameron. Daniel took her hand in his, startled by her firm grip, and immediately pictured her holding a sleek black handgun. She seemed too delicate for an FBI agent. Although he didn't really know any FBI agents personally and his only concept of one came from the movies or TV, total Hollywood hype.

Everyone returned to his or her seat. Daniel slumped into the red wingback chair at the end of the coffee table wondering what the hell he was doing here.

"Daniel, Rob asked me for a rather unusual favor and you immediately came to mind." Daniel shifted uncomfortably in his seat trying to imagine how he could possibly be of service to the FBI. Before his mind got very far down that road, Jack continued.

"As you're an expert trainer in the lifestyle and you already have a playroom in your home, I thought you might be the perfect consultant to help him out."

Daniel bristled, sitting up straight in his seat and leaning forward, his forearms resting on his thighs. "Jack, I'm not really comfortable discussing my involvement in the lifestyle with outsiders. You know that, and especially not in front of this young woman. Besides, you know I've left that life behind."

"I know, but this is important and it concerns Agent Cameron."

Agent Cameron's gunmetal blue eyes locked onto his. He couldn't read her, which annoyed him. He usually had no trouble assessing a woman's mood and considered himself sort of a female mind reader.

"I'll let Rob explain," Jack said.

Agent Scarborough cleared his throat and began, "We have a line on a human-trafficking ring and we plan to put decoys in all the clubs in the area in hopes of attracting the spotter who will lead us to the base of operations. I'm not sure if you're aware, but several bodies have been discovered in a shallow graveyard at the end of Gull Road. At first, we classified them as prostitutes but recently we discovered they were women who frequent BDSM clubs. We're fairly certain each was kidnapped by this group and then sold at the auctions they hold every few months. Usually they target women with few personal ties. No family in the area, no boyfriend or Dom to watch over them; and in a job where it might be a few days before someone noted an extended absence."

Daniel had read about the recent findings in his neighborhood. He still fancied himself a newspaper junkie, his favorite way of relaxing between surgeries. Embarrassed, he had to admit to himself that the fact they were reported to be prostitutes might have caused him to dismiss the crimes a little too cavalierly.

"This group of slavers," Agent Scarborough continued, "sells women to men who are serious sadists. The women are used so brutally they often wind up dead, then they're simply replaced with new merchandise. We believe we've stumbled on the graveyard they've been using for disposing the bodies."

Daniel cringed inwardly at the thought of such incredible horrors. However, he still had no idea what any of this had to do with him.

"Agent Cameron has volunteered to act as a decoy here at the club," Agent Scarborough said, "but she has no experience in the lifestyle and will need some training in order to be believable and attractive to the organization. An auction's coming up and we're hoping she might be able to lead us to the site if she gets picked up."

Little Miss Special Agent? I don't think so, thought Daniel. However, he decided to play along for the moment. "When is this auction?" he inquired.

"Two weeks from Saturday," Agent Scarborough said with a straight face. "But, we need to get her into the club as soon as possible so there's enough time for her to be noticed."

Daniel bellowed a laugh. "Right. And you think your innocent little agent here will get her PhD in bondage that fast? I don't think so. And I'm not interested."

Agent Cameron spoke, her voice angry, "Dr. Taylor, my stature may be somewhat diminutive but I assure you I'm no lightweight in anything I do. I'm committed to saving these women from both torture, and eventual murder, at the hands of these bastards."

Agent Scarborough said, "Dr. Taylor, I understand how you might…"

Agent Cameron poked the air with her finger. "Aren't you in the business of saving lives, Doctor Taylor? I'm willing to do whatever it takes here and nothing you say will dissuade me. Furthermore, if you won't help me and more women end up dead, well, that's on you."

He hadn't anticipated Little Miss Special Agent getting her nose out of joint. And she certainly had spunk. He'd give her that much. Honestly, she had no clue what would be required. Perhaps a little shock therapy was in order. "Unfortunately, Agent Cameron, I fear you have absolutely no idea what you're asking."

She cut him off, "I've done my homework, Dr. Taylor. I know what's involved and I'm ready to jump right in."

Yeah, I don't think so, missy. Time for a reality check. "You do, do you? You realize I'll have to fuck you, and not only the vanilla stuff, but all sorts of ways. How about restraints and floggings, how about hot wax and nipple clamps? I could go on and on, but what's the point? You're jumping into the deep end of the ocean without a life jacket."

She stood up, her face flushed. "Continuing with your metaphor, I'm a fully certified ocean lifeguard, Dr. Taylor, and instead of jumping to trite conclusions, perhaps you should give me a try and then decide. If I don't live up to your high standards, or should I say low, then you can criticize me to your heart's content." Her fists landed on her trim hips.

Annoyance fueled him and he walked over to face her. "All right, little Miss Smart Ass, let's see you put your money where your mouth is." He grabbed her by the arm and tugged her toward him. They faced off. "You'll keep your mouth shut and do whatever I tell you without one second of hesitation. And you will answer me with 'Yes, Sir.' Is that clear?"

"Yes, Sir," she snapped.

Her sarcastic tone pissed him off. He halfway expected her to punctuate her agreement with an impertinent salute. Reaching to the back of her head, he removed the clip, taking the tortoise shell clasp hostage and placing it in his pants pocket. Running his hands through her long dark hair, he arranged it behind her back. "Take off your jacket," he ordered. She ripped it off, and one arm briefly got stuck in the sleeve. She tugged on it violently and heaved it forcefully onto the floor. His anger eased and he struggled not to smile. She was having a tantrum. When his eyes fell on the weapon at her waist, he froze. He had no idea if he should touch it.

Alyx unhooked the holstered weapon from her waistband and tossed it into Agent Scarborough's lap. Quick hands caught it before it would probably have hit him in the nuts. Daniel tried to regroup.

"Shoes off," he ordered. She kicked the right one free, then the left, and they hit the wall behind him with two loud thuds. Turning to Jack and Agent Scarborough, "Really? Look at her, there isn't a submissive bone in her goddamned body." They didn't answer him. *Come on.* They had to know he was right. He fumed. Okay, he thought, let's see how far I can go with this. "Eyes on me," he commanded. Unbuttoning her shirt one notch, he loosened it at the neck and gazed at the hollowing of her clavicle. He put a finger in the tiny indentation, filling the gap. Their eyes locked together in a battle of wills as he slowly worked his way through the tiny pearl buttons. He left the last two closed, but opened the white fabric as wide as he could. She didn't flinch, her eyes blue fire.

The lacy bra surprised him. He'd expected something plain and practical, perhaps a sports bra. She had magnificent full breasts and he felt himself harden. Immediately he realized he'd been the one to let his eyes drift and quickly returned them to where they belonged. Hooking his index finger through the center of her bra, he pulled her close and leaned in, grazing his lips over hers. He took a kiss from her. The sweetness of her scent filled his head and he inhaled deeply before taking another kiss. This time he put a hand behind her back, securing her against his chest, and plundered her mouth. She responded with an eagerness that threw him off kilter. He opened his eyes and gazed into those big baby blues. *Fuck.*

He circled around behind her and pressed his chest to her back. He pressed his erection against her ass, then grabbed her long dark hair in his fist and jerked her head back, exposing her neck. Her sharp intake of breath set his pulse racing. Facing her, he kissed her again, their tongues wrapped in a lustful embrace. He ended it by biting her bottom lip before pulling away. The roughness of his kiss left her lips swollen and glistening and he struggled to control the urge to throw her over the arm of the couch and fuck her right in front of Agent Scarborough. Somehow, he didn't think Little Miss Special Agent would allow anything even close to that. Not yet.

She was nothing like the women he used to play with. And for some strange reason, he was incredibly turned on. "Feet apart," he growled. She moved them to shoulder width. "How do you answer me?" he barked.

"That wasn't a question, Sir." Her face showed no emotion he could read.

"You're a real smart ass, aren't you, Agent Cameron?"

"Yes, Sir," she answered and he knew she told the truth. He put a foot between her legs and kicked them farther apart and she landed her hands on his shoulders to steady herself. Holding her tight against his chest, with one hand against her back, he thought about working his fingers between her legs to see if she was wet, his urge to dominate and take what he wanted rearing its ugly head like a Grizzly bear reawakening after a long hibernation. Instead, he squeezed the muscular cheeks of her ass and focused on her face. Her crystalline, ice-blue eyes blazed, her cheeks slightly flushed and he thought maybe a glimpse of arousal flickered behind her angry facade. He smirked inwardly and then released her.

He still had doubts this would work, but what the hell? He could have a little fun before he flunked her out of sex school. She wasn't overly shy, he'd give her that much. He found her incredibly attractive: her body trim and well-toned from what he could tell, and those fascinating eyes. She had the most beautiful face, with full pouty lips and high cheekbones and long dark eyelashes that curled to unfathomable lengths. Her skin was flawless and slightly tanned. He guessed she liked the outdoors and wondered how she'd gotten so brown. He hadn't noticed tan lines on her body and wondered if she'd been sunbathing nude somewhere. He tried to imagine what her smile might be like and what she sounded like when she laughed. Jesus. Where was he going with this? *Get a grip, Daniel.*

Okay, back to the matter at hand. He had some vacation time he could arrange, let his partners handle his cases for a week while he put her through her paces until she finally ran from his house screaming. And, he rationalized, he'd be doing a service for his community at the same time. Perfect.

Daniel forced himself to avert his eyes from Alyx's flushed face and returned his attention to Agent Scarborough. "She's brave, I'll give her that. I'm not sure she has what it takes to be convincing as a submissive, but I guess we can give it a try."

He re-buttoned her blouse, fully expecting her to smack his hands out of the way and do it herself, but instead she remained perfectly still as he worked his way down the line of tiny buttons. He retrieved her jacket from the floor and held it out for her, as if they were on a respectable date and he was helping her with her coat. This whole thing seemed really messed up for some reason.

"My hair clip?" she said with too much attitude, extending her upturned palm.

"I'm keeping it." He flashed her a smug grin. "You can get it back tomorrow—maybe. I'll send my driver to pick you up. Be ready by 7:00 p.m. sharp. Pack a small bag with essentials, but no clothing except workout clothes. I have a gym and we'll be using it. Other than that, I'll provide whatever I want you to wear and it won't be much." He heard her sharp intake of breath. Now he had her attention.

Alyx huffed, then retrieved her shoes from the far wall and

slipped them on. Removing the wallet from his back pocket, he extended his card and waited for her to come to him. "Here's my number, when you need to call and tell me you've changed your mind and you're not coming."

Alyx bit her bottom lip and her cheeks flushed, Daniel knew it wasn't desire, but anger again. "Don't worry. I'll be ready and on time." She jerked the business card out of his hand and shoved it into the pocket of her jacket.

"Oh, I'm not worried, Agent Cameron, but *you* should be. You have no idea what you're in for, even with all your research." She glared at him but kept her pretty pink lips shut.

"All right then," Agent Scarborough said, slicing through the room's tension. He stood and handed Alyx her service revolver. "Thank you for agreeing to help us, Dr. Taylor. I'll tidy up some details with you tomorrow and we'll keep in touch each day so you can apprise me of Agent Cameron's progress."

Jack flanked Daniel as the two agents exited. Nobody shook hands on the way out. Jack walked over to the bar and poured himself two fingers of bourbon, extending the bottle toward Daniel. "No thanks."

"That was entertaining."

Daniel glared at him. "You better hope you never find yourself on my table, Jack, because I might have to think twice about literally ripping out your heart. Right about now, I'd like to kill you." Daniel shoved his hand into his pants pocket and Alyx's hair clip poked into his knuckles. He wrapped his fingers around it and felt his erection harden.

Alyx got in and slammed the door of Rob's black Escalade. Rob sat beside her and didn't say anything. He turned the key in the ignition and the engine purred to life. Unexpectedly, he threw his head back against the headrest and broke into hysterical laughter. Alyx faced him and glared, but of course he couldn't see her expression in the darkness. Rob laughed for at least an entire minute, while Alyx fumed.

"Are you quite done?" she finally said.

Rob wiped the unseen tears from his eyes and let out an audible sigh. "Shit, Alyx, I nearly split a gut in there. I thought for sure you were going to deck the guy. And under normal circumstances you should have." Rob struggled to catch his breath.

Alyx beamed in the darkness. "What an asshole, but I did have him going there for a minute, didn't I?" She started to laugh.

"You definitely did. When he told you to answer him, and you said he hadn't asked you a question, I thought he was going to blow a gasket."

"I know," Alyx said, letting out a chuckle. "He was getting pissy."

"Although, I'll admit he got one thing right, you certainly are a smart ass." Regaining his composure, Rob put the car in gear and headed down the long driveway turning left onto Old Montauk Highway. Alyx wished the trip were shorter, anxious to be home and in bed. In the height of the summer tourist season the ride back to the city could take upwards of several hours. However, the day after Labor Day, which the locals affectionately nicknamed Tumbleweed Tuesday, traffic instantly evaporated. They'd be back to the city in an hour. Of course, Rob would take advantage of the unwritten law enforcement privilege of driving well over the speed limit. Hell, they might make it in less than an hour.

Finally in her bedroom, Alyx stripped off her clothing and threw it on the floor. Picking up Jason's tee shirt, she studied it long and hard, then walked to the kitchen and grabbed a garbage bag and heaved it inside. Back in her bedroom she donned a pair of sweatpants and a camisole, then searched her closet and every drawer in her bedroom, ridding herself of any trace of him. She bagged it all and walked it out to the incinerator door and shoved it inside. Why she'd kept any of his stuff around mystified her. They'd had a terrible break up and he'd even gotten violent at the end. Dating a cop always carried added risk, especially with a temper like Jason's. Somehow, she seemed to only remember the good times when she broke up with a guy. Delusional about her relationships with men. Nothing ever changed in that department.

Teeth brushed and faced washed, she climbed into her queen-sized bed and switched on the TV, but she was too wound up to fall asleep. What had she gotten herself into? That pompous ass would be sending someone to pick her up tomorrow night and take her to his house where he'd do terrible things to her. The thought made something in her belly clench. Well, not really her belly, farther down. She decided to consider the bright side. He could have been an ugly son-of-a-bitch, something she hadn't considered when volunteering with her unbridled enthusiasm, and before thinking the whole thing through. He was probably the best-groomed and best-dressed man she'd ever seen. That black pinstriped suit he wore had to be more than the mortgage payment on her apartment and the royal blue tie perfectly complimented his pale blue shirt. She'd always been a sucker for a guy in an expertly tailored suit. Tall, broad-shouldered, lean, his wavy brown hair framed a face that could knock your breath out at twenty feet, not to mention those smoldering dark eyes. They looked downright dangerous. And the kissing, she hadn't expected that. But her thoughts soon settled on other things—floggers, restraints, clamps, hot wax? Yikes. Well, restraints didn't bother her, she'd let a boyfriend or two tie her up before, that was fun. Clamps? Definitely not. The other stuff? *Perhaps in an alternate universe.*

Sleep continued to evade her. Even Jimmy Fallon couldn't distract her from thoughts of kinky sex and what the perverted Dr. Taylor would do to her. Frustrated, she jumped out of bed and ran to the kitchen to retrieve the folder Rob had given her. Sliding under the covers again, she switched on the bedside lamp and flipped through the background info inside. There: the required negotiation between a Dominant and a submissive. They would have to agree on what was acceptable to both of them. Well, she thought, he probably liked the most extreme *everything*. Ugh. There were definitely things she had no intention of trying. Some of them she couldn't even say out loud. How much stuff could he make her do in a week? Well, twenty-four hours in a day, times seven days, that's 168 hours. Gulp. That's a lot of sex, or whatever. But they had to sleep and he had to go to work, so that would probably cut it in half. Maybe there would be a lot of people in need of emergency heart surgery and she'd get lucky. On the other hand, she did need to learn enough to be convincing for her debut at the club next weekend. Oh, boy. Catch 22.

Whichever way this went she was fucked, literally and figuratively.

Chapter 2

Saturday

The morning found Alyx in bed with three of the Seven Dwarfs—Grumpy, Sleepy and of course, Dopey—for having volunteered for this reckless assignment in the first place, and she was off to see Doc, although he was most definitely not a dwarf in any way, shape, or form. She'd probably take a turn as Bashful when she arrived at his den of iniquity, but hopefully she'd have a few moments as Happy. Sneezy? Maybe she'd catch cold from being naked too much. Well, she'd officially lost her mind.

Alyx reminded herself to keep her eye on the prize, seeing those slavers in handcuffs. She'd managed a few hours of restless sleep, haunted by nightmares of whips, chains, nipple clamps and spreader bars, although the one where the illustrious Dr. Taylor dripped hot wax on her had actually awakened her with an orgasm.

Shit. Could she really be into this stuff? Could she be some sort of sex-crazed pervert? Hell, no. What would her parents have said if they'd ever known she was doing this? Good thing they were both dead, because it might have killed them. Did she really just say that? She was glad her parents were dead? Well, she wasn't entirely sure her mother was six feet under.

Fuck, she was losing it and she hadn't even stepped into Daniel's dungeon yet. *Holy Crap.* Did he really have a dungeon? She'd read about them and seen pictures online. Some people called them playrooms. Yeah, playroom, she liked the sound of that much better than dungeon. She thought she remembered Jack, the club owner, saying Daniel had a playroom in his house. A shiver ran through her and her belly clenched in that weird-wonderful way again.

Alyx scoffed down her usual breakfast, Greek yogurt with granola—blueberry today, and then ruminated over her coffee for at least an hour. Perhaps she should spend some time grooming her body. She had the distinct impression she wouldn't be wearing much clothing during the upcoming week of scheduled torture under the iron hand of Dr. Taylor. Grabbing the phone, she called the salon to see if she could get a mani-pedi. Three o-clock. Perfect. She'd save her shower for later.

Dressed in jeans and a navy tee, she threw on her short white denim jacket and walked the three blocks to the shop. Another beautiful autumn day greeted her and she soured over the fact that she wouldn't be able to attend the get-together with her hometown buddies. She'd been excited about seeing everyone this weekend and catching up on local gossip. Riding a few waves if the weather held out.

Someone shouted, "Alyx!" His tall lean frame came at her. Jason. Ugh. She waited and watched, hoping a car might hit him as he crossed 9th Avenue against the light.

"Hey, babe, what's new?" His good looks dazzled her, like they had when she first met him. Too bad he was such a prick. He had an ego the size of the Empire State Building and made sure he spread it generously around most of Manhattan, the bodies of fawning women (and maybe even a few men) strewn thoughtlessly in its wake. She still couldn't believe she'd fallen for his act, blaming it on his GQ looks and his well-honed *sexpertise*. Momentary insanity she pleaded to herself and perhaps a tad too much alcohol on countless occasions.

"What do you want?" she said tersely. He pulled her into a hug and she felt her body go stiff. He promptly let go.

"You look great. How are you?" he said as if they hadn't been through the worst break-up ever.

"Why do you care?" she said, her expression dour.

"What's with the cold shoulder? You on the rag or something?" His glare unnerved her and anger lurched up from her gut.

"In case your memory fails you, the last time I saw you things got pretty ugly between us."

"I was a jerk. It wasn't intentional. I just got a little carried away with the game we had going. I didn't mean to hurt you. You totally overreacted."

"Overreacted? You left me tied up for hours. I was so numb I thought I'd never walk again."

Jason leered at her. "Such a drama queen."

"I have somewhere to be." She shook her head in frustration and walked around him. Stopped. Jason still had a set of keys to her apartment. Shit. She had to get them back, or change her locks. She'd already let this go on too long. "Jason," she said, turning toward him. "I need my keys. I've asked you like a dozen times."

"Sure, I'll bring them over one night. Maybe tomorrow?"

"Absolutely not," she said emphatically. "I'll be out of town until next weekend. I don't want you coming over, just drop them in the mail."

"Come on, I'll come over and we'll have some fun. We were good together."

"What? We were awful. You cheated on me at least five times."

"Whatever." He walked off in a huff. Well, she'd definitely have to get her locks changed the minute she finished this assignment.

Alyx returned home with bright red toenails glaring up at her from her flip-flops. She usually picked a more demure color but apparently her inner harlot had already surfaced.

She emptied the duffle bag of clothing for her cancelled weekend with friends and repacked if for a week with Mr. You-Won't-Be-Wearing-Much-Clothing. Zipping it shut with a forceful tug, she stripped out of her clothes and headed for the shower. The buzzer on her intercom sounded, startling her. She wasn't expecting company. Fearful she'd lost track of time and Daniel's driver had already arrived, she glanced at the clock on her bedside table. Only 5:30 p.m. Safe.

She wrapped herself in a terrycloth bath sheet and went into the living room. Pressing the intercom button, she heard Matt's voice and buzzed him in. Opening the door a crack, she peered down the hallway at the elevator. Matt greeted her warmly and they shared a quick hug before she ushered him inside.

"Sorry, you caught me as I was getting into the shower," she said, a touch embarrassed.

"Good thing I love my wife." Matt flashed her a wicked smile.

Alyx slapped him on the back in playful admonishment. "What are you doing here? Everything all right?"

Matt removed his denim jacket and slung it over the couch. "I wanted to check on you. I'm worried about what you're doing with this guy, this Dom dude."

How sweet, she thought. "I'll be fine. Don't worry. Please."

"But I do. This is way over the top, if you ask me. I can't believe the Bureau even asked you guys to do something like this." Matt's brow wrinkled up. "Go take your shower, I'll help myself to a beer and then we can talk." Matt headed over to the refrigerator and opened it wide. He leaned in and grabbed a Corona from the top shelf. "Got any lime?" he called, his head still inside the fridge and his cute butt perched in the air.

"In the bottom right-hand drawer."

She let the hot water cascade down her back, banishing the invading chill of anxiety. She shaved everything smooth. Jason had talked her into going sans pubic hair; actually, he'd done it for her, having come up with the idea one night in the middle of foreplay. He'd pushed her knees open wide and secured them to the frame of the living room's pullout bed using scarves he'd scrounged from her closet. A little foam and a razor and well, the whole thing had been pretty hot and the added sensitivity during sex had surprised and elated her. There she went again, remembering the good parts of a relationship when this one belonged clearly in the loser column.

She towel-dried her hair, rubbed her skin with coconut oil and threw on yoga pants plus a white camisole. Matt sat on her couch with his legs sprawled across the coffee table. His alma mater, Michigan State, scored a touchdown and he hooted loudly, slapping his knee. "Yeah, baby."

Alyx sat on the over-stuffed chair and propped her bare feet on the table. She wiggled her garish red toes and chuckled.

"For your new sexy persona?" Matt pointed the neck of his beer bottle at Alyx's toes. He smirked.

"Might as well go whole hog if I'm going to be convincing."

"You're scaring me. Who are you and what have you done with Alyx? I think some sex-crazed alien has snatched her body."

"It's kinda weird. I waver between terror and excitement."

Matt chuckled. "I came over because I was worried about

you, but it seems like you've got this under control. But having kinky sex for a week with a total stranger." Matt seemed to consider the situation carefully for a minute. "Although, I could see where it could be kinda *interesting*. Like a fantasy."

"Exactly. That's kind of where my head's at. It'll be for the greater good. I have to admit; his body is like a god's." Alyx blushed.

Matt laughed out loud. "Shit, Alyx, you're hysterical. I think you're actually looking forward to it."

Matt drained the last of his beer and slammed it down hard on the coffee table. "I'm glad I stopped by. You've put my mind at ease, mostly. But if this whole thing goes south, call me. I'll drop everything and come get you."

"Thanks, Matt. Sure, I know you always have my back. I'll be fine. It's only for a week. How much stuff could he do to me in a week?" Well, she'd already done the math on that and had concluded, a lot.

Matt slipped on his jacket, hugged her, landing a kiss on her forehead. "Do you need me to keep an eye on your apartment?"

"No. My neighbor, Hilda, has a key and she'll water my plants. After this week, I figure there'll be another week or so while I'm working at the club and I'll be staying at the place they rented for me to crash at."

"All right then, I'm outta here. Jillian is going out with her girlfriends tonight and I'm on baby duty. Sure is nothing like my old Saturday nights. At least there's a good game on tonight."

They shared a wave goodbye as the elevator doors closed. The clock on her kitchen wall said 6:30 p.m. Yikes. She only had a half-hour to finish drying her hair, put on a little makeup and throw on some clothes.

At seven o'clock on the dot the buzzer shrieked. She gasped. A short man in a dark suit and thin black tie greeted her when she opened the door. His graying hair formed a perfect semicircle around the back of his head, the hallway lights reflecting off his shiny bald top. "Ms. Cameron?"

"Yes," Alyx croaked. Where had her voice gone?

"My name is Mason, Dr. Taylor sent me to pick you up."

"Hello, Mason. You're very punctual." Alyx reached for her overnight bag, but Mason beat her to it.

"I'll get that, miss," he said, turning toward the elevator. Alyx locked her apartment door and followed him. Mason pressed the bottom button marked LL. Her mind wandered. LL— Loser, Loser or Lucky Lady? Alyx settled into the rear of the silver Lincoln Navigator and laid her head against the seat. She'd offered to sit shotgun next to Mason, but he insisted she take the back seat, like some privileged rich bitch with a chauffeur. Retrieving her phone from her purse, she plugged in the ear buds and swiped her finger across the screen until she found *Adele*. She closed her eyes and let the music carry her away to someplace sad. Perhaps she fell asleep, because they arrived at the beachside mansion fairly quickly. Actually, too quickly.

Mason popped open the door and waved her out with a bit of a flourish. The three-story Victorian structure seemed to glow with the light of a thousand candles. No lawn, just tufts of beach grass with their flouncy fronds bowing to and fro in the night breeze. It stayed cooler near the ocean and she hugged herself for momentary warmth. Her eyes peered up to the top of the huge manor where an oversized tower loomed. She immediately thought of shackles and whips. Could there be a dungeon on the high turret of the massive house? No, a dungeon would be underground, in the basement. She shuddered, but not from the chill. Her thoughts ran through scenes from scary movies. *God, Alyx. What have you gotten yourself into?*

"Coming, miss?" Mason said, interrupting Alyx's thoughts

of bondage and pain. She hadn't taken a single step away from the car yet.

"Of course. It's quite an impressive home, Mason."

"You'll like it. Dr. Taylor has taken this old house and made it quite a showplace. Yet, as my wife says, it's rather homey." Somehow Alyx seriously doubted that.

Mason opened the colossal front door and stepped back, his hand upswept in a welcoming gesture. Alyx crossed over the threshold and held her breath, the foyer alone was bigger than her entire apartment. A double staircase arched upward to the second floor, the white spindles in stark contrast to the dark oak banisters. The chandelier above belonged in a haunted mansion with its dark wrought iron filigree frame that enclosed glass globes. Gleaming wooden floors welcomed her feet and a giant circular table with a marble top held a replica of an old-world schooner with its intricate rigging and starched white sails. Soft jazz sounds wafted and she felt transfixed in this completely unfamiliar world.

"Can I take your jacket, Miss Cameron?"

"No thank you. Please, call me Alyx." She wondered what the kindly old man thought of this whole arrangement. Did he know why she was really here? Did he know she worked for the FBI?

"Very well. Dr. Taylor said to meet him in the main living room," Mason announced. "Come, I'll show you." He left Alyx's duffle at the foot of the majestic staircase and she trailed him through a huge, well-appointed kitchen and a short hallway to the right.

The doctor sat on the far side of a U-shaped sectional couch facing a massive stone fireplace with a giant TV screen mounted above. A fuzzy beige rug lay beneath a square wooden coffee table. The black and taupe striped cushions surrounded him in a comfy embrace. Newspaper pages masked his face and only his faded jeans and part of his black tee were visible. He'd crossed one leg over his knee, his feet bare.

Did he know she was standing there? She waited. Mason had vanished soundlessly. She wondered if he expected her to start acting like a submissive already. Especially after she'd gotten all up in his face about being willing to jump right in. Or perhaps she was the one who'd been a pompous ass. Panic grabbed her gut. Maybe she should kneel in front of him. Or, or, or. *No way that was happening.* However, she didn't want to piss him off in the first five minutes of her arrival either.

Slowly, methodically, he folded the paper in half and laid it on the cushion next to him. He folded his arms over his broad chest, making his biceps bulge. His gaze fell on her. "Agent Cameron, you came." Alyx didn't say anything. Anger warmed her face. She thought she'd been clear about her commitment. Apparently, he hadn't taken her seriously. Her number one rule in life was not to jump to conclusions, take each situation on its own merits and assess its worth. It had served her well on the job and in her personal life. Well, except for Jason the Philanderer. Her radar had definitely been malfunctioning then.

"I told you I was in. I thought I'd made that crystal clear."

"You did. However, I've found people frequently don't say what they mean."

"Or," she countered, "they mean it when they say it, but they change their minds." Alyx pursed her lips. "I prefer to believe people don't choose to lie."

"That's an odd statement coming from someone in law enforcement. Not only are you a professional liar, I would think you deal with many, many liars in the sordid world of crime."

Alyx thought a minute. True. Matt had often chided her for being too sympathetic in their line of work. However, she'd never actually been wrong in her assessment of a suspect, or a witness. She believed in people, but she wasn't stupid either.

"Just as I suspected," Daniel said. "You're overthinking things already. We're going to have to switch that brain of yours off if you're going to get into the proper mindset."

Switch her brain off? Had she landed in Dr. Frankenstein's lab? Did he plan on giving her a lobotomy? He was a heart surgeon, not a brain surgeon.

"Care for a glass of wine?"

Oh, God, yes. She needed alcohol. "Please," she said, demurely, hoping to mask the trepidation in her voice. Daniel rose and gently touched her elbow, ushering her out of the oversized living room and into the kitchen.

"Have you eaten?"

"Yes," she lied. When Matt showed up unexpectedly, she'd totally forgotten about dinner. Now that she thought about it, she hadn't eaten anything since breakfast. Whatever, maybe she'd lose a few pounds this week, what with all the physical exertion she'd be putting forth, and working out in his gym. Definitely a positive sidebar to this ridiculous situation.

He opened the professional-grade refrigerator and selected a bottle of chardonnay, a label Alyx didn't recognize. The corkscrew popped the bottle open and Daniel set it in a bucket with ice, placing it on a tray with two stem-less wine glasses. "Come." He motioned toward the back of the kitchen. "Let's sit out on the deck and talk."

Alyx followed him outside, closing the French doors behind her. Ocean waves crashed onto the shore, reminding her of the years she'd spent on the beaches here. Every summer since she was sixteen she'd guarded this ocean. Growing up, she'd only known the life of a beach lover and surfer. As soon as she and her friends came home from college each semester they immediately made their way to the ocean just to let it know they were back. And before they left, they came to say goodbye. The beach felt like home.

Daniel set the tray on a table next to a cushioned double lounger. Alyx walked to the end of the decking and gazed at the black sea, the white froth of the cresting waves contrasting sharply against the backdrop of the dark night. The ocean acted calm, the complete opposite of her mood.

"I grew up on this ocean," she said.

"You did? I had no idea. I assumed you were a city girl." Daniel came and stood beside her and handed her a glass.

"Thank you." She sipped the cool, crisp wine. Perhaps she could fantasize this into something that would get her through the week without being totally traumatized. Maybe.

"I grew up in Westhampton Beach. I lifeguarded every summer in high school and college."

"So, you were serious the other night? You really are a certified lifeguard?" Alyx frowned, but didn't cast any aspersions his way as he continued, "I'm impressed, being an ocean guard is no easy feat. Did you make many saves?"

"Enough. It's funny though. I can barely remember the people I saved, but the one I didn't is burned in my mind as if it were yesterday." Daniel stared at her.

"I'm sorry. That must have been awful."

"It was three people. All from out of town, out of the country, actually. Three young Asian men. There was a serious rip current that day and we had signs up prohibiting swimming. But they were out of the supervised area. When we heard trouble, three of us went to find them, but too late. I was only seventeen and I took it really hard. We all did. We used a human chain outside the breakers to search for the bodies. We found them. I'll never forget what their faces looked like as we laid them out on the sand."

"I know how that feels. I, too, don't remember the ones I've saved as much as the ones I've lost." Daniel's arm pressed against her shoulder and his body heat surged through her. She cringed at what would follow and her spine shivered. And yet, something inside her burned a little too warm. Already, she knew this would be a long week. Really, really long.

"Are you cold, or maybe afraid?" he said in response to her obvious shudder.

"Neither." His handsome face distracted her. This wasn't going anything like she thought. "Where did you grow up?" she said, hoping to shift the focus off her.

"Right here, in Hampton Shores."

"In this house?"

"No. I bought this house and renovated it. We lived closer to town. My parents aren't really fans of the beach, which is absurd since this is an ocean community."

Alyx felt off-center. Was this the same man she'd met the other night? The one who acted so pompous and bossy? Surprisingly, he seemed sort of kind and compassionate, like he could be a friend. *Stop it, Alyx. You're working overtime on some delusion. Stop now before you get yourself into serious trouble.*

"So," Daniel said, interrupting her ridiculous thoughts. "Why don't we sit and negotiate our arrangement?" He escorted Alyx over to the lounger by her hand. His touch surprised her, like he was already in charge. Well, duh. Of course, he was.

Alyx sat and leaned against the beige cushion, her feet splayed in front of her. This *chair* was the size of her bed. Daniel settled in alongside her. She peered up at the starlit sky and held her breath. This felt entirely too romantic for what she'd envisioned. Exhaling slowly, she took a long draught on her wine and settled the glass on the side table. She sucked in a deep breath and held it again.

"Breathe," Daniel said. She turned her head and he was staring at her. "In and out, slowly."

Like sex? She thought. Well, maybe not all that slowly.

This would be fucking he had in mind. Hard and fast, well, maybe not so fast. She'd have to fake her orgasms, if he was expecting that. That's if he even cared, which he probably didn't.

"Let's start with the basics." Daniel sat up and faced her, his legs crisscrossed. "Your experience. How many men have you been with?" His expression seemed way too serious and she couldn't hide her shock.

"What does 'been with' constitute?"

"It means whatever you want it to mean."

Alyx retrieved her wine glass and took a sip. "Five," she announced, "one high school boyfriend, two in college and two after that. No sex with the high school guy, yes with the others."

"And what do you mean by sex?" he said too casually.

"What do you think I mean?" The sound of her voice made her flinch, too screechy.

"Look, sex is a very broad term and easily misunderstood if two people aren't thinking along the same lines. So, I'll make it easy, I'll give you a checklist and you simply say yes or no." Daniel seemed as if he was trying not to laugh at her. Anger rose in her chest.

"Fine." She huffed.

"Okay, I assume we can check off vaginal sex."

"Yes."

"Oral sex? Given?"

"Yes. Although, I've been told I'm not that good at it." *Holy shit. Did she really say that?*

Daniel chuckled, but didn't comment. "Swallow semen?"

Geez. "Yeah, a few times, can't say I loved it." God, she'd never get through *this part*, so how would she get through the real live stuff?

"Oral sex, received?"

"Yes." Cold sweat started to collect on the back of her

neck. Her mouth had gone dry and she slugged down another gulp of alcohol.

"Anal sex?"

"Good God, no." Well, she'd definitely said that out loud. Another swig.

A V formed between Daniel's brows, but it didn't appear like he was really annoyed, but sort of, bemused. "Okay, but you'll never get by in the club with that attitude. That's something we'll need to address right away."

Another gulp. No way was she letting anyone in her back door. She'd have to figure out some way around that. She drained her glass.

"When's your period due?"

The change in direction caught Alyx off guard. Well, he was a doctor, but really? He wasn't *her* doctor. "Why is that important? I don't have my period this week, you're safe."

He laughed. She didn't think she'd said anything even remotely funny. "No, it doesn't bother me sexually, I'm concerned about birth control."

"You needn't worry about that, I'm very responsible." This line of questioning had started to bother her. She wasn't a sixteen-year-old. She'd never taken chances when it came to birth control. The first time, well, not really prepared and her boyfriend had used the pullout method. Not exactly full proof, but the one and only time she'd had sex without taking precautions. She wasn't a risk-taker in that department. Ever.

"Okay, I've heard that before. What are you using?" Daniel inquired, sounding way too much like an M.D.

"I'm on the pill."

"And you have them with you?"

Shit. Did she remember to bring them?

"I don't like that expression on you face. What's wrong?"

"I'm not sure I packed them." Alyx chewed on her finger, then remembering her new manicure, abruptly dropped her hand. She thought for a minute, retracing her packing sequence. Dr. Taylor's expression made her anxious. She remembered grabbing them along with her toothpaste and toothbrush. "I'm pretty sure I have them."

"If not, I can manage a prescription for an emergency refill if necessary." Daniel leaned his chin on his hands and added, "So, since our medical forms certify us healthy and you're protected, then condoms are optional. Your choice." He raised his eyebrows and tilted his head slightly, waiting for her response.

This was so weird, like negotiating a business deal. Well, she was at work, so that wasn't particularly farfetched. Truthfully, she hated condoms, and she figured if she did, then she could most assuredly understand how a guy would detest them. "No condom."

"Excellent," he said, a little too enthusiastically. "Let's continue. Since you've never been a participant in the lifestyle, I take it you have no experience with any of the other practices. You claim you did your homework so I'll assume you're familiar with many of the things I'm referring to."

"I guess so. But I only need to learn enough to get by at the club, so let's not overdo it," Alyx said, hoping he might show some restraint. *Restraint?* She better not say that out loud.

"Have you ever used restraints? Played any bondage games with your boyfriends?"

Shit. Was he reading her mind? "A little," she offered. "With boyfriends three and five."

"Did you enjoy it?"

"Mostly." Well, not with Jason, he'd gotten too carried away with the idea of making her his prisoner.

"That doesn't sound particularly convincing, Alyx." Daniel reached across her, brushing over her breasts and plucked the bottle of wine from its icy nest. "Hold out your glass," he ordered.

Alyx realized she'd downed her wine too quickly. "I'm not sure I should drink anymore."

"Trust me, Alyx, you're going to need a second glass for what I have in mind." Her pulse rate sped up and she swore he'd hear her heart pounding. He poured the chilled Chardonnay into her glass and she struggled to keep her hand from trembling. Although she wasn't exactly sure it was fear having this effect on her.

"Now, explain to me about the bondage experience that went bad."

"Uh, my last boyfriend, Jason, he tied me up and, well, I never should have let him. He'd been drinking and when I changed my mind we argued and he huffed out of the bedroom and passed out on the living room couch. It took me a while, but I eventually freed myself and, well, I kicked his ass to the curb."

"Good girl. But just so we are clear, rule number one in bondage play is that a Dom never, and I'll repeat that, never, leaves his sub unattended when she's bound. Not even for a split-second."

"Safety first?" Alyx said, trying to lighten the mood. She couldn't believe what a totally different person this man was from the one she met at the club. Dr. Jekyll and Mr. Hyde, or would that be Dr. Hyde?

"Absolutely. The motto should always be: Safe, Sane and Consensual." He flashed a zillion-mega-watt-smile at her and a wave of heat ignited her skin. God, he sure was a looker.

Daniel placed the tray with the empty wine bottle and glasses on the kitchen counter. He led Alyx out of the kitchen by her hand, flicking the lights off on the way out. Her petite hand felt cold in his and he laced his fingers through hers, holding her firmly, fearful she'd run out the front door.

"I'll show you to your room and give you a few minutes to settle in." Daniel glanced back at her face as he tugged her up the staircase. Damn, he still couldn't read her. Why was she such an enigma? She seemed too calm, but every once in a while something dark flashed across her face and he couldn't decide what it was. Fear? Anger? Loathing? Maybe she really despised him. He had acted like a total ass in Jack's office, letting his anger get the better of him. And she'd just told him about a bad experience with an old beau who had anger issues. He never let anger find its way into a scene with a submissive. However, he didn't like being challenged by anyone, especially not her. And it wasn't because she was a woman. He had great respect for women. Both his mother and sister were accomplished professionals, his mother a prominent psychiatrist and his sister owned her own invest-ment firm. And he didn't degrade women. He was in awe of them and definitely considered them the stronger of the sexes. It was just *this woman* who unnerved him for some reason. Perhaps because she wielded a gun?

Daniel opened the door to the green bedroom. He always identified a room by its dominating color. Sometimes he thought it made him sound like an asshole, too much like a rich bastard, but he couldn't seem to break the habit. His hand touched the small of her back and nudged her inside. "Whenever you come in here and close the door I'll assume you want to be left alone. On the other hand, you can't hide in here either." He grabbed her upper arm and made her face him. "I'll outline our arrangement in more detail at breakfast, but for now, you may have free time from noon until four to do as you wish, although you may not leave the premises. The remainder of time you will be under my control and I will do with you as I see fit." Her azure eyes blazed and he braced himself for her refusal.

"I didn't sign up to be a slave," she said, her voice almost a growl.

"Actually, you did. As my submissive I say what you eat, what you wear, when you sleep and when you can have free time. From my vantage point that is your biggest problem, Alyx, following orders. I need to break you of that as fast as I can. There can be no topping from the bottom. If you do that for even a single second at the club they'll know you're a fraud. Do you know what I mean by that?"

"I read about it. As the Dom, you're the top, and as the sub, I'm the bottom. If I tell you what to do in a scene, then I would be 'topping from the bottom'."

"Exactly," Daniel said. She grinned, proud of herself, he thought, and he felt calmer than he did when she arrived. "I'll return for you in fifteen minutes and we'll get started. Take care of whatever you need to in the bathroom. Lose the jeans. You can leave the tee shirt and underwear on for now." He smirked at her shocked expression, then walked out and shut the door. His smile broadened. She was fucking adorable.

In his bedroom, he shrugged out of his clothing and pulled on a pair of black cotton pajama bottoms. He brushed his teeth, gargled with mouthwash, ran a brush through his hair and then studied his face in the mirror. His blood rushed with excitement. He did crave training new submissives. Pure innocence in his hands; so pliable, nervous. He leaned on the counter and fretted. Maybe those adjectives didn't really apply to Alyx. He had to keep reminding himself she wasn't a real submissive, but instead, a well-trained FBI agent used to making others follow *her* orders. She restrained people for a living, handcuffs one of the tools of her trade. Worry struck him. He hadn't considered all the ramifications of her law enforcement training—the complete opposite of being a submissive. Shit, half the Doms he knew were cops, even the women Dommes. Could he really break her? Bend her to his will? His heart rate increased. Did he want to?

Returning to her bedroom door, he knocked twice but didn't wait for a response and entered. She sat in the bed's middle, her legs crossed, her fingers toying with the hem of her pink tee. She looked pretty in pink; he'd have to remember that. The crotch of her black panties taunted him and he couldn't wait to get them off her.

Unsettled by her annoyed expression, "Ready?" he said cheerfully, hoping to bring her mood around to something more pleasant. She bit her lip and seemed to consider her response.

"As I'll ever be, I guess." He put out his hand for her and she scooted off the bed and accepted it. They walked toward the hallway's end, to an unseen door across from his master bedroom. Daniel pressed against the seam in the right-hand corner and the secret entrance sprung open to reveal another staircase.

"Secret torture chamber?" Alyx mumbled, her eyes as large as light-bulbs.

"Something like that," he said, flashing her a wicked grin. Daniel flicked on the light and led her up to the third floor and into an enormous square-shaped room. The wall overlooking the ocean was composed entirely of glass and shielded from the outside by a series of slatted bamboo blinds. Daniel let go of Alyx's hand and walked over to raise the shades. The starlit night sky came into view like the background in a science fiction movie: astronauts rocketing their ship through outer space. He turned toward Alyx but she wasn't checking out the panorama. Her wide eyes surveyed the array of equipment. He waited for her to adjust to the surroundings.

"So, it's not a dungeon. Good," she said and then sighed mightily.

"Dungeons aren't my style."

"Something tells me I wouldn't like a dungeon."

"And how do you feel about this room? I call it the rec room."

"Do you spell that with a W or an R?" Alyx seemed bemused, but trepidation vexed her voice.

Daniel's throat rumbled with laughter. "I would say with an R, but the other word will also work. We'll have fun but you might also be wrecked by the time I let you out." He arched his eyebrows threateningly.

Alyx's expression appeared stoic. "It's pretty high up, so there's certainly no escaping your torturous ways even without being tied up."

Daniel furrowed his brow. "Alyx, this is all about pleasure. I have no intention of making you suffer anything you won't enjoy."

"I'll admit it's not as scary as I thought. You don't have any whips and canes. That makes me feel a teensy bit better."

"No, I'm not into hurting anyone. I fix bodies for a living. I have no interest in doing damage to them. Some women I got involved with early on were into pain, but I didn't have the stomach for it. I couldn't even fake it."

"Well, that's reassuring."

Her fingers twisted the hem of her tee into a tight knot. She seemed lighthearted enough, but he sensed her underlying anxiety and tried again to reassure her. "Alyx, this is all about giving over your body to your Dom, to show you how many ways you can experience indulgence."

"What do you get out of it, if it's all about me?"

"I get off on pleasing you. Literally."

Was that a smirk? "Sounds rather altruistic to me. Guys are usually more concerned about themselves."

"Then, Alyx, you haven't been with the right men." A question mark flashed across her face. "But here you are again, overthinking things. If you spend too much time in your head you'll prevent your body from feeling what it needs. My expectation is that you *will* give over control. To me. Although I fully understand this could be difficult for someone like you."

"I'll do my best, I swear."

"Good girl. I've trained many submissives, but this will only work if you trust me to give you what you need, which isn't necessarily what you may think you want."

"I don't know. Trust is a big word."

"That's an honest response and I appreciate honesty. I will earn your trust." He stepped toward her and she retreated against the wall. He needed to proceed with caution.

"All right, let's get started. First, I want you to walk around the room and touch everything as you go. Ask me any question you want. Then we'll start with protocol."

Her big eyes gazed up at him. "Fine," she said softly. He gave her a little nudge and she tentatively stepped toward the giant wooden X on the wall to her right.

Daniel lit the oversized candles scattered around the room then seated himself on the overstuffed chair at the foot of the king-sized bondage bed. He propped his feet up on the ottoman, crossing his arms over his bare chest. This chair was probably the most important piece of equipment in the room, for it was where he administered aftercare—the time he spent with a submissive once she hit subspace, when she'd be disoriented from endorphin overload. Most Doms wouldn't admit it to anyone other than another Dom, but this was often the most satisfying part of the relationship with a submissive. If one weren't in the lifestyle and only knew how sordid movies and erotic novels depicted it, true understanding of how important aftercare was would never be gained. It flourished in the space in which a Dom and a sub would talk, really talk, and learn to trust in each other. Trust, the most vital bond between a Dominant and submissive. Without her full faith, he wouldn't be able to move Alyx forward into nirvana. Daniel swallowed, realizing how little time he had.

His mouth salivated at the image of his little subbie leaning her chest against the St. Andrews Cross, her hands and feet in place near the arm and ankle restraints. Standing spread eagle, her black bikini barely covering her cute little derriere. She turned around and repeated the pose. With her arms over her head, the hem of her pink tee hiked up to reveal her navel. "I like the way you look there."

She actually pursed her lips. "This isn't so bad. What would you do to me once you had me tied up?"

Hmm, thought Daniel. Let me count the ways. "It's the perfect place for a flogging, which I think you'll find quite thrilling. Most women seem to. And, of course, I could certainly fuck you on it. As you so aptly demonstrated, I can restrain you either forward or backward."

Per his instructions, she worked her way around the room's perimeter, running her hands first over the restraining bench and then the spanking horse. Stopping at the bondage bed, she smoothed a small wrinkle from the silky black satin sheets, then tugged on the foot restraints for durability. Facing the black-lacquered cabinetry, she hesitated a moment, then swung the double doors open in one quick motion. A gasp filled the air, but Daniel couldn't see her face hidden behind the door. He smiled at her apparent shock. She closed the doors quickly and then moved around him, facing the rack where he'd hung plastic bags of rope, floggers were also arranged in a neat row. She flicked the fronds of a lash with her middle finger and he covered his mouth with his hand to keep from revealing his amusement at her innocence. Pivoting toward him, she attempted a smile. Daniel would give anything to hear her thoughts, but he'd have to wait until she decided to share them.

Alyx reached up and hit one of the shackles hanging from the ceiling. It swung back and forth, a pendulum singing a silent sexy song.

She'd completed her trip around his world. Well, his former world. He couldn't remember the last time he'd been in here and had spent a good part of the day getting it in shape. Cobwebs might add to the atmosphere of a dungeon, but not here.

"Any questions?"

"Too many, so I'll take your advice and stop overthinking this."

"Good girl." Daniel got to his feet and beckoned Alyx forward with a crook of his finger. "Come here, little one." Terror flashed across her lovely face. Oh yes, he was the spider luring her into his web and she knew it.

She padded toward him slowly, like a prisoner walking to her execution. He held her by her upper arms and fixed his eyes squarely on her face. "We will start with protocol, Alyx. There are three basic positions you must learn and be able to execute without thinking: the inspection position, the slave position and the surrender position."

Alyx's face crumpled. "I really don't like that word."

"Which word?"

"Give me a break. You know which word."

Well, he wasn't quite sure. His best guess would be either slave or surrender. If she hadn't been a law enforcement agent he might have overlooked the word surrender. "Alyx, it's important we have open and explicit communication, so please make sure you express yourself clearly when I ask. This is not the place for miscommunication. You could get hurt."

"Fine, I get it. The word slave, I hate the word slave."

"Trust me, I fully understand that, but you need to realize the word has a very different meaning in the lifestyle. It's a loving relationship, and one a woman chooses, not one forced upon her. Some women want their Dom to make all their decisions for them, from what they eat to what they wear. They find it very liberating, which of course sounds distinctly like an oxymoron. Many women who choose the slave lifestyle are powerful and dominant in their careers. I could name several who would surprise you, but once they are home with their Dom, they enjoy the freedom of letting someone else be in charge."

Bewilderment expanded Alyx's countenance. "Have you ever had a slave?"

"No, Alyx, that's not a relationship I'm interested in. Truthfully, it's way too much responsibility. My job is intense enough and riddled with important decisions on a daily basis. I don't need to come home to a woman who needs me to tell her what to do."

"But, isn't that what you're expecting from me?"

"That's only so you can play the part at the club and to get you used to obeying. I wouldn't expect that if we were in a *real* relationship."

"Oh."

Daniel pondered this for a second. A real relationship with Alyx? She was so fucking hot.

"All right, let's move on or we'll be in here until sunrise. The inspection position. You will do it with clothes on first." Daniel grabbed her by the shoulders and pulled her closer. "Stand tall, shoulders squared, chin up, eyes down." He waited as she got her body into position. "Good girl. Now lace your fingers behind your neck, elbows out straight." She glimpsed up at him. "Eyes down," he corrected her. "Now spread your legs, put your feet a little past your shoulders." She complied and he stepped back and shifted to her side, checking the planes of her body. The position pushed her magnificent breasts out and up. Gorgeous.

"Perfect," he said, and she exhaled. "Some Doms prefer

your hands clasped behind your back, but this way is acceptable without earning you a punishment. Your Dom will correct you if he has a different preference. While in a scene, as we are now, you are not allowed to speak to me unless I ask you a specific question. Your response shall be either 'Yes, Sir' or 'No, Sir.' Only say more if I ask you to explain yourself. Understand?"

"Yes, Sir," she said, staring up at him.

"Ah, there you go again. In the inspection position, you need to keep your eyes to the floor unless I give the command, 'eyes on me.' Now I will explain the use of punishment to teach you compliance with my commands."

Her eyebrows scrunched together.

"Punishment comes in many varieties and differing levels. Sometimes humiliation is used at the club, in the form of openly displaying a naked sub for all to view. At the club you will see many subs without clothing, some on leashes attached to collars and couples engaged in open sexual practices. You need to be prepared for that."

Fright distorted Alyx's lovely face and made his stomach clench. He didn't want to freak her out, but she needed to be prepared for anything, everything. Perhaps he should bring her one night before her debut to acquaint her with the intensity of the festivities. He had no idea whether she'd entered the club at the front door or through Jack's private entrance. Either way, he doubted she'd gotten the opportunity to experience the club in full swing, which probably would have put her off this mission in a New York minute. Maybe that would've been a good thing. He still had serious reservations about putting an S&M neophyte in the hands of these sadists for any period of time, even a trained agent like Alyx.

"You look absolutely terrified, Alyx. Let me put your mind at ease about my use of punishment. I'm not into humiliating a woman, nor am I into excessive pain, although some women are seriously into pain. I usually use spanking, and truthfully, most of my subs have found it to be stimulating to the point of orgasm, so I'm not sure how effective it is as punishment. I consider it more of a reminder than actual punishment. So, you might actually enjoy it." Most likely she wouldn't believe him until he forced her there, and tonight wasn't the night. "And, while we are on the subject of punishment this is probably a good time to introduce safe words." Her eyes widened. "Again, if you did your research I assume you know what those are."

"Yes."

He barked, "Yes, what?"

Alyx hesitated then managed to blurt out, "Yes, S*ir.*"

"Good girl. Your safe words will be yellow and red. When do you use your safe words?"

"I say yellow if something is becoming too intense or too painful, and you'll slow down. If I say red, then you stop immediately, Sir."

"Correct. I don't anticipate you'll need them with me, but you may need them at the club if you're with a Dom you don't know very well. The club safe words are the same, yellow and red. If you say red then everything stops immediately and your Dom will sit and talk with you about your limits. Understand?"

"Yes, Sir," she said too quietly.

"Since we're mostly role-playing here and I don't know you very well, I may ask you for a color to be sure I'm reading your response correctly. So if I ask, respond with green meaning you're okay, yellow if you're becoming uncomfortable or red, for stop right this second. Got it?"

"Yes, Sir."

"Good. Now, I'll forgo the punishment tonight, but know that you've already earned five swats on your ass with my hand for forgetting to keep your eyes down and not addressing me by my title. Something to look forward to tomorrow." He arched his eyebrows in anticipation, then said, "What do you say to me, Alyx?" This was killing him. How would he ever get her through this? Striking a healthy balance between keeping her calm and keeping her on edge was going to be a serious challenge.

Alyx opened her mouth, but no words crossed her lovely pink lips. He wanted to ravage those lips, and he fully intended to speed this up so he could get there.

At length, she muttered, "Uh, thank you, Sir?"

"Good girl. Next we'll do the slave position, again with clothes on for now. Kneel at my feet."

He gave a gentle push atop her shoulders and she dropped her elbows and sunk to the floor, much more gracefully than he'd anticipated.

"Good. Now, sit back on your heels, then chin up, eyes down, back straight, like before." He waited while she conformed. "Excellent. Now spread your knees apart, farther than your shoulders." She opened her legs partway and he put his bare foot between her knees and shifted them farther out. "That's it. Now, place your upturned palms on your thighs."

Perfect posture, and he wondered if she would learn everything this quickly. Many subs he'd trained over the years were clumsy and awkward, but Alyx moved with the grace of a dancer. He wondered if perhaps she was, or, more likely, she'd had intense martial arts training. Once he got her into his gym, he'd find out what skills she possessed.

He squatted so they were eye level. "Eyes on me," he said softly. Alyx's cool blue eyes drifted upward until they found his. "Excellent, Alyx, you've done well so far. Now, the last position is the surrender position."

"I don't think I like the word surrender either, it's for criminals or prisoners."

"You are my prisoner now, aren't you? And for the entire

week, I might add." Okay, she'd engaged him in conversation, breaking the rules. Again. He needed to shut this down, and fast.

"The surrender position," he reminded her. "Lay your upper body over your thighs and place your forehead on the floor, clasp your hands behind your neck like before."

Alyx's vision flared. "Come on. You've got to be kidding me. Women actually do this shit?" She bit her lip after the outburst. Then added, "Sir."

Daniel didn't allow himself to scoff at her impudence. But she was seriously trying his patience. He rubbed his face with his hand and sighed. What had happened to his Dom personality? He was seriously out of practice.

"You. Do. Not. Have. Permission. To. Speak. And you've earned yourself five more swats for tomorrow's spanking. Now, put your fucking forehead on the floor, Alyx." *Patience, patience...* he reminded himself. He never got angry at a sub.

Alyx set her jaw, grabbed her long mane of hair and flung it over her shoulder and landed her head on the floor. Under her breath, he thought she said, "Fuck."

Time to step it up, she was way too comfortable and he needed to amp her anxiety or he'd never get her anywhere tonight. He thought this would be fun and a bit of a challenge, but now he realized this might be a long week, too long. He decided to leave her there for a few minutes, hoping to get her into the right frame of mind.

After watching the clock for a full minute, he barked, "Sit up. Time to lose the clothes." Her sharp intake of breath echoed across the room. He'd gotten her attention. He offered his hands and jerked her to a standing position. Her eyes fell to the floor. He laughed inwardly at her abrupt bashfulness, she'd been so eager to keep eye contact before, but now when he expected it, she chose to avert her gaze.

"Eyes on me," he snapped. Her eyes lifted and he beheld

nervousness. "Hands over your head," he commanded. She threw them in the air and he grabbed the hem of her shirt and pulled it quickly over her head. She gasped.

The room felt too warm. Alyx swore her heart would burst out of her chest and hit the prominent heart surgeon in his incredibly handsome face. How apropos.

She thought she had things under control until he'd gone all mean and scary on her. She wondered if he could sense her arousal. Standing before this unbelievably sexy man, clad only in her underwear, was a huge turn-on. His naked chest looked delicious and she wanted to run her fingers over those sculpted pecs and rock-hard shoulders. If she didn't know better she'd have thought him a personal trainer rather than a heart surgeon. She wanted to jump on him, tear his flimsy pants off and fuck his goddamned brains out. But, that would definitely be topping from the bottom and would likely earn her a major punishment. She had to admit the idea of the promised spanking had unleashed a slow burn between her legs. How could she have become such a perv in just one day?

"Turn around," Daniel ordered. Complying quickly to his command, she focused on the restraining table. She pictured herself sprawled across it, secured and vulnerable, totally at the mercy of a Dom. Daniel didn't immediately touch her as she'd anticipated. Instead he walked to a corner and she stole a glance, but couldn't see what he was doing. Her heart rate soared. What was he planning to do next?

Music abruptly filled the room and she recognized it right away. Howie Day, she loved this CD. He padded back to her, his bare feet slapping lightly along the hardwood. His body close, his warmth on her back as he moved to her bra clasp, unhooking it in one quick move. His hands slid up her back, over her shoulders, and the straps drifted down her arms, her bra vanishing from sight.

"Breathe, Alyx," he whispered near her ear. She hadn't realized she'd been holding her breath, and exhaled slowly. "That's my girl." His fingers moved over her arms in a comforting gesture. He gently massaged her shoulders, then let his hands drift to her sides. Slipping his index fingers into her panties' elastic, he slid them slowly down her legs. "Step out," he said, crouching behind her.

Making the same motion up and down the sides of her legs, he rose, wrapped his arms around her waist and pulled her against his body. His smattering of chest hair prickled her naked back. She couldn't breathe, even if he ordered her to. With one hand, he grabbed her hair and twisted it over her shoulder then tugged on it, pulling her head to one side and exposing the soft flesh of her neck. His warm lips grazed over her skin and she struggled not to moan. He grasped her chin in his firm grip and kissed her mouth gently then nipped at her bottom lip before plunging his tongue inside. She tried unsuccessfully to stifle another moan. She shouldn't be enjoying this so much. Yet the thrill of anticipation over what awaited had her pulse pounding. And oh, her whirling mind.

He turned her body to face him, capturing her hips in his grasp. "You have a beautiful body, little subbie," Daniel said as his eyes traveled to her toes and back again. "And I like that you're shaved bare."

Oh, God. Her eyes fell to the floor and she gulped. Nobody had ever said anything to her like that. She thought she could easily drop ten pounds and still not be thin. She never handled a compliment very well either. Thankfully, he expected her to keep her mouth shut and her gaze on the floor, so she didn't have to acknowledge his statement. She thought this whole experience would be less intimate, less personal, more like working out at the gym. But Daniel's probing questions and off-hand comments kept distracting her.

"Come," he said, taking her hand. "We'll start with a flogging." Alyx felt her body tense and she gave herself a pep talk. You can do this. Don't let him see your fear, or would that be excitement? She still couldn't decide.

Daniel walked her over to the large wooden X bolted to the wall. Grabbing her by the shoulders, he directed her away from him and positioned her up against the polished wood. She startled at the coldness against her chest and stomach. Raising her right hand, he buckled her wrist into the padded leather cuff and slid a finger underneath to check if it was too tight, repeating the motion with her other hand. He slid his warm hands over her body, spread her legs wide and shackled both ankles into the mounted restraints, again making sure his finger fit between her flesh and the leather straps.

Howie Day's voice sang out, *"Brace yourself, with all that you have."*

"Perfect song," Daniel whispered in her ear and she arched her back in response, like a feral cat. "Brace yourself, sweetheart." He ran his hands up and down her arms, massaging her lotioned skin, then drifted over the sides of her torso and across her hips. His hands were soft and agile as they moved over her flesh, not the calloused hands of a laborer, the hands of a skilled man intimately familiar with the female body. He stroked upward under her arms and she cringed, giggled.

She felt his smile on her neck. "My, my, are we ticklish, little subbie?"

"Yes, Sir," she said, squirming, while he continued running his fingertips along the undersides of her arms.

"There will be *no* laughing in the rec room," he admonished.

"Yes, Sir," she said, chewing on the inside of her cheek to stifle herself.

He tugged on her makeshift ponytail again, exposing her neck and leaned in. His lips nipped at the seashell curves of her ear, tickling her lobe and making her wriggle. "Are you okay, Alyx? Are the restraints too tight?"

"No, Sir," her voice raspy.

His arms circled her waist and his hands traveled up between the wood and her breasts. He squeezed them gently. His voice came low and rich, "I think you'll be surprised at how much you'll enjoy this, my Alyx."

"I'm trying to believe that."

"Silence," he snarled. "You do not have permission to speak." He pinched her nipples hard and she inhaled sharply. Grasping her shoulders, he massaged them a few times, then traced small lines toward her bottom. "I like the feel of your bare skin, Alyx," he mumbled into her ear and again she cringed at the tickle creeping across her skin. Goose bumps erupted. He cupped her bottom and squeezed her butt cheeks, then stroked up and down the sides of her torso again. Any part of her that wasn't already scorching, thawed under his touch.

"Are you ready?" he said against her nape.

"Yes, Sir," she mumbled. He bit her earlobe gently and then ran wet kisses across her neck. She recoiled and a small giggle escaped her.

"Laughing again, Alyx?" he said gruffly, and she feared she'd angered him.

"Uh, no, Sir. I mean, well, y-yes, Sir. Maybe a little."

Daniel struggled not to laugh out loud. "Now, now, little pet, nothing is funny here. This is all carnal, dark. I thought I made that clear already. I've never punished a sub for laughing before but I'll gladly add this to your list of infractions. And there most assuredly will be no humor during a flogging. Understood?"

"Yes, Sir. Absolutely not, Sir. I totally get it."

He worried this whole thing was about to blow up in his face. He needed to get his game face on, and quickly, before this turned into a bad Saturday Night Live skit. "Enough," he said, using his most intimidating tone. "Your only response is yes, or no, Sir."

Jesus, she was delectable, but really. *Focus man.* He had to make this painful enough so she wouldn't fold under the hand of another Dom, or he'd be doing her no service at all.

Selecting a medium weight, deerskin leather flogger with no knots at the end, he snapped it a few times in the air to get her attention. She jumped at the sounds. Good. He needed her tense in order to make this rewarding. He moved in close and let the strands of soft leather trail across her naked back, down over her bare buttocks. "This will be painful, but not too. What are your safe words, Alyx?" he said, his voice stern.

"What?" she said and he knew the anticipation of a lashing already had her distracted.

"Wrong. How do you answer me?"

"Uh, what was the question, Sir? I forgot," her voice shrill.

"I said, what are your safe words, Alyx?"

"Y-yellow and red, Sir."

"Good girl. Use them if you need to." And with that, he stepped away from her and let the lashes fly. The fronds hit her skin with a gentle thud. She jumped and then stilled. He kept the pace steady at first, then increased the rhythm moving right and left across her back, eventually drifting downward to caress her beautiful behind and then her muscular thighs. He wondered how long she would last.

Stopping, he moved in, leaning his body against hers, his

massive erection strained against his cotton pants. He pressed it into her backside. In a low growl, he said, "You look so beautiful like this, little subbie. Still with me?"

"Yes, Sir," she said, breathless. The heat from her reddened skin against his chest burned like a shot of warm scotch sliding down his throat. He reached around with his free hand and grabbed a breast, pinching the nipple hard. She gasped. Sliding his hand between her legs he ran his fingers through the slick moisture and pressed two fingers inside her. "So responsive to the flogger. *Sooo* wet," he hissed into her ear and gooseflesh rose on her skin. "And we've only begun." Obviously, her breath sat trapped in her lungs. "Breathe, Alyx. I don't want you passing out." When he heard her release a breath he stepped back, bereft at the loss of her body heat.

Changing the stroke so only the tips struck her, the lashes made little pelting noises, like freezing rain against a windshield. He knew this would sting more and kept a close eye for her response. When her hands fisted in the restraints he decided she'd had enough. Dropping the flogger onto the bed, he moved in quickly and circled his arms around her waist, her breathing rapid and her skin glistening with sweat.

"You did well, darling. I'm proud." He decided she deserved a reward. He pressed his body into her back and ran his hands over her heated skin, trailing his fingers over the inside of her thighs, then slid them into the moistness between her legs again. Her head fell backwards onto his shoulder. Her arousal quickened his pulse and he kissed her gently behind her earlobe. "You're so worked up, sweetheart." He placed a fingertip at her opening and slipped a finger inside. She quivered under his touch, sucking in a ragged breath. His tongue traced circles around her ear and she keened loudly.

"Shush," he chided. Circling the sensitive nub between her legs, her hips flexed into his groin and he knew her climax wasn't far away. "Not yet, baby, you will not come until I give you permission."

"Please, I can't control that," she mumbled.

"Oh, yes, Alyx. This is all about control. You will wait until I allow you to come." Thrusting two fingers deep inside her over and over again he felt her backside writhing against his erection and her vagina clenched in response to the relentless penetration of his fingers.

"Daniel, please," she begged, groaning loudly.

"How do you address me, little subbie?" he snapped. Removing his fingers, she groaned at the loss of his touch.

"Oh, God, I mean, Sir, please, Sir."

"Good girl." He reached up and released her wrists from the restraints, then undid the ankle cuffs. He quickly reattached her so she faced him and continued his assault on her vagina. Kissing her deeply, he used his other hand to massage her breast, pinching a nipple until she cried out. His mouth drifted downward and he clasped the other between his lips and nipped at it with his teeth, then sucked. She whimpered.

"Not yet, baby," he reminded her. He pulled his fingers out of her, his palm resting up against her pelvic bone. She opened her eyes and gave him a wanton stare. Sure, she struggled to stay quiet, obedient, but he made her wait a moment longer, then drove in three fingers to the hilt. "Fuck," she yelled. He covered her mouth with a kiss to shut her up. Tongues danced, pulses raced, breathing became panting. His fingers curled inside her, toward her pelvic bone, and he began massaging the bundle of nerves that sat against her vaginal wall, while his thumb ravaged her clit. He increased the stroking and pressure until he had her at the crest, and she'd be unable to hold back.

"Come, sweetheart," he whispered through a kiss. His tongue plunged into her mouth, imitating the action of his fingers. She moaned into his mouth as her soft folds clenched around his fingers. He waited until the spasms ebbed, then slowly withdrew his fingers, pinching her clit to draw out the last few shudders.

Kneeling, he quickly unbuckled the ankle cuffs, then reached up and undid her wrists. Her body went limp and her head fell onto his shoulder. He scooped her up into his arms and headed for the oversized chair at the foot of the bondage bed. Taking the soft flannel blanket from the chair's back, he settled her against his chest and draped the blanket over them. He tucked her head under his chin and held her tightly, shifting her off his painful erection.

Slowly, her breathing eased and her body mimicked sleep. He stroked her hair and kissed her forehead gently, enjoying this moment of closeness. They sat that way for a while until her breathing changed. Her head popped up.

"Oh, Daniel, I'm sorry. Did I fall asleep?" Her eyes blazed in the candlelight and damp tangled tresses of hair fell over her eyes. He pushed the long locks off her face and kissed her lips gently.

"No, little subbie, you hit what we call subspace. Honestly, I'm shocked you got there on the first try. I'm delighted." She sat up straight and the blanket fell from her shoulders baring her beautiful round breasts.

"Subspace? I did read about it, but I wasn't exactly sure what it was. It felt like that orgasm took me outside of my body. Damn awesome."

"From my vantage, I think you liked it well enough." Even in the dimness, Daniel could see Alyx flush.

"But, what about you? Aren't I supposed to return the favor?"

"I'm pleased you offered, but no, not at this point." She shifted on his still-hard dick and contemplated.

"But you must be uncomfortable?"

"I'm not a teenager Alyx and my body doesn't get everything it wants whenever it wants it. I will wait until you are properly prepped." Alyx seemed confused and Daniel decided she'd had enough for one night. He reached over to the small refrigerator and opened the door. Retrieving a water bottle and a plastic container of cut watermelon, he popped each lid and handed Alyx the bottle. "Here, you need to hydrate." Alyx emptied half the bottle. "Good girl." He settled her back onto his chest, snuggling her tightly. "Open your mouth." He fed her chunks of watermelon, alternating between her mouth and his.

"Wow, I've never loved watermelon as much as I do this very minute."

She gaped at him with her beautiful azure eyes. "You're a rare beauty, Alyx." She definitely blushed that time and his heart galloped.

Danielle led Alyx back to the second floor, still wrapped in the soft flannel aftercare blanket. Opening the green room's door, he flicked on the light and two bedside lamps blazed to life. He pushed gently on the small of her back and ushered her inside. "Take care of what you need to in the bathroom. I'll wait and tuck you in."

Daniel sat in the jade-green wingback chair in the corner. He leaned his head back, crossing his arms and legs. The toilet flushed, water gushed from the bathroom faucet and a moment later Alyx returned to the room, still wrapped in the subbie blanket. "Lose the blanket, you're to sleep naked," he ordered. He turned down the covers and waited for her to slide in between the crisp white sheets.

He gazed quickly at her flawless body and had the urge to climb in next to her. Pulling the covers up to her neck, he sat on the side of the bed and leaned over, placing a hand on either side of her shoulders, effectively trapping her between the sheets. She appeared so innocent, contented. She rewarded him with a dreamy expression.

"You okay?"

"I'm just so, *wonderful*."

"Good. I enjoyed tonight. You did really well."

"You're a good teacher," she said, her smile widening.

"Honestly, I'll admit I was worried. This isn't exactly the way it usually works. I had to keep reminding myself you aren't really my sub." He brushed the hair back from her face, leaned in and stole a kiss from her. The warmth of her lips, and the sensation of her tongue dancing with his, threatened his control. He'd better leave before he got in trouble.

"I'll come for you at eight," he announced. "We'll throw some weights around in the gym and then go for a run. I usually do three miles, how about you?"

"Three is fine."

"Good. Sleep well." He gave her a quick peck on the lips and made his way out of the green room. He turned before shutting the door and they shared a silent knowing interlude.

Readying himself for bed, he gazed into the mirror over the master bathroom sink and sighed deeply. His mind was still in the rec room. He'd been surprised and pleased at both Alyx's enthusiasm and responsiveness. When he met her at Jack's last night he never imagined tonight would play out the way it did. Remembering how much she'd struggled to keep her mouth shut made him grin. Perhaps he should introduce her to the gag. He wasn't all that fond of gagging his submissives, but she might force him into it with her smart-ass mouth. He pulled on his dick, still struggling with his erection. And her sweet offer to give him some relief, shit, he hardened even more. He should have taken her up on that offer. Tomorrow. Tomorrow he'd take her. From the front, from the back, shit, every way he could.

Okay, he needed a shower. He needed release.

Exiting the bathroom, he pulled down the covers on his bed and sat on the edge. He leaned his forearms on his knees and stared at the parquet floor. *Eyes on me*, he said in his head. The memory of her gazing at him made his arteries throb. He wanted to touch her slick skin again, hold her in his arms. He pushed himself up off the bed and ambled toward the French doors leading to the balcony overlooking the ocean, and flung them open. Leaning on the railing, he inhaled the briny night air and closed his eyes. Her vanilla scent lingered in his head.

The sounds of waves rolling onto the shore spoke to him, the tide's ebb and flow like chapters of his life. He'd never thought very far into the future. He'd always fixated on the immediate; school, football, his career, his patients. Daniel inhaled deeply, the cool ocean breezes clearing his head. What would his life be like in twenty years? He had so much and yet sometimes he felt his life had no meaning. He shook his head. Jesus. He was getting morbidly philosophical. What brought that on?

Lying in bed, he stared up at the ceiling's black abyss, then his vision drifted rightward. The moonlight coming through the panes from the balcony doors made square patterns on the far wall and he counted them, like he did every time, even though he knew exactly how many were there. A little ritual he couldn't stop no matter how many times he tried. Rubbing his face with his hands, he inhaled deeply and let it out slowly, then parked his palms behind his head. He wondered if his little subbie had fallen asleep, and how beautiful her face would be in the throes of dreamland. The thought of her so close, and yet so far, felt like pure torture.

Chapter 3

Sunday

Daniel's phone alarm pulled him from the rec room, where his dreams had him fucking Alyx on the bondage bed all night. He'd run his tongue over her glistening skin, her breathing labored, her luscious mouth screaming his name when they both climaxed. His heart pounded in his chest and he was drenched in sweat. His dick stood at attention, again… or still. He couldn't remember.

He glanced at the clock: 7:45 a.m. A fast shower.

Dressed in a gray wife-beater shirt and black gym shorts, he raised his knuckles to the Green Room door and knocked, but walked in before she said, "Come." Boy, did he ever want to, and right inside her sweet spot. She stood in the bathroom doorway, her toothbrush all sudsy in her mouth. "Just a minute, Sir," she mumbled through the foam, putting a finger up.

He stared. Everything she did was delectable. Her cute little ass was hidden under tight black spandex shorts, her breasts molded into perfect mounds inside a fitted purple tank-top. A pair of tortoise shell sunglasses sat wedged in the V-neck of her shirt. Exiting the bathroom, her open shoelaces trailed across the beige carpet. "Almost ready, Sir," she said, now seated on the bed and reaching to tie her shoes.

Daniel walked over and knelt. "Here, let me do that." He placed her sneakered foot on his thigh and tied the lace into a perfect bow. Both shoes tied, he pushed himself between her legs and pulled her in for a kiss. A surprise expression crossed her face. "Come on, let's go." He secured her hand in his and led her from the bedroom.

Daniel pulled two water bottles from the fridge and handed one to Alyx. "Let's hit the gym for thirty minutes, then we'll go for a run. Do you need to eat something first?"

"No, if I eat before I work out, I'll puke."

Daniel grimaced. "Let's try to avoid that. I've seen enough vomit to last a lifetime."

"Sorry, I have a habit of being rather blunt sometimes."

A blonde, older woman walked into the kitchen, shrugged off her jacket and hung it in the kitchen closet. She smiled brightly. "Good morning, Sir."

"Good morning, Lydia, how are you today?"

"Very well, Sir, thank you."

"Lydia, this is Alyx Cameron, the houseguest I mentioned."

"Of course, so pleased to meet you, Miss Cameron." Lydia extended her hand.

"Nice to meet you, Lydia," Alyx said, shaking her hand.

Lydia wrapped an apron around her waist. "Breakfast, Sir?"

"A bit later."

"Very well, Sir."

Daniel ushered Alyx from the kitchen, down a hallway on the east end of the house, then through a dark paneled door to reveal a well-appointed gym. A Cybex circuit, including a leg press and a squat rack occupied the room's right side. Weights stacked on a metal rack waited on the far wall and a large open area with bright red matting filled the center of the room. Black and yellow TRX ropes hung from the ceiling.

"My other torture room," Daniel said, raising his eyebrows in amusement.

"Oh joy. I just crave torture, Sir."

"Don't tempt me. I could have you naked and trussed up in here before you knew what happened."

"No, thank you, Sir." Although the flush in her cheeks said differently. "I prefer to torture myself for the moment."

"That could be breaking one of the rules I planned to outline at breakfast. No self-pleasuring." For her, that is, he'd already jerked off twice since her arrival. Thankfully, that would change shortly as he planned to have his dick buried inside her before noon.

"Why would you make such a ridiculous rule?" she said sardonically.

"Because I want you frustrated and I want to control all your pleasure while you're under my whip."

"Fine, you're the boss." Alyx huffed and went to the squat rack, putting two twenty-pound plates on each side.

"That's a lot of weight," Daniel observed.

She ignored him, obviously displeased with his comment. "Is Lydia your housekeeper?"

Daniel stacked weights onto the leg press across from the squat rack. "Yes, Lydia's married to Mason and they live in the cottage on the east end of the property. Lydia manages the inside of the house and Mason handles the outside and takes care of the cars. They're both off duty by eight, with few exceptions."

Daniel watched as she got into position, resting the bar low on her neck and then dropping her sweet ass toward the floor. Her thighs proved seriously muscular as she pressed them into service, although, at rest, and last night, he hadn't noticed them to be overly large. Daniel couldn't take his eyes off her. "I think tomorrow I'll have you do that without your workout clothes." Alyx gazed intensely at his image in the mirror. She did a set of twelve and he let her finish, not wanting to distract her further.

She clanked the bar back onto the hooks securing it and exhaled loudly. "Like hell," she said to his image in the mirror.

"What did you say, little subbie? Need I remind you that other than between the hours of noon and four you are completely under my command?"

Well, she'd momentarily forgotten that. But no way in hell she'd be working out naked. How could she distract him from this thought? He loomed behind her, his expression angry. What had she said to make him mad? Then she noticed he wasn't observing her image in the mirror, instead his worried eyes focused on her bare shoulder.

He touched the spot with his forefinger. "What's this?" he demanded, his voice too harsh. Uh-oh. She'd forgotten about it because she really couldn't see it unless she forced herself to look in the mirror. She bristled.

"Please. You're a surgeon, I'm sure you know full well what it is." She guessed he hadn't noticed it last night under the rec room's dim lights. Or perhaps he'd been too involved with other things. Her belly clenched in that weird way just thinking about their evening session. On the trip here she'd tried to distract herself with music and mundane thoughts, and although she'd never admit it to anyone, she'd been downright terrified. But then he'd been so gracious, a gentleman—offering her wine and talking with her like he actually cared about how she felt. The whole night had been filled with the forbidden. And then, in his playroom, the first lesson in being a submissive, well, *off the charts hot!* And that amazing orgasm! And she'd thought she'd have to fake it.

Alyx released the bar from the safety rack again and let it fall onto her shoulders, but Daniel grabbed it, returning it to the metal latches. He put his warm finger on the mark again and pressed.

"Of course, I know what this is," he snapped. "What I really want to know is how you got it?"

Alyx sighed. "I don't want to talk about it."

"Was I not clear about the honesty issue between a Dom and sub?"

"Well, Daniel, I'm not really your sub now, am I?" her voice too loud. "We're just playing some kind of sordid game, aren't we?" The pain darkening his face hit her like a club to the solar plexus. Holy shit, she'd hurt his feelings. He pulled his finger away from her shoulder as if he'd touched a hot stove. Their gazes met in the mirror. "My bad," she said. "I didn't mean for that to sound the way it did. I-I, just, well, after this week we'll both go back to our lives and this whole thing will fade. You'll probably have a huge laugh about it with your buddies at the club."

He reached out and turned her to face him, the cold metal bar between them. "Is that what you think? That I don't give a shit about what we're doing? I take this stuff seriously, even if you don't."

She might as well be adrift at sea with no way of finding her way to dry land. "Daniel, we've only known each other for one day. Most people wouldn't even consider us acquaintances." He didn't respond, not that she'd actually asked him a question. Silence hung between them.

"Alyx, it's not like we simply bumped into each other at a coffee shop and struck up a conversation about the weather. I think the quality of the time we've spent together in the last twenty-four hours moves us up a few rungs on the friendship ladder, don't you?"

Alyx knew he was right. How had she gotten herself into such an uncomfortable situation? Daniel had been nothing but wonderful to her and she had to confess that, so far, the sex had been absolutely mind-blowing. She'd miss it when the week ended, well, maybe not the anal stuff, they hadn't gotten to that yet, and she still hadn't figured out a way to avoid it.

"You're right, Daniel. I didn't mean any of that. I guess, when this whole assignment is over, I'd be glad to consider you a friend." Geez, now, maybe she'd gone too far? What if he misunderstood and thought she liked him as husband material or something? She presumed him to be commitment phobic, being still single at his age, which she guessed had to be mid-thirties, and if he felt her closing in on him he might freak out. Good God. Why was she having this conversation in her head? She'd only just met the guy.

Daniel sighed and ran his fingers through his hair in obvious frustration. "Are you going to tell me how you got shot, or not?" His dark brown eyes were sad and emotion welled up inside her. He reached underneath the bar separating them and pulled her into his chest. "Please, Alyx," he mumbled into her hair, "tell me."

She cringed inwardly before pushing away from his embrace. He held onto her shoulders, refusing to let go. "It was a huge fuck-up and got my partner killed," she said quietly. Gathering her emotions into a tight wad, she tamped them back into her gut. "A raid, sort of like Waco, only on a smaller scale. We closed in on a skinhead gang and things quickly got out of control. There had to be at least twenty agents involved and even with our body armor we lost an agent. Four of us got hit. My partner took a bullet in the side, under his vest and it pierced a lung and lodged in his heart. I ran for him and took three shots myself. If not for my vest, I would have taken two bullets square in the chest. The third one bit my shoulder."

Daniel clutched her tight. "It's out? The bullet? It's not still in there?"

"They got it out."

"Fuck, Alyx, the thought of you injured is ripping out my guts."

"Could've been worse. I was out of the hospital in a few days. The rehab was a bitch, however." Daniel squeezed her so hard she couldn't breathe and she finally pushed herself away from his warmth. "My boss was pissed. Not only did he lose an agent, but he reamed me for breaking protocol." She hesitated. "You probably find that ironic." She peered up into his face. "At least he didn't spank me," she said trying to lighten the mood.

"Perhaps I'm doing Agent Scarborough a favor then. Look at how disciplined you'll be when I send you back to him." Turning her back around, he slapped her hard on the ass and pushed her back under the bar. "All right, little subbie, enough talk, back to work."

They finished their workout and then headed out into the bright fall sunshine. The unseasonably warm weather portended another beautiful day and Alyx inhaled the briny ocean air and sighed. "I love the ocean. I forget how much I love it sometimes."

"I feel exactly the same. Sometimes I spend so many hours in the hospital I don't get a chance to breathe fresh air enough. Coming home to the ocean refreshes my spirit."

"Couldn't agree more."

They headed east on Dune Road, passing the occasional biker or runner waving a friendly hello. Their footsteps pounded the macadam and Alyx had to run at a faster pace than usual to match Daniel's long-legged stride.

Back in the kitchen, the wonderful aroma of coffee greeted

her. Lydia was setting the outdoor table. Daniel led Alyx onto the deck and pulled a chair out for her. "A true gentleman," she said, seating herself under the umbrella. Daniel sat beside her, picked up the coffee carafe and poured Alyx a steaming cup. "Oh," she chirped, pouring the hazelnut concoction into her coffee. "My favorite creamer."

Lydia asked Alyx what she would like for breakfast and she settled on peach Greek yogurt with granola, her favorite. Daniel had scrambled eggs and dry whole-wheat toast. They both had fresh squeezed orange juice.

"Everything to your liking?" Daniel said as they dug in.

"Perfect. I can't believe you have all my favorites."

"You see, Agent Cameron, like you, I do my homework." Daniel flashed her a mischievous grin.

She narrowed her eyes. *What did that mean?* Her thoughts drifted to the rec room last night, had it merely been coincidence that he played her favorite music? And now the yogurt and creamer?

"What do you mean, homework? You found out my favorite foods? And what about the music? Was that part of your spying, too?"

"Yes, I confess to it all."

"But how?"

"Your boss put me in touch with Matt. He sent me these…" Daniel picked up his phone, scrolled through the screens and handed it to Alyx. Photos of the inside of her refrigerator clearly showed hazelnut creamer, yogurt and granola. The next photos included images of her iPhone playlist. Top 25 Played had its own photo. "He also told me you wear the same size as his wife, which he knew from the time you fell in their pool and she lent you clothing."

Daniel winked and disappeared behind the newspaper. The same image she had of him on arrival. Alyx grabbed the top of the paper and pulled it down, forcing him to pay attention.

"Are you fucking kidding me? You sent Matt on a 007 mission? That's pretty bold, Mr. Hot-shot Detective."

"*Dr.* Hot-shot Detective, if you please," he corrected her playfully.

So, Alyx thought, Matt had visited her house that afternoon under the guise of being concerned, when in truth, he'd embarked on a sleuthing mission for the illustrious and bossy doc. Wait until she got hold of Matt, she'd kick his adorable little ass all the way down 9th Avenue. But her anger quickly faded and she glowed inwardly. She knew Matt really had been worried about her and this gave him an excuse to check on her. She should be flattered Daniel had gone to these lengths to assuage her.

Daniel reached for the chair beside him and retrieved a gift-wrapped box. "Here, for you."

Alyx accepted the package and stared at Daniel, open-mouthed. "What in the world?"

"Open it."

She untied the pink ribbon and tore at the paper imprinted with fuchsia rosebuds. Carefully unfolding the delicate paper, her eyes fell on a scanty red bikini.

"For our swim later," Daniel said. "The ocean's still warm in September. I know how much you enjoy swimming in the big blue. I believe you had to cancel a certain outing with friends this weekend."

And how did he know that? Alyx shook her head. She didn't want to know who else in her inner circle had spied for Daniel. Alyx didn't know what to say. She'd never had a boyfriend who moved heaven and earth to please her like this. And he wasn't even her significant other. As a matter of fact, this whole thing had gotten weird and way too personal, something she hadn't anticipated at all. She wanted to ask him why-

why-why, but didn't know how to phrase it without coming off like a bitch.

"Thank you, it's lovely," she said through tight lips. They finished breakfast and Lydia cleared their dishes.

"Okay," Daniel said, folding the newspaper in half. "I said at breakfast I'd outline my other expectations and protocols. So, let's get that taken care of."

Alyx swallowed the last of her orange juice, when the lump lodged in her throat. She gripped her coffee mug and leaned back in her chair, pulling her knees into her chest. Perhaps last night had been a ruse to lull her into a false sense of security. And things were about to take a severe left turn toward Painville.

"I promised we'd work on your attitude about anal sex," his expression serious, scary even.

"But," began Alyx.

"Exactly, your delectable butt. We need to get to work on that right away if you're going to be ready by Saturday." Daniel crossed his arms over his muscular pecs and his heated glare made her insides somersault.

"I don't think I want, what I mean is there are limits to what I can…"

Daniel interrupted her whiny plea. "Let me pay you the favor of being blunt. You have no idea how dangerous this could be for you if you go into this decoy situation unprepared. Have you ever seen the results of anal rape?"

Actually she had, what a horrible sight. She mumbled, "Only once. The guy was dead."

"In some ways that might be a blessing. The amount of damage done by forcible anal rape is devastating. And the surgery to repair the damage is worse. Anyone who's had rectal surgery will attest to the fact that it's about the worst pain imaginable. My mother had a simple rectocele repaired during her hysterectomy and she was screaming and biting towels in the bathroom for a week. There wasn't enough pain medication I could give her to thwart that kind of pain without totally knocking her unconscious."

Alyx winced at Daniel's words. This wasn't doing much to get her interested in letting him shove anything up her ass. The blood drained from her face.

"I didn't tell you this to frighten you."

"Yeah, well I'd hate to hear what you'd say if you wanted to scare me," she snapped.

"I want you to think past this moment. You plan to put yourself in the clutches of some serious sadists. I don't think the club will be much of a problem unless you're there for an extended period. But the minute those slavers have you, you'll be at their mercy. There's no preventing them from assaulting you the minute they have you. And if you're not prepared you're going to get seriously injured."

Alyx remained silent, still unconvinced.

"Okay, let's move off that tack and head in a different direction. We'll take it slow and I'll bet you a hundred bucks that by the end of the week you'll be singing a different tune. Trust me, in my capable hands you'll find it much more pleasurable than you imagine."

"Well, it's not like I have much of a choice now, do I?"

"Finally seeing the light," he said, rising from his chair and extending his hand, "it's only eleven, that's one more hour on my time and I intend to make good use of it. Let's go."

Daniel tugged Alyx by the hand and up the stairs to the second floor. "I'd prefer to take a shower before we…"

"No shower," he said cutting off her attempt to stall. "We'll take a swim after, that's if you want to. By then, we'll be on your time so it's up to you. We'll shower after that."

We'll shower? He didn't plan on showering with her, did he? That certainly shouldn't be part of the required training. This whole situation confused the hell out of her. She hadn't anticipated all this personal stuff. She thought she'd just have to submit to his torturous attentions in the playroom, but then he'd go about his business and she'd be left alone. She'd downloaded a bunch of books on her e-reader and figured she'd catch up on her reading. It was Sunday, so by tomorrow that would most likely be the case. He'd be off to work and all this weird uncomfortable attention would vanish.

"Let's leave our sneakers and socks here," he said, slipping his off and parking them inside his bedroom. He knelt and untied the laces on hers, "Up." She lifted her foot off the floor and he yanked one sneaker off, then a sock, then proceeded to the other foot. He set her Nikes next to his. For some reason Alyx couldn't take her eyes off the paired shoes on his boudoir's floor. They seemed so *normal*, like they belonged together.

Daniel opened the magic doorway to the rec room and pushed Alyx in front of him, nudging her derriere up the stairs. It felt like a hundred degrees from the intense morning glare flooding through the glass picture window. Daniel ambled toward the window and pulled the shades down. He walked over to the thermostat and rotated the knob to the left.

"It'll cool off in a minute."

Plummeting the temperature to zero wouldn't cool the blood boiling in Alyx's veins.

"Off with those shorts and go stand by the bondage table," he said, giving her a scornful look. Exactly what she didn't need. She already feared she might combust. "Don't look so terrified. Trust me."

Alyx wanted to. Hell, she did trust him. But she still couldn't seem to move her bare feet toward the bondage table.

"Alyx," he barked. "We're effectively doing a scene here. I need you back in protocol."

"Yes, Sir." But she still hadn't moved.

Daniel pivoted to the black lacquered cabinets and

dropped mystery items into a metal bowl. Her stomach did that somersaulty thing—again. He faced her. "Are you a child? Must I undress you myself?"

"No, Sir," she said, reaching for the waistband of her shorts. She slid them down and stepped out, then tossed them onto the chair where Daniel had held her and fed her watermelon last night.

"Might as well take off the shirt, too. I intend to take you up on last night's offer."

Her offer? What had she offered? She couldn't remember. Damn.

Alyx pulled the fitted top over her head and dropped it onto the chair alongside her black spandex shorts. Totally naked. In broad daylight. Yikes. The room, still unpleasantly warm. Daniel grabbed the bottom of his gray tank top and pulled it off in one quick motion and cast it atop her workout clothes. Alyx feasted her eyes on his well-toned chest and muscular biceps. He looked just scrumptious.

"Let's go, little subbie, over by the bondage bench. Face the wall and bend over."

Everything between her legs *clenched*. She faced the slatted blinds and settled her upper body over the black leather upholstery. The leather's coolness felt good on her inflamed skin. Daniel came up behind her, still wearing his shorts. He placed the metal bowl on a small table. Alyx couldn't see what was in it, which was probably for the best. Her pulse raced, her heart pounded. Dampness formed between her legs. This shouldn't be turning her on, should it? Let's just get this over with.

Daniel caressed her bare buttocks. He pinched and rubbed her skin and her vagina tightened in response. "You've got the cutest little ass, pet." Her arteries contracted, expanded in a cadenced beat. Good thing she was sprawled across this bench, she doubted her knees would have supported her. Her nerves careened, a tremor prickled through her.

"I'm going to restrain you. Remain still." Daniel leaned over her, his warm chest flush against her back's bare skin. Grabbing one hand he placed it over her head and buckled it into the restraining cuff attached to the table's right-hand corner. Then moved to her left hand and snapped the cuff shut around that wrist.

"Good girl," his lips near her ear. He nipped the sensitive lobe, raising a tingle inside her. "Give me a color, sweetheart."

"Gr-ellow," she mumbled. "Green, halfway to yellow."

"Do you think humor will save you from my evil ministrations?"

"Unlikely, Sir. Something about you seems to bring it out in me." She squeezed her eyes shut, too tightly, expecting admonishment, maybe even a swat on her ass. Daniel kept quiet and she wondered if he thought she was making fun of him. Perhaps she was. She had to stop baiting this man, her teacher.

Standing, she felt him slide his warm hands down her thighs, then grab her ankles and spread them wide. He secured them in the leather restraints on the table's legs, leaving her exposed and vulnerable.

Powerful hands caressed her bottom, his touch light. "People often make jokes when they're afraid of something. But you'll enjoy this, Alyx, trust me," his voice low and rich. For some strange reason the sound of his words relaxed her. "First you'll feel my finger." Her throat went dry and her stomach flipped over.

"You're thinking too much," he said softly. "Let yourself feel, Alyx, clear all thoughts." He gripped her hip with his hand and held her firmly. She felt the cold drizzle of lube between her cheeks and stiffened. The muscles of her anus puckered tightly and she squirmed. A stinging slap made her jump.

"Do. Not. Move," he said. His hand stroked the place he'd slapped. Her arousal dampened the insides of her thighs. The touch of his finger up and down the crack of her ass made her shudder with excitement. His thick finger pressed against her anus. She wanted to escape, and as if he could read her mind, he clutched her hip tighter. A warning. "Now push back against my finger, you need to relax, Alyx, or this will become a bad, bad memory." He swirled the tip of his finger around the tight ring of muscle and then slipped it in. Alyx gasped. "Hush." His finger slid inside her, in and out before the shudder had left her body. Pushing his finger in and out a few times, he added another finger, continuing the thrusting motion. She tried to twist away, but his other hand said no.

"I'm going to enjoy taking your sweet ass before the week is out, little subbie." A shockwave of arousal ran through her. He pulled his fingers out and something cool touched her skin. "Push back," he instructed. She whined as the butt-plug stretched her open. His grasp on her hip kept her from moving away and he eased it slowly inside. Wider and wider. She groaned and pushed her forehead into the cool black upholstery.

"Almost there, baby," he said, twisting the plug in a circular motion. And was it? Could it? It was in! He rubbed her bottom reassuringly and her clit throbbed. She groaned too loudly. Never would she have thought anything back there would arouse her, and embarrassment rushed through her.

Daniel laughed and his sneering notes delighted her. She squirmed under his grasp. He wiggled the plug and sparks of electricity shot straight to her clit.

"You're a lovely woman, Alyx. I like the feel of your bare skin, so soft." She felt the stroke of his hand and the heat of his body as he pressed his groin into her backside. "And now we'll have some fun with this inside you."

He leaned over her again and unbuckled her wrists, then crouched and released her ankles. Sliding an arm under her stomach, he flipped her over and reattached her wrists. In one swift move, he clutched the undersides of her knees and positioned her feet on the table, spreading her legs wide. All the breath fled her lungs.

"Keep your legs in position or I'll restrain them," his authoritative voice said. He removed his shorts and his erection sprang free. Her eyes widened and her brows shot up. She prayed he didn't notice. Impressive, she thought, *too* impressive. Just like the rest of him.

He traced lines up and down the insides of her thighs with his long fingers. Her stomach fluttered. "Look at me," he said ever so softly. He smiled wickedly. "I've wanted to bury myself inside you since you smart-mouthed me in Jack's office the other night. I nearly bent you over the arm of the couch and fucked you right there in front of your boss."

Alyx released a pent-up breath and then bit her lip. She wanted to say something smart-alecky but refrained. She needed to stay in protocol and stay quiet unless he asked her a question.

He grabbed his dick and placed it at her vaginal entrance, swirling it around in her wetness. Slowly, he pushed inside her. Huge. She didn't know if it was simply him or because she had that thing inside her. "You're so fucking tight, baby." Leaning over, he kissed her, then pushed all the way into her with one brutal thrust. Alyx yelped. He felt so good inside her. The warmth of his mouth, the flick of his tongue, distracted her from the odd feeling coming from the plug. Reaching down he pinched her clit as he slowly moved in and out. Incredible sensations. Indescribable. Her clit blazed with ecstasy. He continued to circle the tight bundle of nerves with his thumb and the sweet agony pushed Alyx toward the crest. Her breathing became ragged, leaving her panting.

Daniel kept up the slow torturous rhythm, driving deeply into her slick center. "Feels so good," he groaned. Alyx's insides quivered. "No, not yet, baby. You don't have permission to come." He rotated his hips in a rolling motion, then pulled out and plunged into her, burying himself to the hilt.

"Please," Alyx cried. "I can't control this any longer, Sir."

"Yes, you will. This is all about control, Alyx. You wait until I tell you," he growled, his breath labored.

Alyx's head hit the wall behind her as Daniel picked up the rhythm, pounding into her. He leaned over and grabbed the top of her head to cushion it from slamming into the wall, then covered her mouth with his and their tongues danced that sexy tango again. Alyx's insides trembled. All control, fleeting.

Daniel continued. Relentless. Her insides burned. He reached down and twisted the plug and Alyx screeched. Would she have to beg?

"Now baby. Go," he rumbled in that sexy-as-hell voice of his.

Alyx climaxed loudly and Daniel followed with two sharp stabs before releasing himself into her. He collapsed on top of her, their hearts pounding in syncopating rhythms. "Fuck," exclaimed Alyx, heaving a mighty sigh and trying to force air into her lungs. "Fuck. Fuck. Fuck. Sir." She'd never vocalized that loud during an orgasm. Never.

"Fuck is right," Daniel murmured, breathless himself. Without looking, he deftly released her from the restraints. Alyx wrapped her arms around his back.

"It's only Sunday." Alyx whimpered. "I'll be dead before the end of the week at this rate," she sputtered. "...Sir," she added as an afterthought.

Daniel chortled. Pulling out of her, he kissed her again

and then stood. "I like a noisy woman. I didn't think you'd be a screamer."

"I'm not," Alyx muttered. "Or, I wasn't." Her face flushed, she averted her gaze.

"Then I would say things are going splendidly. So far." She still couldn't make eye contact with him.

"Stay," he said, then walked to a wall-mounted square white box next to the black cabinets. He popped open the door and grabbed something. She felt the warm washcloth between her legs as he gently cleaned her. He folded it and then wiped himself. He landed the cloth inside the metal bowl, then sat her up. The plug pushed deeper inside her and she squirmed.

"Oh, geez," she mumbled, punctuating her words with a squirm.

"Don't worry, you won't be thinking about it for long."

"You mean I have to leave it *in*?" Alyx's eyes widened.

"Until I replace it with a larger one."

"No way," she screeched. "What if I have to go to the bathroom?"

"No need for embarrassment. Tell me and I'll remove it and then, put it back." Words evaded her and she knew she had absolutely no recourse. Daniel picked her up by the waist. "Do you know how fucking adorable you are right now?" Well, again, no words.

"How's your head?" he said, rubbing the top affectionately. "I didn't mean to knock you into the wall like that." He kissed the top of her scalp.

"Like I said, at this rate I'll be dead by Friday." Alyx smirked at him. "Sir," she added.

"Aren't you a riot? Come, let's take a swim and we'll shower later."

There was that 'we'll shower' again. She must be mistaken; he probably meant they'd each shower in their own bathrooms.

Although, the thought of running her hands over his soapy broad shoulders and massive biceps, over his taut stomach and steel-like buns, threatened to arouse her all over again. What the hell was happening? She'd become some kind of a sex-crazed slut.

Like an exotic tropical vacation, far away in another land. She and Daniel swam in the deliciously warm ocean and sunbathed on the deck. Lydia served them grilled shrimp on arugula for lunch and she'd made fresh lemonade plus roasted peaches for dessert. Daniel spent a few hours away from Alyx as he attended to phone calls and messages in his at-home office. Four o'clock, and her free time neared its end. Her skin prickled at the thought of what he'd demand of her tonight.

"I'm going for another swim," he said, his deep voice coming from above. "Care to join me?"

"Definitely," she said, rising from the cushioned lounge chair.

"I think you've had enough sun for one day," he chided. "I don't want you to get burned. Did you put sunscreen on?"

Oh, she was getting burned, but it wasn't from solar radiation. Too much sex. So much screwing had scorched her to a crisp. "Yes, I used sunscreen," she answered snidely. Throwing her sunglasses on the chair, "I'll race you in," she screeched, and sprinted for the shoreline. He had to take off his tee shirt and topsiders, which gave her a few seconds edge. Just as her toes hit the ebbing water she felt two arms around her waist and he tossed her over his shoulder. Alyx squealed. "You son-of-a-bitch. Put me down."

"I'll never let you beat me, little miss I-can-do-anything," he yelled playfully. He crashed through the surf then heaved her into the air and she fell screaming into an oncoming wave.

Alyx wiped the water from her face as she surfaced. Daniel's happy face popped up in front of her as they bobbed up and down in rhythm with the rolling sea. She felt sixteen again, romping in the ocean on a beautiful summer day, frolicking with her surfing pals. For a moment, she almost forgot where she was and what lay ahead.

Her chest rose and fell rapidly, her breath labored. "I almost beat you."

"Not even close," he said and chuckled. They floated blissfully on the waves for a while, the bright sky and brilliant sunshine only added to Alyx's contentment.

Returning to the deck, they toweled off and Daniel reminded her, "Back on my time, little subbie." He flashed that sexy smile of his and Alyx's insides swirled into a mass of jingling nerves.

"Yes, Sir."

"Let's shower and I think we'll play in the TV room tonight."

"Fine, Sir." The TV room? Was that the room she'd first met him in? Maybe he'd make her watch porn. She'd watched some with Jason, and the first ten minutes were usually kind of hot but then it got gross. No doubt in her mind these movies weren't made for women. They had no storyline, no excitement of the chase. Just lots of genitals going in and out of various holes, and in really unflattering light. Not romantic in the least.

"I need some time to wash and dry my hair. Is it all right if I'm back in say an hour?"

Daniel furrowed his brow. "You're showering with me."

Alyx gave a matching frown. "But, surely that isn't part of the training I need for this assignment."

"I know. It's just for me." His smile made her squirm. Again, she thought this weird. Why was he doing this to her?

Daniel grabbed her hand firmly and marched her through the kitchen and up the stairs to his bedroom. Definitely not going the way she'd planned, thought Alyx. His behavior had become entirely too familiar, too intimate, in a different kind of way.

In the middle of his huge bedroom, she wore her damp red bikini. Daniel went directly into the bathroom and she heard the spray of water from the shower. He waited in the doorway, "Come," he beckoned. Alyx remained transfixed. She should tell him no. Except, technically, she was on his time and under his control. But, this seemed too much like a relationship and just, well, *wrong*.

Slowly, she inched toward him. He stepped in her direction and pulled her into his chest. He deftly released the string behind her back and slipped her bathing suit top off, letting it fall to the ground. Her nipples hardened. "You have magnificent breasts, my dear," he said in a throaty voice. "I could play with them all day." Each hand cupped a breast and he massaged and squeezed them until it became almost painful. His touch ignited flames on her skin. "I love seeing you naked," he murmured near her ear and she sucked in a breath at the touch of his lips. Her core kindled into a furnace and she tilted her pelvis toward him reflexively. She wrapped her hands around his shoulders and let them drift down his taut back and over his firm backside.

Their lips met in an urgent kiss, and she felt herself sinking into the deep end of the ocean, the swirling rip current threatening to drown her in a sea of emotion. She shouldn't be letting herself enjoy this so much. Her heart swelled with desire, but also something else. Something terrifying. Thankfully he broke their embrace and tugged her toward the shower. Using both hands, he pulled the side strings of her tiny bikini bottom and whipped it off her. "Ta-da," he said with a boyish grin.

Alyx laughed. She hadn't anticipated him being so playful. He did keep calling it play, when she'd totally expected mean and scary. *Pain.*

"In you go," he urged, opening the glass doors of the shower and shoving her inside. Alyx had never seen a shower like this. The jets came from every direction, assaulting her body with stinging precision. She screeched, covering her sensitive breasts with her hands.

Daniel immediately came to her side and wrapped her in his strong arms. "Too much stimulation for your tender skin?"

"Torture," she squealed and Daniel reached and moved the knob to the left so the water's intensity decreased. She inhaled deeply and let it out, then relaxed.

"Better?"

"Much." Daniel grabbed the body wash from the shelf and squirted it into his hand. He came around behind her, and pushed her hair off her back, slinging it over her right shoulder. Massaging the soapy lather into her shoulders and neck, his expert touch worked the muscles until she felt like her body had turned to jelly. He continued slathering her body with soap, moving over her backside, down her thighs, circling around her stomach, eventually landing on her tits. Alyx pushed them up into his wide palms, her head falling back against his chest.

"You like my hands on you," he mumbled.

"Yes," she said in a throaty voice, "Sir."

"And I like them on you." He nuzzled her nape.

"Mmm," she murmured. She could sense the dampness between her legs even in the shower. His erection poked into her butt and the thought of him entering her from behind made her pulse thrum.

"Breathe, Alyx," he reminded her for like the twelfth time since she'd met him. She was afraid to breathe, she was so close to coming she feared if she didn't hold everything tightly together she'd shatter into a million pieces.

He turned her around twice, letting the spitting jets remove the soapsuds from her skin and a small wave of dizziness set her off balance. Daniel trailed his hand down her stomach and rammed two fingers into her vagina. Alyx gasped loudly and everything inside her exploded in a rush of heat.

"Bad girl," Daniel growled into her ear. "You did not have permission to come." Alyx couldn't answer as her body trembled with the last shudders of her orgasm.

After she calmed, she muttered, "Sorry, Sir. I-I, you snuck up and I couldn't concentrate."

"Hmm… well, I'll have to add a few more swats onto your spanking tonight."

Ugh, she'd forgotten all about the promised spanking. And she'd totally lost count of how many swats she'd supposedly earned. No way. She wouldn't let herself be subjected to that humiliation. Although isn't that what she'd said about shoving something up her butt?

Daniel washed her hair and his finger's soothing strokes on her scalp felt incredibly erotic. Shit. Was there anything this man did that wasn't sensual? Other than at a salon, no one had washed her hair since she'd been a little kid. The only one she could remember doing it was Greta, their housekeeper.

Alyx returned to her room in one of Daniel's white tailored shirts. He wouldn't allow her underwear for the rest of tonight, he'd said. Alyx protested, saying she didn't want to walk around in front of Lydia and Mason without any underwear on, but Daniel had pretty much told her to stop whining. She dried her hair and applied blush and mascara, and left her hair down, arranging it in curls that cascaded over her shoulders. She felt feminine in a way she'd never experienced before.

Lydia made them Fettuccine Carbonara for dinner with cold asparagus in a light vinaigrette dressing. Daniel lit the candles on the table then poured two glasses of a delightful Pinot Noir, which he actually served slightly chilled. They ate at the outdoor table and watched the sun set together. Seagulls soared across the darkening sky, their discordant cries disrupting the ocean's peaceful mood.

Finished with dinner, Lydia cleared their places and they sat a while longer, sipping their wine and talking about the general state of world politics, getting into a serious discussion about the absurdities of America's dysfunctional Congress. Lydia came back out and said her goodnights. Alone with the handsome doctor now, she wondered what playing in the TV room would entail. Not knowing what he was going to do to her raised her anxiety level up to red. He was so damn good at keeping her on the edge of arousal.

"Ready?"

"Yes, Sir."

"Good girl," he said, rising from the table and extending his hand.

Daniel escorted Alyx into his den. She looked sexy as hell in his white shirt and yet he couldn't wait to rip it off her. She was so fucking responsive and he needed to teach her more control. She'd climaxed too easily in the shower and her orgasms wouldn't be as satisfying if he didn't let the tension build sufficiently before allowing her release. Any Dom worth his salt knew that, and it would be his challenge tonight.

"I thought the room where I met you was the TV room? There's a TV in there," Alyx said.

"That's the living room. This is where I usually hang out on the rare occasions when I have time."

"Oh."

"I recorded *60 Minutes*."

Relief was on her face, as she said, "I thought you were going to make me watch porn."

"Why would I be interested in porn when I have the real

thing to play with?" As soon as the words left his lips he knew he'd screwed up.

Her face flared with anger. "What the fuck?" she began. Daniel put his fingers over her lips before she gave him a huge tongue-lashing, one he totally deserved, and besides he had other intentions for her tongue tonight.

"I'm sorry. That was a terrible thing to say. I meant it as a joke but I realize it was totally insulting. The reason we're doing this is for the greater good. I promise I won't lose sight of that."

He secured her hands in his, uncurling her fisted fingers, lacing his through hers. He tucked them into his chest. "Please, Alyx, don't be mad. It was an asinine thing to say, even in jest."

Her eyes softened and she sighed. The fire in her eyes quelled. "Fine. But be careful, mister. You're in sensitive territory. As much as I'm a willing participant, don't for one second compare me to a hooker or porn star. If we were in a real relationship, none of this shit would be happening."

"I get it," he said, pulling her hands to his mouth and kissing her knuckles one at a time. But he wasn't entirely sure truth lingered in her words. Perhaps she enjoyed this more than she was willing to admit to herself. Her eyes had darkened, but quickly lightened and his heart sped up. He needed to move away from this line of thought and fast.

"I'm going to have a scotch. Want one?" Daniel released her and walked behind the bar. He pulled out a bottle from the shelf and perched it atop the shiny gray marble.

"Why not?"

"How do you like it?"

"Lots of ice and a little water," Alyx said, perching herself on a bar stool.

"Great minds think alike." He poured about three fingers of the golden liquid into old-fashioned cut-crystal glasses and filled them with ice. He splashed in an inch of water from the nearby tap and swirled the contents of both glasses with his long index finger. "Suck," he said, putting his finger on her sexy full lips. Alyx wrapped her lips around his wet finger and slurped the oaky liquid off. "Practice for later," he said with a wink. Alyx flushed crimson.

Handing her a glass, he ushered her toward the black leather sectional couch facing the sixty-inch television screen. He picked up the remote and selected the title from the DVR menu. Daniel sat and patted the cushion next to him and she complied. "Normally, as a submissive, you would kneel at my feet."

Alyx sipped her drink. She placed it on the brown leather-topped coffee table a little too forcefully, her brow knitted. He knew she was about to give him a ration of shit about what he'd just said. Great, he'd pissed her off twice already tonight, things were going downhill faster than a speed racer. "You have permission to speak freely until we start the scene, then you're back in protocol."

"Seriously?" she began.

Here it comes, thought Daniel. He braced himself.

"At your feet? On my knees? On the floor? While you sit comfortably on the couch? That's absurd. Who would find that acceptable behavior?"

"Alyx, I'm not going to keep arguing with you about why these behaviors are satisfying to both parties, and I'll emphasize that again, *both parties*, it simply is, and either you're going to comply or not. When you're at the club, you will most likely be kneeling at your Dom's feet whenever you are not actively participating in a scene. When you're not, and your Dom wants to leave you alone for a few minutes, he'll chain you to the floor in the submissives' waiting area."

"What are they? Cavemen?" she said, then added a sigh. She hung her head in her hands.

"Be quiet," he said too seriously, "the show has started." He put his arm around her and pulled her in close and their debate ended for the moment. He'd decided one thing for sure, he had to bring her to the club one night in order for her to grasp the significance of what would be expected there. He didn't seem to have much success convincing her what acceptable behavior would be for the club. Tomorrow, he'd call Jack and Rob Scarborough and inform them of his plan. The club only opened Thursday through Saturday, and he wanted to give her a wake-up call, fast. Thursday, it would be then.

Alyx snuggled under his arm, her head on his shoulder, occasionally reaching for her drink and then returning it to the table. "Oh," she said, abruptly sitting upright in response to a commercial. "The new James Bond movie. I'm dying to see it. It just opened."

Daniel was thankful her mood had improved. "A fan of the Bond man, huh?"

"I love spy movies. They're my favorite. *The Bourne Identity, Mission Impossible*. I can never get enough."

Daniel marveled at her childlike enthusiasm for the movies, then settled her back on his chest with a hug. She felt so right in his arms, so flawless, the perfect mixture of lethal woman and errant child. The closing credits scrolled across the screen and Daniel flicked off the television with the remote. He picked up a different control and pointed it at the wall's red electronic eye. The lights lowered and music emanated from the surround-sound speakers. Alyx startled, then composed herself.

"Smooth move, Sir."

"Lose the shirt and I want you on your knees in front of me. You're back in protocol. Is that clear?"

Alyx swallowed hard and the pulse in her neck throbbed in response to his commands. This was the key, he needed to keep her off kilter, a little more fear, she definitely responded appropriately to his authoritative tone.

"Answer me," he barked.

"Yes, Sir," she said and jumped to her feet. She reached for the hem of his white shirt and quickly pulled it over her head and tossed it on the couch. Sinking to her knees, she immediately assumed the slave position, her hands upturned, her eyes fixed to the floor.

"Excellent. Do not move." Daniel rose and walked to the entertainment center and opened the drawer where he'd stashed his toys and a towel earlier in the day. She turned her head slightly to catch a glimpse of him. Nervousness oozed out of her. Perfect. He stopped behind the bar and ripped a paper towel from the dispenser.

Behind her back, he laid the over-sized white bath towel across the coffee table, then reseated himself on the couch and placed his toy bag on the floor. He pulled his blue polo shirt over his head, placing it on top of his tailored white shirt. He opened the top button of his jeans, his erection threatening to escape the confines of the denim. Alyx's eyes remained focused on his bare feet. The heat wafting off her felt like a smoldering fire.

"Eyes on me," he commanded, sitting on the edge of the cushion. Her sweet face shifted upwards, her eyes dark blue again, like the ocean. He rested his chin on his steepled fingers.

"First, you will get the spanking I promised, and instead of it being a punishment spanking it will be for fun and should heighten your arousal for what comes next. Tonight we're going to play with toys, Alyx, and then I will fuck your mouth." Her body stiffened. Somehow he doubted what she said about not being good at oral sex. He couldn't imagine her lips on him would be anything but divine. Taking hold of her shoulders, he ran his fingers over them and then down the outsides of her arms. A tremble passed through her.

"When you are at the club, spankings and the use of butt plugs are common practices, so there will be no way to avoid them, the same goes for oral and anal sex, which I explained to you earlier. Toys are also popular and I will attempt to introduce you to as many as I can before the week is out. I will also tell you which ones to avoid. And that goes for ball gags and the use of anything sharp—no blood or chemical play, you're too inexperienced and I doubt you'd like them anyway. Those should be hard limits for you. Understood?"

"No problem with that, Sir," she affirmed.

"Right answer. Do you have a vibrator at home?"

"No, Sir."

"Why? I thought most women had one in their nightstand."

"I don't know, Sir. I just never got around to getting one."

"Then this should be quite a treat and I'll let you take it home with you." He couldn't read her expression. Terror or excitement? Perhaps both.

"But first you get a new plug, which will enhance your enjoyment when I spank you." He knew her anxiety level was peaking. Good.

"On your feet," he commanded. She rose slowly. Grabbing her by the hips, he faced her away from him and pushed her toward the knee-high table. "Hands and knees on the table. Rest your head on your forearms, ass in the air."

Alyx climbed onto the towel atop the hard table and got into position.

"Excellent, now spread your legs." He helped her move her knees apart until her butt cheeks were open far enough. "The new plug is bigger than the one you have now," he explained. Using the paper towel he grasped the old one by its tail and pulled it out. "I think we only need to go one size bigger before I will be able to take your ass."

Squirting the cool lube along her crack, he gently stroked the slick gel around her hole. He ripped open the wrapper and drizzled lube over the plug then grasped it by its flat tail and pressed it against the ring of muscle. "Push back," he reminded her. He twirled it slightly and pushed it inside. Her gasp excited him.

"Good girl," he said, rubbing her beautiful ass cheeks with his hands. He could barely wait to see the red glow on her bottom from his imminent spanking.

He stood and slipped an arm around her waist and lifted her off the table. "Up you go, pet," he said. On her feet, facing him, he searched her face for signs of her mood. "You okay?"

"Uh-huh," she said unconvincingly. "Sir."

"Give me a color."

"Uh, gr…een.

"Good girl."

Daniel sat and took Alyx with him, slinging her over his lap and trapping her legs between his. He positioned her adorable ass squarely on his thigh and pushed her head toward the floor with his other hand. "Like Howie Day said in his apropos song last night—brace yourself. Put your hands on the floor." She squirmed and writhed on his lap and he placed his left hand over her back, pinning her in place.

"Sir," she yelled. "I don't want to do this. Please let me up."

"No, Alyx, this is something you have to endure. Trust me, I think you'll feel differently when I'm done." He rubbed and squeezed the soft skin of her beautiful ass to bring the blood to the surface. Alyx continued to squirm under his firm hold. "For a punishment spanking I would normally make you count. But since I've changed this to an erotic spanking I will decide when to stop."

He continued to massage her soft skin, running a finger down her ass crack, and giving the plug a little twist. Alyx squeaked in response. He rubbed his palm back and forth across the backs of her thighs.

"Please, no, Sir," she pleaded. "I don't want you to spank me."

His hand came down on the right cheek of her ass and she screeched. "Ow, that hurts."

"It's supposed to, Alyx. There's a fine line between pleasure and pain and I will find that line for you. If you relax into it, it will hurt less." His palm rested on her lower back, his legs immobilizing her. A whimper escaped her as she continued to struggle. The next swat hit her on the left butt cheek. She yelped. The third hit across both cheeks on the under curve. This time she stayed quiet. In between swats he rubbed her warm skin lovingly, letting her recover from the sting of each slap. After ten swats, he figured she'd probably had enough and he slipped his finger between her soft folds. Soaking wet. Delicious.

"See, baby, you're incredibly turned on. You're so wet, so slick. I can hardly wait to bury my dick inside that sweet spot of yours." His palm on her ass, he fanned his fingers out, tiny touches of his fingertips teasing at her quivering core. Rethinking his original plan, he decided she deserved a reward for enduring her first spanking. "I'm going to allow you to come now, Alyx." He worked his fingers over her clit, stroking and pinching the tiny nub until she purred. Thrusting two fingers inside her he felt her clench around his fingers and her panting breath told him she was there. "Let it go, baby." Her arms wrapped around his leg and she pressed her face against his calf and groaned. The heat of her mouth nearly sent him over the edge.

Drawing out the last few shudders from her, he pinched her clit once more and then placed his hand on the flaming skin of her ass and gently massaged her cheeks until she calmed.

"Fuck," she muttered against his leg and the hairs on his calf prickled.

Reaching an arm around her waist, he settled her on his lap. Tears drifted down her face and he rubbed them away with his thumb, then kissed her wet cheeks.

"I'm so proud of you." He hugged her tightly to his chest and kissed the top of her head. He waited a minute then reached for her chin. Tipping her head back, he kissed her. The salty taste aroused him further and he probed the depth of her lush mouth with his tongue. *Shit.* She made him so hot. He didn't know how long he'd be able to last before driving his dick into her.

Alyx's heart pounded so fiercely against her chest it threatened to erupt. First the butt plug and now a spanking. If anyone had tried to convince her either of these would be such a turn-on she would have laughed. Well, probably not actually laughed. But Daniel had been right. He'd sent her to heights she'd never attained. She had no idea. There were orgasms and then there were *Orgasms* with a capital O. Shit. With two of her past boyfriends she'd never even had one tiny orgasm and faking them had gotten tedious.

"You, okay?" Daniel whispered against her eyelashes. Alyx shivered at his warm breath. She pulled back and clasped his face and drew him in for another kiss. The man sure could kiss. She could spend all day with their tongues intertwined.

Breaking their kiss, he said, "I'll take that as a yes." His face wore a playful frown. "Be careful, sweetheart, you're topping from the bottom."

Well, that was the problem with this Dom/sub stuff, she thought. When did the woman get a chance to do what she wanted? Admittedly, blindly following orders was a huge turn-on, but on the other hand she'd like to be in charge once in a while. "Sorry, Sir."

"Okay, up you go. I want you on your knees again." He placed one of the throw cushions from the couch in the space between his bare feet and pulled her down to face him.

"Unzip my fly and take my cock out," he ordered. Alyx blanched. This wasn't a skill she felt all that confident about. And he was fucking huge compared to the last guy she'd done this for, and that had taken so long she'd nearly gotten lockjaw. She braced herself for disappointing Daniel. She'd give it her best shot, but doubted it'd end happily.

The thought of having her luscious mouth on his dick was all Daniel could think about right now. He gazed upon her pretty pink lips. So fucking sexy. Images of her hot mouth on him had him reeling. Alyx managed a shaky smile, then slowly slid down his zipper and reached in with her hand, freeing him. He suddenly realized he'd skipped the toy lesson. Overanxious. He should be ashamed of himself, but he decided to shelf toys until later.

"Start with your hands. However you like." Since his little subbie wasn't all that secure about her oral skills, rather than tell her what to do, he decided to wait and see what she'd do on her own.

Alyx's saucer-sized gaze stared at his erection's length and thickness. She furrowed her brow, then wrapped her small hand around his girth and applied the slightest pressure. She brushed her thumb over the bare head. *Sweet Jesus*, her hand felt so good on him. She squeezed him and stroked her thumb around the head's ridge and his dick pulsated. Her other hand grabbed him lower and she began a rhythmic stroking, up and down, increasing the pressure until he nearly came. He had to reach out and stop her. Must slow things down.

"No more hands, baby, just use your mouth," he said with what little oxygen he could find. He concentrated on slowing his breathing down. *Pace yourself, man.*

"Yes, Sir," she mumbled, but didn't move. She looked deeply into his eyes and made him wait. Insane torture. He didn't know if it was intentional, but the girl was fucking tormenting him.

She leaned in and braced her hands on either side of his waist and he slid down farther on the couch, resting his head against the back. The dark waves of her hair cascaded over his thighs and he grabbed it and twisted it into a spiral and held it. He didn't want anything to interfere with his vision of her lips devouring him. The tip of her tongue licked him and he groaned. His hips lifted toward her face and sweat broke out on his forehead. He closed his eyes, her sweet warm breath had him straining toward her. Balling his free hand into a fist, he struggled to keep from thrusting his hips up and ramming himself down her throat. Her tongue stroked the sides and over the tip until the relentless tempo of her attentions had him writhing. She sucked hard and he feared he'd explode in her mouth.

"Jesus fucking Christ, Alyx. Enough." He grabbed her by the shoulders and pushed her off him. Her glistening, swollen lips nearly sent him over the edge.

"I'm sorry, Sir," she began.

"Jesus, woman, don't say you're sorry. You're fucking great at this. Whoever told you that you weren't should have his head examined. And he didn't deserve you."

Her face softened and her eyes brightened. "Come here, you little vixen," he said, pulling her to her feet. "Straddle me."

He held her hands and she settled herself over him, a knee braced on either side of his hips. "Now, down. You're in control of how fast and how deep you take it."

Their fingers laced together tightly and the sight of her lustful eyes on his face made his dick throb more. She made him wait again, her hot wet flesh poised over him. *You're killing me here, Alyx.* She didn't seem particularly innocent at the moment and he worried that giving her control might encourage her to top him even more than she had already. When had he lost control of this scene? This had the makings of a tactical disaster. But what the hell, let her have a little control. He certainly didn't want to dampen her enthusiasm now that he had her more confident. Of course, if this was for real, instead of this ridiculous game they'd subjected themselves to, he'd be more than happy to give her the reins. *Well, once in a while anyway.*

Lowering herself, she didn't hesitate, sinking her weight onto him with one quick thrust. His dick pulsed as she squeezed around him. Their clasped hands tightened as she moved up and down, the rhythm building. She paused momentarily at the top, then followed with a hard-downward thrust.

"Fuck," he groaned, closing his eyes to concentrate on the sublime sensation of her velvet sheath surrounding him. "Hold onto my shoulders," he ordered. Her small hands gripped his flesh, her fingernails biting into him. He reached behind her and gave the plug a twist.

"Fuck," she cried. He twisted it again as she continued riding him. Daniel seized her hips and pulled her down, down, thrusting himself deep inside her. They moved in a pounding rhythm that seemed to go on forever. She had stamina, and a warmth, no, a heat, a fire, that threatened to consume his sanity.

He opened his eyes and found her staring at him. Her pupils dilated and she grinned. "Oh, goddamn," she yelled, her breaths short and ragged, her cheeks flushed the same pink color as her ass.

"Come for me, baby." He gasped, and she clenched around him and cried her release. With one final plunge, he exploded inside her. Daniel growled as the shudders from his orgasm roiled through him. An incoherent mewling escaped his little subbie's sweet lips. Jesus, she fucking blew him and then she blew his mind. His dick twitched inside her as the spasms from her soft core sucked him dry.

"Jesus, Alyx, you're killing me," he sputtered. She collapsed against his chest, circling her arms around his back. Her heart fluttered against him like the wings of a humming-bird. He stroked her hair with one hand and her back with the other. His dick still throbbed inside her and she pulsed around him with tiny intermittent aftershocks.

He didn't want to let her go. Ever. Wrapping his arms around her tightly, he held on as if someone was about to swoop down and steal her away. *Sweet Jesus, he was in serious trouble here.*

Alyx decided she was dead. Yup, he'd finally killed her. She'd never walk again. Yet Daniel's arms around her felt so safe, secure. No one had ever made her feel like this before.

"You okay?" Daniel said near her ear.

"I'm either in heaven," she said. "Or hell."

Daniel's robust laugh rumbled in his chest, making her smile. "I'm not sure this was much of a lesson. I think maybe I let you have too much control." *Oh yeah*, she thought. *That'll teach him that I, too, am a force to be reckoned with.* But she decided to keep her mouth shut, for once.

Removing her head from his chest, she pulled back and put both hands on either side of his face, then leaned in for a kiss. Daniel eagerly responded, his tongue searching and caressing the inside of her mouth. His dick twitched inside her and he pulled her down tightly to his lap. He stroked the side of her face, smoothing her sweat-soaked hair. She almost purred.

When their breathing arrived in the normal range again, he scooted them both to the edge of the seat cushion. Taking the towel from the coffee table he pulled her off his lap and used it to wipe them both clean. He settled her against his chest and leaned back, perching his feet atop the coffee table and Alyx settled her legs on top of his. The soft crooning of Frank Sinatra floated on the airwaves.

"You like Ol' Blue Eyes?" Alyx asked, draping her arms over his as they trapped her breasts in a sort of embrace.

"I do, not all the time, but in the right setting. You?"

"Couldn't have said it better myself."

They sat quietly like that for a while, basking in the after-glow of what seemed more like lovemaking than it should have. Alyx's mind swirled in a whirlpool of scenarios. Could she really be falling for this guy in just a few short days? She needed to rein in her emotions and guard her heart. She knew enough biology to understand that all the orgasmic oxytocin and dopamine flooding her system could easily trick her into believing more was going on here. When it was business, a temporary arrangement.

Daniel settled her into bed like he had the night before. It left her with an odd confusion. Sort of like when her father used to tuck her in, so tight she could hardly breathe. Her father made it a challenge each time, telling her he'd secure her so tightly that no one could steal her away in the night.

This entire experience with Daniel overwhelmed her in so many different ways. His authoritative, controlling, almost fatherly demeanor was kind of fucked up, while other times he acted playful, childlike.

What game was he playing?

Chapter 4

Monday

Daniel knocked three times on her bedroom door and entered. She should have set an alarm. "Time to get up, sleepyhead," he chided her. Sitting on the bed's edge, he slid his hand under the covers and tweaked her nipple, making her yelp. "You're sleeping on *my* time, little subbie," he said, leaning down and giving her a quick kiss on the lips. "Time to get our blood pumping, then we'll have breakfast."

His dark eyes seemed playful, happy. She wanted his body on top of her, the weight of him pressing her against the mattress, like an electric blanket on a cold winter day. But then she frowned in confusion.

"Two spankings for your thoughts?" he said, mirroring her expression.

"Isn't today Monday?"

"Yes, why?"

"Don't you have to go to work? Save a few people?"

"No, I took the entire week off. Did I neglect to tell you that?"

"Yes, you most certainly did," she said, thumping her hands against the bed.

"Oh, so you thought you'd have a respite from my attentions during daylight? Well, little subbie, I hate to disappoint you, but you're wrong. I'm here for you twenty-four, seven. I bet you can't wait to see what torturous activities I have planned for today." He peaked his eyebrows playfully and every nerve ending south of her navel clenched.

Well, she hadn't calculated him taking vacation time. 168 hours of Dr. Taylor's ministrations. Well, originally, she'd considered that a nightmare, hours upon hours of pain-laden kinky antics, and she'd been terrified. But now her insides trembled for a different reason.

"Ten minutes," he snapped, getting up. "I want you in the gym, stat. Don't be late, or I might have to lash you right there on the inclined bench."

"Oh, hell no," she screeched as he tore the covers off her, exposing her naked body to the cool morning air. Her nipples hardened, but not only from the sudden chill.

"Not only will I, I'll thoroughly enjoy it." His smile exuded wicked eroticism. "Countdown's started," he warned and then left, closing the door behind him.

Alyx jumped out of bed and beelined for the bathroom, grooming and dressing while keeping a close eye on the clock. She made it into the gym with about twenty seconds to spare. Daniel glared. "Close call, little subbie. Now that you've ruined my fun, I'll have to think up some other rule for you to break. The consequences will be delicious."

"I think last night convinced me to stay on the straight and narrow, Sir."

"Bullshit. You can't convince me you didn't like it. Every.

Single. Minute. I distinctly recall your arousal. Besides, I'm the Dom and I can do whatever I fucking want."

Alyx shook her head but kept her mouth shut. She couldn't bring herself to admit that on some fucked up level she sort of enjoyed getting a few swats on her ass. Yet she really didn't want him to do it again. Did she?

They finished their workout, then ran the agreed upon number of miles before a leisurely breakfast on the deck. The day proved a bit cooler than expected and Daniel gave her one of his Boston College sweatshirts to keep her warm while they ate. He told her that he'd attended Boston College on a scholar-athlete award for football. Halfway through his sophomore year, however, he'd decided the school was too small and the remote location depressed him. He eventually transferred to Boston University.

Daniel's phone rang. Rob Scarborough was checking on Alyx's progress. Daniel explained that outside of her tendency to top him every now and again, things were going reasonably well. He explained that it was imperative to give Alyx some sense of the club before her debut because when she observed what really went on there it might be too much. They agreed on Thursday night and Daniel said he'd call Jack and arrange for her to get one of the "meet and greet" tours for interviewing new members. Daniel would be there, but they'd make it seem like they met at the club. Daniel handed Alyx his phone, "You have an admirer."

"Hi, Rob. Yeah, so far we haven't killed each other. Yet." Alyx laughed and winked at Daniel. "No, you don't need to come on Thursday. Daniel said he'd keep an eye on me. I'll see you Saturday." She handed the phone back to Daniel.

After breakfast, they swam in the ocean and sunned themselves on the deck for a few hours. "I never take this kind of time to hang out and enjoy life," Daniel said. "It's a bit strange, almost like I'm on vacation."

Alyx removed her sunglasses, gazing at the beautiful man lying next to her on the cushioned lounger. Right on, doc, this felt weird and wonderful. "Honestly, this is nothing like what I thought spending a week with you would be like."

Daniel gazed at her. She put her sunglasses back on. "You thought you'd be tied up in my dungeon like a prisoner?"

"Some version thereof," she said. "I don't know, I'm not sure what I expected. Definitely more pain."

"You see, Alyx, again this is all about pleasure, pain is just another aspect of pleasure, providing it's used properly by an experienced Dom."

Alyx still wasn't sure about that. The flogging had been intense but she didn't find it distasteful, actually it had heightened her excitement more than she wanted to admit. Although, she was beginning to think that reading the phone book with Daniel would ignite her erogenous zones.

After spending the afternoon swimming and lounging on the deck they showered separately and Daniel told her to meet him in his study. She found him behind his desk, staring at his computer monitor. "Come here, doll face," he said, crooking his finger. Daniel called her so many nicknames she couldn't keep up. She'd never been a real fan of those cutesy monikers people used. Her father had never called her anything but Alyx, or Alyx Lynn, which he invoked mostly in a fit of annoyance.

She stood alongside Daniel as he casually leaned against the backrest of his chair, his white tee shirt stretched by his incredible musculature. Before she could see what he'd booted up on the screen, he pushed his chair back and pulled her onto his lap. "We're going to go through the things you will refuse. Obviously, these are things I don't approve of, so I don't have them in my playroom. Therefore, I can only show you this stuff online."

They spent about an hour surveying really twisted paraphernalia and she couldn't understand why he'd have to tell her this, she'd never go along with such creepy and dangerous things.

"Of course," Daniel said, "no whips, no canes, and there's this device that holds your mouth open so you can get face-fucked for a good long time, don't let anyone put this on you." The image made Alyx cringe, reminiscent of the facemask that Hannibal Lector wore. She nodded as a shudder wracked her body.

He shifted her on his lap and looked her in the eye, holding her tightly. "Do not let anyone suspend you from the ceiling unless you can bear some weight on your toes, it's too much stress on your shoulders, no blindfolds until you're more experienced, hopefully you won't get that far, and absolutely no ball gags. They strain your jaw and make you drool, which means your Dom has to keep wiping your chin unless he gets off on the sight of you slobbering."

"Sir," she said, her voice soft. "I'm glad you didn't show me this stuff the first minute I arrived or I would have been out the door so fast your neighbors would have sworn the Roadrunner just flew out of your driveway." She smiled weakly.

"Now, now, little subbie, that would have been unwise of me, wouldn't it?" He gave her a reassuring squeeze around her shoulders.

"I guess Rob picked the right trainer, it scares the shit out of me to think who I could have gotten stuck with."

Daniel's laughter rumbled, soothing her. "Now I'm worried that you consider me too soft. I just might have to do something about that tonight." He gave a dark, wicked grin and her insides tightened.

He warned her that the slavers could very possibly secure her in a dog kennel. Realization hit. So many ways this could go bad. He warned her again that if she spent any length of time in these slavers' hands they could brutally assault her and she began to suspect he might be trying to scare her out of completing her mission.

No way, doc. These women must be saved.

Lydia made them skirt steaks smothered in sautéed mushrooms with stir-fried broccoli and potatoes stuffed with ham and onion. A heart surgeon eating red meat? But Daniel convinced her that it was only a problem if you had cholesterol issues. He didn't.

Eating in the dining room tonight, she felt seriously underdressed in Daniel's white shirt. He didn't allow her much clothing and at first, she'd found it awkward, but now a certain liberated vibe expanded in her, especially with the no underwear rule. Hmm, if she lived like this all the time, laundry would be an afterthought.

"Wine?" Daniel said, bringing her back to the present.

"Please."

"So, tell me about your parents. You said you grew up in Westhampton Beach as a kid. What did your parents do?"

Alyx sighed. She didn't want to get into this. Too many bad memories that she'd long ago buried.

"Did I say something wrong?" Daniel said, taking a sip from his wine glass.

"You? No. It's just that… I don't know…"

"You don't have to tell me, but I'm here."

Alyx considered his offer to avoid tumbling down her rocky memory road, but then she went for it, "Well, honestly, I didn't know much about what happened between my parents until my father died. I was eighteen. My mother left when I was three and I never got a straight answer from anyone about what happened. They simply said she'd run off. No reason why, not that she ran off with another man, or she had a nervous breakdown or anything." Alyx cut a slice of steak and put it in her mouth, chewing, swallowing.

"So it was only my dad for all those years. We had a live-in housekeeper because his job took him away for long periods and sometimes he had to leave on the spur of the moment. He told me he worked for an oil company and he was the guy they called for global emergencies.

"I was a freshman at Columbia when one night a man showed up at my apartment and said he needed to speak with me. He identified himself with CIA credentials. Probably unwisely, I let him in. I'd no idea what he could possibly want. He told me he worked with my dad and had sad news. My father had been killed while on assignment in Libya and my dad had made him promise that in the event of his death he'd personally deliver this letter to me. I took it pretty hard, and this man, his name was David, stayed with me all night and talked to me, explaining as much as he could. He let me cry on his shoulder and held me for what seemed like hours.

"The letter explained so much. My mother left because she couldn't stand being married to a man who was away so much and who, one day, might not come home at all. Originally, she thought she could handle it, but once I was born the reality of being hitched to a covert agent paralyzed her and she simply packed up and left.

"He left me a ton of money and I used a good chunk of it to buy my apartment in the city."

"That must have been hard. Growing up without a mother and then losing your dad, too." He placed a hand on top of Alyx's and his pained expression saddened her.

"Twelve years is a lot of time. I've let it go." Alyx slipped her hand out from under his and sipped at her glass of red wine. Silence, like a dark cloud, hung over them.

"So, you went to Columbia University. What did you study?"

Alyx smiled at him, glad to be exiting her parents' sad story. "Actually, I started out as pre-med but got tired of memorizing all the formulas and scientific names, bored actually. My sophomore year I got interested in computers and considered systems engineering. Then I enrolled in a criminal justice course to fulfill my social science requirement and my professor got me all hot and bothered about a law career. I went on to Columbia law school and in my last year both the FBI and CIA courted me."

Daniel raised his eyebrows. "You have a law degree?"

Alyx glared. "Why does that surprise you? I'm not a stupid woman."

Daniel put down his fork. "I never assumed you to be stupid. Not for a minute. I admire you. I think you're smart and brave, perhaps too brave for your own good."

Alyx let her gaze fall into her lap, then picked up her fork and returned her attention to the delicious dinner Lydia had prepared, before continuing, "Well, anyway, both of the recruiters gave me the same line. I had areas of expertise in science, computers and law, which they found unusual and desirable. Plus, I spoke four languages. Languages came easy to me even before I went to college. My housekeeper wasn't your garden-variety maid. She spent a lot of time teaching me Russian and Chinese. Spanish and French I learned in school." Alyx laughed, recalling her crazy life with Greta, her surrogate mother, and a secret agent for a father.

"What's so funny?"

"I was thinking about my life with Dad. He was a crazy dude. He used to play this stupid game with me, our own version of *Mission Impossible*. I didn't know at the time how prophetic it was, or how close to reality. He must have had a ton of these ridiculous scenarios set up before he left, because sometimes, literally, he would get the call and be out of the house in fifteen minutes. Whenever he'd phone me, the music from MI would be the first thing I heard. He'd call me Agent Cameron and do the whole "should you decide to accept this mission and this message will destruct in the next five seconds." Alyx waved her hand in the air.

"My heart would start pounding. He'd give me instructions and I couldn't write them down, I had to remember them in my head. He'd send me all over the house and sometimes the neighborhood, on some ridiculous scavenger hunt, complete with clues, riddles, invisible ink, breaking into locked cabinets, all sorts of crazy. I loved it. In the end there'd be some surprise. A new article of clothing I wanted, or a book, or a video game. Something totally cool."

A certain sadness invaded Daniel at the tale of Alyx's childhood, one so different than his own. His parents sent him to a private high school and he found that many of his best friends didn't live anywhere near his home. He had friends here, but the difference of being a local who came home to his house after school every day he hadn't experienced. He'd gone to the Ross School during his elementary years and that was okay. In some ways his life was similar to Alyx's during those early years, he, too, came home to the housekeeper. His mother worked long hours at her practice and his dad, a busy corporate attorney, spent most weekdays in their New York apartment. He often wondered how his parents stayed together so long. Perhaps the cliché was true—absence made the heart grow fonder? When his father passed away last year his mother had been devastated. The diagnosis of pancreatic cancer had hit them both hard, and watching his father whither, with no hope of recovery, took its toll on Daniel.

"You're quiet all of a sudden. Did I depress you?" Alyx pushed her plate away.

"No." Daniel inhaled, exhaled. "Maybe a bit, but mostly I was thinking of my own childhood." Daniel explained his home life and his father's recent death. He hadn't really talked about it with anyone other than his mother, and Lacey. But somehow he found it easy to be honest with Alyx.

Lacey. If she knew what he was doing she'd kill him and he'd deserve her wrath. When he agreed to this he hadn't really considered it cheating, but more like a job. Lacey didn't tolerate anything about his former interest in the lifestyle and made him promise to dismantle the rec room. In fact, she'd levied that threat before she left for her Dubai business trip. But she'd be gone for another week and by then Alyx would be nothing but a memory. When he agreed to this arrangement he didn't have a clue that it would be like this. He'd originally thought Alyx was a pain in the ass, and truthfully he didn't think she'd actually show up, and then he predicted she wouldn't last a day.

Now what could he do? He'd just have to get through the week and then banish Special Agent Alyx Cameron from his psyche.

Daniel set his iPod into the rec room's speaker system and selected Alyx's *Top 25 Most Played* list. He stood in front of her and pulled her naked body into him for a kiss. He didn't recognize the song. As the lyrics filled his head, he said, "How appropriate. You taste like sugar. Who is this?"

Alyx smiled sweetly. "Match Box Twenty. The song is titled *Like Sugar*."

"Slave position," he ordered, pulling back from her warm, luscious body. Her smell drove him absolutely insane, to the point where he never wanted to shower again. Alyx sunk to her knees, shoulders squared, back straight, her upturned palms atop her thighs. She lowered her eyes and waited for his next command. *Perfect.*

"Tonight will be about endurance, Alyx. You need to have enough stamina to endure a scene for as long as your Dom expects. Think of it like acting in a play." Daniel crouched in front of her. "Eyes on me." Alyx raised her sparkling blue orbs to meet his. "I've been thinking about this a lot, and I've had a lengthy conversation with Jack. We're going to try and make it so that you work only with Doms we know. Since we can't blow your cover, we'll make it appear as if you're in training and will only work under the supervision of the guys employed by the club. If you're in training, there'll be more tolerance for any screw-ups, but you still have to be convincing."

She stared at him but didn't respond. Good, she was learning. "You may speak."

"I appreciate that, Sir, it eases my anxiety."

"I'm glad. Tonight I'm going to flog you again. But it will be more intense and last longer. This will most definitely be something you'll do at the club and do often." He got to his feet and extended both hands to help her up. The grasp of her warm fingers already had his pulse thrumming wildly. Why did she have such an effect on him? Almost unbearable. He wanted his hands all over her, his mouth following in the trails of his fingers.

He slowly positioned her heated body against the St. Andrews cross, his bare chest making contact with her back. Caressing her arm, he slid her petite wrist into the soft leather cuff and buckled it. His other hand slid up the outside of her thigh and followed the pathway to her breast. He squeezed and tugged on her nipple and she gave a little yelp. He smiled to himself. "You're so responsive, my sweet. I confess I had no idea you would be like this." She obediently remained silent. *Perfect, again.*

Grazing her nape with his lips, he nipped and licked his way to her ear. This time, she outright squealed and his dick twitched and pulsed. "Shush," he ordered. Jesus, he didn't think he would ever have enough of her and the thought that she'd soon be gone from his life nearly spiraled him into full-blown depression. He distracted himself with buckling her other wrist into the leather shackle. Pressed tightly against her, he pushed her body flush against the hard wood with the weight of his own. Sliding his hands up her restrained arms, he mimicked her pose. With her, he felt oneness. Or maybe he was merely a shadow, a shadow of her. Because he was nothing like this woman, she was too good for him. Was this admiration, or worship?

Peeling himself away from her warm flesh felt like he'd cut off his own skin. Gripping the flogger in his right hand, he snapped it in the air a few times. She didn't even flinch this time.

"Ready?

"Yes, Sir."

And he heard no fear, no apprehension, no anxiety. "Let's see how long you can last, baby."

He started out slow and easy, bringing her along gently. When the pace picked up and her muscles tightened. He moved in to assess her level. "Give me a color, baby."

"Green," she said breathlessly. He stroked her hair affectionately and gazed into her half-lidded eyes. He'd bring her there slowly, deliberately, passionately.

"Good, girl. Relax into it. Keep your muscles loose," he said before inching back and beginning anew. He worked her up to yellow, but had to stop. Not because she needed it to cease. He did. He couldn't make it through another minute of this torture. He needed inside her. *Now.*

The sound of the lash's snap, the feel of the stinging pain, the heat spreading across her skin. The startle… the thrill… the excitement… the arousal… the tingle… the breathing… the racing pulse… the sweat moistening her skin.

Heat. Snap. Sting. Searing fire. Snap. Sting. Heat. The pain, the pleasure, all blurred together. *Impossible to tell the difference.*

His soft hands soothed her flaming skin and the heat of passion became unbearable. His thick fingers pushed inside her and her cry of pure ecstasy escaped.

He let her come and she was grateful, because otherwise she'd have disobeyed when she exploded into a million pieces.

"Oh, baby, you were spectacular. I'm so proud of you." Alyx couldn't believe how satisfied she felt, both from the amazing, mind-blowing orgasm and the fact that she'd pleased Daniel. She couldn't let herself think how fucked up this was and how much she needed to make him happy. Yeah, fucked up, blissfully fucked.

"I need to be inside you, baby. I need it so bad." His lips pressed against her ear, his tongue slipped inside and she shivered. He groaned. "Right here, I'm going to fuck you right here strapped against the cross."

"Please, Sir," she whimpered, speaking without permission. She didn't care. She wanted him to force himself inside her so badly she'd beg.

Her legs still shackled into a wide V against the hard wood, he rammed his hard shaft into her. He held her wrists and thrust into her in violent pushes. She couldn't keep silent. "Oh, God."

"Yes, baby, let me hear you. Let me know how much you like this." His words shoved her near the edge and she didn't know how much longer she could hold back. Her vagina started to tighten and she sensed the wave coming, a tidal wave of pure ecstasy and she wanted it so badly.

"Please, Daniel, let me come. I can't hold out any longer."

"Not yet, baby. Resist." Their breaths came in a pounding syncopating rhythm, their cries merging into one lustful utterance. He pounded into her and she gripped the metal hooks, melding the shackles to the cross to anchor herself. She needed to hold on for dear life before she rocketed into the ceiling and disappeared into unconsciousness. Death by orgasm. What a way to go.

"Now," he ordered. "Come now, baby." And she did. And he did. It was the most incredible eruption of passion. Rivulets of sweat streamed off her body as every part of her throbbed. His breath landed heavy on the side of her face. He caught her chin in his hand. His tongue plundered her mouth as they both struggled to draw air into their lungs. The kiss ended, but his face stayed close, his nose pressed against hers. They remained silent like this for a pseudo-moment, suspended in time. And then he chuckled, little exhalations tickling her nose. She could sense his smile against her cheek.

"Fuck, Alyx, what are you doing to me? You've bewitched this jaded man."

Alyx struggled not to grimace. What the hell *were* they doing? This couldn't be, could it? Her heart fucking with her head.

They'd showered separately because Daniel needed distance after that mind-blowing sex. He'd said too much, sounded too much like Mr. Relationship. A bad move, and he knew it. Returning to her room, he tucked her into bed once again and headed toward his bedroom. A heaviness filled his chest. Thoughts of Saturday started to depress him. He couldn't decide what pained him more, the thought that she'd be gone from his house or fear of placing her into the slaver's sadistic murderous hands. Running his hand across the back of his neck he realized he'd been holding his breath, his pulse pounding. He should talk her out of this beyond-crazy danger.

He settled under the covers and stared into the abyss of

dark ceiling, his hands laced behind his neck. No moon tonight and he couldn't count the bright squares that usually dotted the wall. He let out a long breath and wondered if his little subbie had fallen asleep yet. The concept of her so close, and yet so far? Pure torture. He wanted her here next to him, but couldn't. This was business. He stared at the clock. Nearly midnight. Eight more hours before he could see her. Unexpectedly, his bed felt too big, too cold, he couldn't identify what had come over him. Until—loneliness. He wanted her warm-blooded body next to him.

Fuck it. Jumping out of bed, he ran down the hall and found himself standing in front of her door. Technically, she was still on his time and she would have to do whatever he wanted. He didn't have to explain himself. He was the Dom.

Knocking softly on the door, he pushed it open, hoping not to startle her. "Alyx, are you awake?"

"Yes," she whispered in the darkness.

Walking directly for her, he threw back the covers, scooped her into his arms and flung her over his shoulder. She gasped and squealed and he swatted her ass gently as he marched down the hallway.

In the dimness, he slid her off his shoulder and eased her into his bed, then snuggled in next to her and stretched the covers over them. She didn't say a word. He heard her every breath. He felt winded, but it wasn't from exertion. "Turn onto your side." She swiveled toward him. "The other way."

Wrapping his arm around her waist, he pulled her into his chest, tucked her head under his chin and inhaled the honeyed scent of her silky hair. Her body felt rigid against his. "Breathe, Alyx," he murmured into her ear. She exhaled slowly and he felt tension leaving her muscles. "And relax, we both need some sleep."

So much for putting distance between them.

Once again, he thought of Lacey. He'd only known Lacey

six months when she asked him to marry her. He'd never mentioned his **BDSM** involvement and had no intention of ever doing so until she'd stumbled on the rec room one afternoon. He'd been in there trying to figure out the best way to dismantle it before she moved in, when she unexpectedly showed up. That had been a nightmare of a day. She didn't speak to him for an entire week until he finally assured her he'd left that life behind.

Guilt pinged against his ribcage. He should've told Lacey what he was doing this week. But she'd already left the country and telling her on the phone seemed too risky. She refused to even entertain an exploration into any aspects of a kinkier sex life and he'd finally conceded that this was as good as it would get. She'd called him twice already, but he blew her off, claiming the connection was bad.

Besides, his little subbie would be long gone before Lacey got home. It was meaningless sex anyway, something she'd never understand.

Lacey was all about plans for the future. That would be good for him, he never mused about his tomorrows, and especially when it came to the wedding. She'd take care of everything and he wouldn't have to do jack. She already had the honeymoon all planned out—traipsing through Europe for an entire month, when actually he'd prefer parking his ass on a beach and playing a little golf or tennis. Lacey would never go for that. Heaven forbid she broke a nail or something equally dreadful.

And now this insanely amazing woman had come into his life and screwed with his head. Fucked his body, fucked it enthusiastically, openly, honestly. He kept trying to convince himself this was only the blush of new lust, the elixir of a sexy, smart, funny woman. Once the thrill of exploring Alyx's body faded he'd feel the same way he felt about Lacey, which was what? Jesus.

Did he really love Lacey? Perhaps he'd agreed to marry her for all the wrong reasons, figuring he'd screwed around long enough and needed to settle down.

The sound of Alyx's shallow breathing calmed him. She could drag him from exhilaration to tranquility so fast it made him dizzy, like free-falling from the stratosphere, rocket fast, then landing on a giant downy pillow. He squeezed her tightly against his chest, inhaling her fragrant scent and it almost sounded like she purred.

Chapter 5

Tuesday

Alyx squinted into the glaring sunlight beaming through the glass-paneled doors and covered her eyes with her forearm. She couldn't breathe, her neck secured under a heavy weight. Something even heavier was slung across her pelvis, pinning her against the mattress, something warm. She put her hand under the covers and felt the sinewy flesh of a man's leg. His slumbering face lay inches away. Little puffs of air crossed his full, thick lips and he seemed to be grinning in his sleep. She wanted to touch him, but chose not to wake him from peaceful slumber. Lifting her head slowly, she searched for a clock and spied one on the opposite nightstand. 8:47. Dr. Taylor had overslept.

In bed with him, both naked, her mind tailspinned and she struggled for oxygen. Gently, so as not to disturb him, she loosened his grip around her neck and sucked in a breath, then slid his muscular thigh farther down to rest across her legs. He stirred and she held her breath in anticipation of his rousing. He mumbled something, but she couldn't make out the words. What the fuck was she doing in his bed? He assigned her a room of her own and couldn't understand why he'd come back and carried her to his room like some caveman waylaying his woman.

She stared at the ceiling and smirked. Kinda hot, actually.

"Good morning, sunshine," he cooed, pulling her close, his arm around her waist. She startled, turned. His smoldering brown eyes made her belly tighten and memories of last night shot her pulse through the ceiling.

"Are you my kidnapper now?"

"I'd never target a federal agent."

"Do you ever answer a straight question?"

"Do you ever listen?" Damn, he had to be the best-looking man she'd ever met and definitely the best-looking man she'd ever shared a bed with. But she couldn't understand why he'd dragged her in here. This was a business arrangement, an assignment, albeit a strange one.

"What am I doing in *your* bed, mister?" she finally asked him.

"I don't know. The thought of you sleeping down the hall has been driving me crazy. I've been trying to talk myself out of it ever since you arrived." He shifted onto his back and stared at the ceiling and the loss of contact with his warm, hard body left her bereft. Pivoting toward her again, he asked, "Have I upset you?" He pulled her close and she felt his erection press into her hip. *Oh, man.*

Selecting her words carefully, she said, "No, I'm not upset. Maybe confused. Honestly, Daniel, when we first met I thought you really disliked me and that spending this time together would be dreadful." She scanned his face for a reaction, but he remained impassive. "But you've been so generous to me that I forgot all about that."

"I apologize for my behavior that evening. I acted like a

complete jerk. I was caught off guard and then you were so, I don't know, in my face, and I lost my wits."

"Well, my boss had a good laugh about it. He thought for sure I was going to deck you and he'd have to find another consultant to help him."

"You were having a bit of a tantrum." His hand moved to her breast and she abruptly lost all train of thought. He pinched her nipple and it hardened. His tongue touched her skin, moving toward her other nipple, trapped in the vise of his heated lips, he sucked. She couldn't suppress her whimper and closed her eyes and let the sensation travel downward, the force of suction pulling her toes into a curl. Abruptly, he withdrew and jumped out of bed and headed for the bathroom. When he returned, he said, "Your turn, and then get your cute little ass back in bed. We're going to have some fun." Pulling her by the hand, he swatted her backside and pushed her toward the bathroom.

She returned with minty breath, compliments of a new toothbrush on the counter, and slid between the sheets. He held her close and his lips grazed her ear. She squirmed away as goose bumps erupted on her skin. She giggled.

"Ticklish, again?"

He was propped on one elbow, his smile revealing perfect white teeth. He grasped her nipple again, taunting and teasing it unmercifully. She bit her lip to stifle a sigh before speaking. "Terribly," she answered. "And don't even think about going down that road. I have access to a firearm."

"My weapon is bigger than yours, Special Agent Cameron, and right now I have every intention of making you feel special, very special indeed." A sexy grin flashed across his beautiful mouth and her insides heated. "You're going to experience Honor Bondage. Ready?"

Honor bondage? In her Internet research she hadn't come across this term and had no idea what it entailed. Everything he'd done so far had made her feel like a lonely house-wife whose favorite movie star magically appeared and fucked her until her entire existence was one continuous *moan.*

"I don't know what that is," she admitted.

"Do you trust me?"

She didn't have to think about this, having come to the realization that she'd do anything he said. Which upset her. Ever since she'd been a toddler, she'd been difficult. She'd carried the "terrible twos" to an uncharted extreme, her father had often reminded her. Following someone else's direction and, God forbid an order, had always proved difficult. She liked to be in charge and do things her way. It had landed her in hot water a few times during boot camp at Quantico. Although on other occasions it earned her points for getting the job done unconventionally. And now she was willing to follow this man's commands without question, a man she'd just met?

Finally, even though she wasn't sure, she said, "I do, yes. Absolutely I trust you."

"Good girl. This is a way of showing that trust." He got to his knees and positioned her in the center of the bed and straddled her hips. His cock stood at attention in a sexy salute. "Honor bondage dispenses with the need for physical restraints. You are bound only by the Master's will."

Here she was again. Trying to assimilate what he'd said about the word slave and she could kind of, maybe, sort of understand what he meant, but the word master transformed her blood into ice. Intent on not spoiling the mood, she kept this thought to herself.

"Give me your hands," he ordered. He grabbed her by both wrists and raised her arms over her head, wrapping her fingers around the headboard's wooden spindles. "Keep them here. Don't let go, or *else.*"

His look darkened and her breath hitched. Another spanking? "Fine. Whatever. Just do it."

"Alyx, we're effectively doing a scene and you need to be back in protocol. Only speak when I ask you a question and address me as Sir. You do not have permission to speak otherwise. Is that clear?" His weight remained on her thighs, his cock brushing against her warm flesh. He'd morphed her into a wriggling mass of molten jelly inside of a minute.

"Yes, Sir," she mumbled.

"Good girl." He moved down farther on the bed and grabbed her ankles, spreading her legs wide. Exposed, vulnerable, restrained only by his voice and that scorching gaze. "Keep your legs here and the same command holds. It will be more difficult to keep your legs in position because you have no way of anchoring them. The trick is to stay completely still. Do you understand?"

Desire spread though her in a violent heated rush. Her voice shrank to a whisper. "Yes, Sir."

"Now, if you cannot stay still then I will restrain you, understood?"

Alyx nodded. The thought of being physically restrained heightened her excitement and she briefly thought of intentionally disobeying him so he'd have to tie her down. But no, she wanted to please him for some strange reason.

"Let me hear you, Alyx," he snapped.

"Yes. Yes, Sir."

"Good girl. Now close your eyes and stay perfectly still." Her eyelids shut tightly, she waited with unbearable anticipation. "Breathe, Alyx," he commanded. Damn, why did she keep holding her breath? Well, duh, because her primal mating instincts overrode the mundane urge to breathe. She forced out a long slow breath.

Daniel slipped a nipple into his mouth and sucked until it stiffened to a peak. Alyx groaned as the sensations sent quivers into her toes. "Quiet," he murmured, his hot breath igniting her flesh. She squeezed her lips together. Being quiet might be more difficult than keeping still. She wondered if being noisy would earn her a punishment.

Daniel's hand grasped her other breast and he pinched it while his mouth continued its assault on her nipple. He moved his mouth to give her other breast a nibble, then his kisses drifted over her stomach. The stubble on his chin prickled her skin and her hips rose off the mattress, squirming under the heat of his lips.

"Do. Not. Move." The vibrations from his words tingled her flesh. Too much like a threat.

Daniel sat up and couldn't take his eyes off his adorable little subbie. Jesus, she was beautiful. Her lips pressed together in an effort to keep silent and her eyes squinting like a little girl waiting for a surprise. And a surprise she would get. Something delectable.

"Pull your knees up." When she promptly complied, he grasped her feet and pushed her heels to either side of her ass. "Lift your hips." He slid a pillow underneath her bottom. Placing his hands on the inside of her thighs, he ran his fingers up and down their length, gently stroking the soft tender skin.

She sighed and mumbled, "Oh, God."

"Silence." Yet his lips quirked upward with satisfaction at her words.

She trembled under his touch. She was close to coming. What? He'd barely touched her. "You do not have permission to come, Alyx." His lips settled between the soft folds of her sex. He fully intended to bring her close to the edge several times before he let her orgasm. He wanted her frustrated until he determined she'd reached the height he wanted, and then, well, she'd be one satisfied lady.

His tongue swept through her throbbing flesh. She tasted so salty-sweet and he nipped and teased her clit until it swelled under his expertise. Adding two fingers, he pushed into her forcefully, rotating them back and forth. He pulled them out and probed her with his tongue. Jesus, he could lap her honey up for hours.

Kneeling over her, he held her head in his hands and feasted his eyes on her lovely face. Her lips had disappeared as she bit into them to muffle her cries. His heart thumped, overwhelmed by her strained expression as she struggled to stay quiet. He placed his finger between her scrunched eyebrows. "You're frowning, my sweet. Relax."

She blew out a slow breath and opened her eyes.

"You're learning, little one. Good girl. You've been silent and still, so now you get your reward." His fingers slid inside her again, he pulled and pinched her clit and her back arched off the mattress. "Come now, baby," he cried. "Let me hear you." Her hips rose higher and pressed into his hand. She growled and his heart soared. "That's it, baby. Look at me. Let me see you fly."

She stabbed him with her gaze and he swore he'd been lanced through the heart. "You're so beautiful when you fly, baby."

Sliding his hand under her right knee, he threw her leg over his shoulder. He sank his shaft in deep. This time she groaned and he let her. Their hips moved in a gentle tempo and built to a frenzied thrashing. Flesh against flesh. His orgasm was seconds away and he wanted her to climax with him. "Fly with me baby, one more time. Come for me."

She did and his release roiled through him like a biblical thunderstorm.

Mother fuck. Holy mother. Jesus H. Christ.

Would he ever soar like this again?

Alyx couldn't believe in these few short days they'd actually settled into a routine. First, they'd work out and eat breakfast on the deck. Rob would check in and the conversation would be to the point, no new news to report on either side. This morning the workout had gotten physical in a different way, but luckily, she'd survived and no one left with bruised egos. Well, not much, anyway.

She'd lagged behind Daniel by about two minutes and found him doing chins and dips on the pull-up bar. Seeing his muscles bulge as they lifted his body weight off the ground was an aphrodisiac in and of itself. She'd groaned inwardly. She didn't need to see *or* feel any more of that testosterone.

"Almost late, little subbie. Stop pushing your luck." Daniel huffed.

"Go ahead and do your worst, I'll kick your scrawny ass, Sir." She was baiting him but somehow couldn't resist.

He lowered himself slowly from the bar, leveling a lethal gaze at her. "Oh? Really? You want to play that game?"

Perhaps she'd made an error in judgment?

"Get your perky little ass over on the mat, sweetheart. Let's see what you got." He sauntered over to the thick red rubber mat in the room's center and waited for her. His breath puffed in and out of him, his upper body glistening with sweat under his gray tank top.

Alyx's breathing accelerated and she hadn't even moved a muscle yet. He had her by a good sixty pounds and at least six inches. There'd be no element of surprise she could use like she could with an unsub. Approaching with a confident stride, she reminded herself that body language spoke volumes. She faced him, hands on her hips, feet shoulder width apart just like he liked them. They began to circle the mat, predators stalking their prey.

He lunged for her. She spun into a tight spiral and slipped away. She came up behind him and thrust her Nike into the back of his knee. He fell. She crouched low, anticipating his assault. He nimbly got to his feet, not making a move.

"Cute," he said. "But that's the last shot you're getting."

She ran at him, throwing her shoulder against his hips. Like hitting the side of a truck. He grabbed her around the waist and flung her to the floor, covering her with his massive body. She struggled to shift onto her side, shoving her leg between his to use as leverage. Flip him, flip him over! He didn't budge. For one frantic moment she considered kneeing him in the balls. Instead, she yelled in frustration.

"Not bad for a girl," he teased. "You had me going there for a sec."

"You ass," she shrieked.

"You started it, little Miss I'll-Kick-Your-Scrawny-Ass, Sir."

"I would have stood a better chance with an unsuspecting unsub." She huffed.

"Unsub?"

"It's what we call a suspect, unknown subject."

He lowered his head, their noses almost touching. Those chocolate brown eyes melted her insides. He searched her gaze like he was seeking something ethereal and astonishingly, she felt more exposed than she'd felt in the rec room, or the TV room or, any room in Dr. Taylor's house. His lips crushed hers, his tongue probing her mouth. Before she could catch a breath, he had them both naked except for their sneakers. His throbbing erection poked between her legs. One quick thrust —he was in. Any residual oxygen flew out of her lungs. He pounded into her, the sound overly loud in the carpet-less gym. Without ever pulling out, he flipped her over onto her hands and knees. His chest pressed against her back and he wrapped an arm around her waist, the fingers on his other clasped between hers. He took her wildly, passionately, crazed.

Their bodies crushed onto the floor together, united in this connection she couldn't interpret. So good and yet, so wrong. Breathing together, their heartbeats thrummed in tandem rhythm. Again.

"I've never had a workout session quite like that," Daniel muttered.

All she could do was pant. Inhale, exhale. Her heart felt like it might rupture.

"Let's skip the run and go for breakfast."

"Agreed, Sir," Alyx mumbled. "I think we've burned sufficient calories to qualify as cardio."

Daniel rolled off her and they lay sprawled with their backs on the red rubber mat. Neither moved. The silence paralyzed Alyx. This had absolutely nothing to do with getting her trained as a submissive. She shifted toward Daniel. His eyes were closed. "What exactly are we doing here, Daniel? We fucked like ten minutes ago. And you can't tell me what just happened here, again, is preparing me for my assignment."

His eyelids opened. He stared at the ceiling. Her eyes traveled across his beautiful, sweat-slathered body. She wanted him all over again. How could that be? This was so screwed up.

"I don't know, Alyx. All I can say is you're like an unreachable itch under my skin, a craving that won't go away. I can't get enough." He turned his head and his eyes looked sad—almost. "I'm sorry. I know I've been taking advantage of you. I'll dial it back. Promise."

Alyx thought long and hard about what he was saying. She didn't want it to stop but some inner voice told her she was treading down a disastrous path. "I'm at a loss too, Daniel. It just seems like there's something wrong with this picture."

He sighed, rubbing his face with one hand. "I'll try to start thinking with my head instead of my dick."

He got to his feet and pulled her up, but quickly ceased all body contact. They picked up their clothes, dressed and went back upstairs to change into swimsuits before breakfast. Daniel remained taciturn and the distance between them stretched exponentially wide, a deep cold abyss.

Seated at the breakfast table, Alyx tried not to make eye contact with Lydia. She wasn't sure why, perhaps it was too much like looking your mother in the eye after you'd had sex. It just felt criminal. So many things unethical about this scenario. Alyx shook her head. Just make it through the week, she chided herself.

Not a second after ending Rob's daily call the phone rang again. This time Daniel looked serious as he talked. He listened for what seemed like the longest minute in human history and then glanced at the clock hanging on the cabana wall. "Okay. I'll stop by this afternoon and check on him." Putting the phone down, he spoke to Alyx, "I need to stop by the hospital and check on a patient. Want to go for a ride? Technically it will be on your time, so if you'd rather stay here that's fine."

The thought of him being gone for a few hours left her bereft. What to do? Her body-mind-spirit yearned to be with him, which was exactly why she must stay here. Time away would prove smart. A little detox never hurt anyone.

She'd reached a decision. She shouldn't go with him. Definitely not.

But her mouth had a brain of its own. "Sure," she heard herself saying, "Taking a ride will be fun." What? Good God, this was the same thing she'd done when Rob asked for volunteers to work this assignment. Why did she keep snubbing her better judgment? Especially after she'd just called out Daniel about them behaving in ways that had nothing to do with training a submissive. She was as guilty as he was. Guiltier, maybe. Yet she couldn't stop herself.

"We'll leave around one," he said, too enthusiastically. "And let's get lunch while we're out. A change of venue."

"Fine." Except nope, it would be too much like a date. Well, maybe not. She had lots of guy friends that she went out to lunch or dinner with. No biggie. Actually, all of her friends had a Y chromosome. Mostly she considered it a result of her job; too few females in her office. Ten to be exact; the seven and a half brunettes who'd been recruited for BDSM duty and two blondes, not counting Rob's boss who was a hotheaded carrot-top.

Alyx threw her white jean jacket over the pink tee and denims she'd arrived in. Daniel wore a long-sleeved white linen shirt tucked into belted pressed khakis. He opened the door for her and she slipped into his black Mercedes. He hadn't put on cologne but in the confines of the car, something about him smelled delicious. Pheromones?

Arriving at the hospital, he parked in a "Doctors Only" space and switched off the ignition. "Want to come in?"

Alyx shivered. "My last hospital trip was when I got shot." She hadn't even recalled that tiny detail when he'd invited her. Another sign that she was in way, way over her damn head.

"Then I truly don't want to leave you here alone. In fact, I won't."

That settled, without her input, they entered the hospital and Daniel nodded to numerous greetings from staff members. The elevator landed at the cardiac unit and he placed his hand on the small of Alyx's back and ushered her to a door emblazoned with his name. He directed her to the chair behind his desk and booted up his computer. "This might help pass the time until I'm done. I don't anticipate this taking very long, but you never know." Daniel gazed down at her, placing his warm hand on her shoulder. "You okay? You're kind of quiet."

"I'm fine. I'll catch up on my emails and Facebook while you're gone."

He headed for the exit, then faced her and winked before shutting the door behind him.

How could he have become so attentive in the short time they'd shared? She'd spent years with boyfriends and never reached this level of intimacy. Scanning her emails, she found messages from her hometown buddies telling her how much they missed her this weekend. And how the surfing had been awful on the too-calm ocean.

Before she knew it, Daniel returned. "Ready for lunch?"

"Yes. Is your patient all right?"

"He will be. Just needed to adjust his medication. Should be home in a few days."

After pulling into a parking space on Main Street, Daniel escorted Alyx out of the car. The sign above the restaurant read Café Jax and the hostess ushered them to a small table near the back. Daniel pulled out a chair and Alyx settled into the seat. Sitting opposite her, he watched as she opened the menu, her long black eyelashes shading her bright eyes, her cheeks pink with pouty lips to match. He thought of their playtime last night and again this morning. *Twice. Could she be talked into a third time right on top of this tablecloth?* His dick hardened in response to the mental images. *Jesus, she was living-breathing, walking-talking Viagra.* He'd never expected she'd get under his skin, not like this. Serious misgivings regarding her following through on this assignment troubled him. Not only her participating in scenes at the club knotted his stomach, but the idea of her actually being kidnapped by these sadists, for even a split-second, constricted his throat.

Two separate nightmares haunted him last night and he'd roused in a cold sweat. Luckily, she hadn't noticed. The first had her suspended from the ceiling while a horrid, beastly brute bullwhipped her mercilessly, bloody welts across her back, buttocks and thighs. She silently endured the pain; teeth clenched, jaw firm. In the next bad dream, an ogre strapped Alyx to a bondage horse and then raped her anally, gore everywhere. Daniel swallowed back his revulsion, trying to erase the vile images.

He should talk her out of this mission. Yes, get her to quit before she wound up hurt, or worse, dead.

"Earth to Daniel," she said, waving her hand in front of his stare.

He refocused, but his eyes quickly darted to the right. "Shit," he mumbled under his breath, rising from his seat.

"Vi," he said, leaning in so she could kiss his cheek.

"Daniel, how are you? It's been forever." Vi regarded Alyx with a smile. The woman's green eyes proved dazzling and her skin glowed, although it bore the wrinkles of wisdom and age. Her sleek silver pageboy fell almost to the shoulders of her tailored ebony sweater.

"Vi, this is Alyx Cameron, a business associate," Daniel announced. Then to Alyx, "This is Violet Soderhouse, she and my mother are in practice together."

Alyx extended her hand to Vi and she accepted. "Nice to meet you, Dr. Soderhouse."

"Likewise, and please, call me Vi. Oh, by the way, Daniel, we'll see you tomorrow night?" He narrowed his eyes. "The hospital fundraiser? Oh, tell me you haven't forgotten. Your mother is receiving her award."

Daniel pinched the bridge of his nose. "Slipped my mind, Vi. Not sure I can make it."

"Daniel, whatever it is I suggest you reschedule. Don't you dare disappoint your mother."

"I'll see what I can do, Vi, but no promises." Daniel dug his hands into his khakis' back pockets and sighed.

"I know you were raised better. Anyway, I'll leave you two to your lunch. Ta-ta, darlings." She gave Daniel another peck on the cheek.

The waitress came over and they ordered. Daniel placed his cell in front of him, drumming his fingers on the table. He stared at the phone.

"Two spankings for your thoughts?" Alyx said.

Daniel held up his index finger. "Wait for it." The phone rang and Daniel grunted. "That would be my mother." He picked up the phone, winked at Alyx and said, "Hi, Mom."

"Of course, it was great to see Vi. Uh-huh, uh-huh. Actually, I did forget and I'm not sure. Yes, Mom. I'll make every effort but extenuating circumstances may prevent… Okay, Mom. I will. Love you too." Daniel replaced the phone in his pocket and leaned his head into his palms. "Damn."

"Hey. Go, please go. I'll be fine for a few hours alone tomorrow night."

Attending some boring hospital event featuring pompous assholes in self-aggrandizement annoyed him on a regular evening. He'd much rather send a generous check and skip the schmoozing. Not to mention trading a night with Alyx in his rec room made it a hundred times worse. Alyx needed all the time he could give her. But he loved his mother and he should be there.

The waitress arrived with a Cobb salad for Alyx and Daniel's Reuben sandwich. They both had iced tea.

He wondered if Alyx was relieved that he might leave her alone for a few hours. Maybe she was sick of him. Although, if he had to judge by the recent festivities, she certainly seemed into it. And he? Well, he'd never enjoyed himself with a woman more.

Alyx stabbed a ripe piece of avocado and pushed it past her full lips. Daniel stopped breathing. Those fucking lips. He wanted those lips on him, everywhere. His pulse quickened and his dick hardened. Which happened more and more often whenever he was near this incredible woman. Hell, even when he wasn't. All he had to do was picture her slowly undressing.

It's only sex, he reminded himself. He'd have it out of his system by the end of the week and then his life, and hers, would return to normal. He'd forget all about her. *Maybe.*

"I repeat," Alyx said, interrupting his musings. "Go to this event for your mother. You must. Won't she be horribly disappointed if you aren't there?"

Daniel bit into his sandwich and then sipped iced tea. "Okay. As long as you're my arm-candy."

"What? That's ridiculous." She shook her head and ate a forkful of salad.

"I'm not taking no for an answer. I'll say that I've been working as a consultant for your company and you don't know anyone because you're from out of town and I didn't want to leave you bored." Daniel hoped he could pull this ruse off. His psychiatrist mother could be a pain in the ass with her unsolicited insights and advice, but he didn't care. He wanted Alyx with him. "By the way, you'll need something to wear."

"Did you hear what I said? I'm not going with you." Alyx said, her eyes going wide when she realized she held her fork in the air, almost like a threat. She quickly laid the utensil down.

"I'm the Dom and you do what I say. The nights are my time and if I want to bring you someplace, you'll go."

"Not our agreement," she said quietly. "We can trade the four hours in the afternoon for four hours at night. What's the difference?"

So sensible. Using her fucking FBI brain to solve his problem. However, the real issue was: he wanted her by his side and he didn't care what anybody thought. *Shit.* Two minutes ago, he'd convinced himself that he only cared about her for the sex, and now he wanted to bring her out in public? He wondered if it would be a problem on Rob Scarborough's end. How could it be? It's not like anybody connected with these slavers would be anywhere near the hospital fundraiser clientele.

"You're coming with me," he said flatly, "and that's the end of discussion. As soon as we finish lunch we'll go pick out your dress."

Alyx leveled her glare at him. "Who died and made you King?"

"Me, of royal blood?" he feigned innocence.

Daniel towed Alyx through Cashmere Shores' doors and accosted a saleslady. "Dr. Taylor," she exclaimed. "What a pleasure."

"Hello, Tory," he said gruffly. "This is Alyx Cameron, a business associate who's visiting me. She's attending an unexpected social event tomorrow night and didn't bring any formal attire. Please take good care of her."

"She's in good hands," Tory said, giving Alyx the once over. "What size, darling?"

"Six," Daniel said. Alyx's jaw dropped. "And she'll need shoes, also size six, and the appropriate undergarments."

"Exquisite," Tory said. "Any particular color?"

"Pink, she looks good in pink."

"I know just the thing." Tory sashayed off to the racks.

Alyx leaned in close to Daniel. "What the fuck? Me, in a pink dress? I'm not going to prom."

"Let me guess. Your FBI uniform is a dark business suit and you haven't worn anything terribly feminine in a while. I want to make you feel as beautiful as I know you are. And I love you in your little pink tee." Daniel tugged on the hem of her shirt. This was the only pink item in Alyx's entire wardrobe and she hadn't given much thought to her attire the night she'd arrived on Dr. Taylor's doorstep. But what he said was kind of sweet. He was correct, too. Other than her workout clothes, neutral colors filled her dresser drawers and closet.

"I can't believe you remembered my size in, in everything. And won't this whole affair, or situation seem a tad odd for two business associates?"

"Let them talk. Gossip. I would, if I were them."

Tory returned, carrying a sleek pink cashmere dress featuring a low-cut neckline and spaghetti straps. The material felt like velvet.

"I like," Daniel announced. "Go try it on and come out and model."

Tory ushered Alyx into the dressing room and zipped her into the luscious creation before telling her to wait. She reappeared with black patent leather stilettos and a pale satin string panty. She knelt at Alyx's feet to slip on the pumps. "I think you should probably remove your underwear for now. I brought a nude thong."

Alyx cringed. She'd tried thongs occasionally but didn't find them particularly comfortable. If she wore them exclusively would she eventually get used to the dental-floss-in-her-butt-crack feeling? But then – shit! She still wore the butt plug. Tory stretched open the tiny string bikini as an offering. Alyx snatched it from Tory's hands a little too quickly. "I'll take it to go, thanks."

"Okaaay," Tory said, eyes wide. She arranged Alyx's hair

stylishly, tucking one side behind her ear. "There you go. You're very stunning, you know."

Alyx blanched. She'd always considered herself second-rate. She was first runner-up to prom queen, vice-president of her senior class, ranked number eleven in her graduating class when only the first ten got to sit on the stage with special honors. One time in college her sorority had submitted her picture as a contestant for the basketball tournament queen. She'd won but only because her boyfriend enlisted his entire fraternity to vote for her. She'd never considered herself particularly attractive and not even remotely beauty queen material.

"Come, let's show Dr. Taylor, I think he'll be very, *very* pleased." Tory nudged Alyx out of the huge dressing room. Daniel sat in a Queen Ann chair with his legs crossed, frown lines crimping his brow. As soon as his eyes fell on her his expression brightened.

"Perfect," he said, glancing briefly at Tory. "Turn around." He made a twirling motion with his finger. The dress had a huge V in the back, nearly to her butt crack, with a string of rhinestones connecting the two sides. She couldn't wear a bra. That should please the oversexed Dr. Taylor.

"On you, it looks like a million bucks," he said. "And the shoes are fit for a princess."

"Thank you, Sir." She flushed crimson. Had she really called him Sir in public? Daniel seemed not to notice, but Tory winced, her eyes a little too wide. Alyx decided to ignore her embarrassing blunder.

Daniel walked over to her, sliding his finger under the thin strap of the dress. "We'll take it. And pick out a handbag and a pair of earrings. Something in silver or white gold. Nothing too gaudy."

"Daniel," Alyx whispered, for his ears only. "The dress and shoes are enough, I don't need jewelry. It's too much."

He put his lips close to her ear, his breath warm on her neck, and ticklish tremors ran down her spine. "No topping from the bottom, little subbie. In case you've momentarily forgotten, I'm in charge."

Well, technically no, she thought. It wasn't four o'clock yet. But somehow, she had no will to fight him about this.

Tory laid everything out on the counter and carefully wrapped the items in bright yellow tissue paper, depositing them in a shiny black shopping bag. The dress remained on its hanger and Tory covered it in a large plastic bag.

"Alyx, go wait in the car," Daniel instructed, his stare narrow, stern. For some reason, she felt compelled to obey.

"All right," she said, accepting the keys. On her way out, she peered over her shoulder. "Thanks for your help, Tory."

"Certainly, please come again." Her too-white smile seemed unconvincing.

Minutes later, Daniel returned, packages in hand. He stowed them in the trunk. Settled into the driver's seat, he paused, gazing through the windshield. Alyx followed his line of sight across the street. What had caught his attention?

"That James Bond movie you wanted to see is playing." The small-town theater's show times were listed under the title. Just like her hometown theater, it had probably been built in the 1950s with shabby red-velour seats and an outdated projection system that occasionally didn't make it to the ending credits. The one in Westhampton even closed for two months in the winter.

Alyx's face pinched. What the hell? Taking her to work, insisting that she attend the fundraiser at the hospital, buying her expensive clothes she could never afford, out to lunch, to the movies? Too much.

"Uh…" Before she could utter a single intelligible protest he had her out of the car and walking across the street to the theater.

Alyx loved the movies. Most of the guys she'd dated weren't all that fond of films and she'd been forced to nudge more than one of them awake after the snoring became overly embarrassing.

They snuggled into the rickety seats, Daniel's shoulder pressed against hers.

It ended too quickly and Alyx wished she could see it all over again. "Wouldn't you just love to be James Bond?" she exclaimed as they returned to the car. "The excitement? The danger? It's positively exhilarating."

"At the risk of sounding like a total wimp, no. Plus, it's totally Hollywood hype. I'm sure the life of a real spy is nothing even close to what the Bond man's life is like."

Alyx settled. "I guess. But it's fun to think about."

Returning home at around seven o'clock, they agreed they weren't hungry after such a late lunch. Alyx carried her packages up to her room and hung the dress in the closet. With the price tags removed, Alyx could only imagine the ridiculous amount of money Daniel had probably spent. She had no need for anything lavish and no intention of taking them when she left. The movie *Pretty Woman* came to mind and a surge of disgust swarmed within. A prostitute. That's what Tory probably thought.

Daniel appeared in the bedroom's doorway. "Rec room. Fifteen minutes." It almost sounded like a question.

"Yes, Sir."

"You know how to open the door?"

She nodded.

"Underwear only and in the slave position in front of the bondage bench."

Her pulse rate quickened at his authoritative tone. "Yes, Sir."

"I promised you toys the other night, but I-I got distracted. We'll focus on toys tonight."

Alyx smirked inwardly at Daniel's embarrassed expression. My, my, she'd *distracted* the Dom. "Your wish is my command, Sir."

Daniel left and Alyx relaxed on the bed, focusing on her bright red toenails. She remembered sitting in the pedicure chair worrying about the future terror that loomed large. Daniel was anything but terrifying. He was a good man, a bit controlling, but, dare she think it? *Sweet.*

Alyx pushed the secret spot on the wall. The door swung wide and she left it open. Clad only in her lacy black bra and matching bikini bottoms, gooseflesh prickled her skin. Climbing the stairs to the rec room, she walked over to the far wall and pulled the cord that raised the shades. The brilliant night sky filled the space. She gazed down to the waves crashing onto the beach. A cold front had moved in last night and although the day proved crisp and clear, the ocean yelled its frustration as unrelenting fury pounded the shoreline.

She sensed his presence before he said anything, her eyes cast downward, her palms upturned on her naked thighs. Her heart beat wildly, the sound of the booming surf unable to drown out her raging pulse.

"You're so beautiful, Alyx." Daniel's voice sounded soft, undemanding, uncommanding. "I like seeing you on your knees, nearly naked, waiting for me." Alyx grimaced, shutting her eyes tightly. She wanted to say something to thwart his need for seeing her in submission, slave-like, even though his definition made sense. Almost.

His bare toes grazed her knees. An unexpected urge insisted that she suck them. Geez. Never had she wanted to taste a man's toes but somehow, she wanted to devour every part of his deliciously wicked body. Daniel had somehow transformed her into somebody she didn't recognize.

"Tonight, I'll introduce you to the spanking horse and the C-clamp and we'll play with a bullet vibrator. I'll remove the plug you have now and you can rest from it until tomorrow. Then I'll give you a new and bigger one. We're ahead of schedule in that department. You should be ready by tomorrow night for me to claim your delectable ass. I'm very pleased with your progress." She briefly glanced up, wondering if she should say thank you. But he hadn't asked her a question and so she stayed in silent protocol. Why did pleasing him make her so happy? "Eyes on the floor, baby."

Well, she'd *nearly* stayed in protocol. Damn.

Daniel moved about the rec room silently making preparations for whatever he had planned. More education, more blessed torture. He made her wait too long, her excitement level was skyrocketing.

His toes tickled her knees again and her breath hitched. "Eyes on me." Locking her gaze on his fetching brown eyes, his face darkened. That smoldering glance made her wet before his first touch. "Stand up," he commanded, his Dom persona rising from the softness he'd showed a moment ago.

He marched her in the direction of the bondage bench. "Bend over," he ordered. She sprawled her upper body across the cool black leather. "This will be quick. I don't need to tie you down. Hold on to the table."

Alyx wrapped her fingers over the edge that butted up against the wall. The wall that her head had smashed into last time she lay here as Daniel pounded her into earth-shattering orgasms.

Daniel hooked his thumbs into her bikini bottoms and pulled the flimsy material down to her ankles. "Step out," he said, removing her panties. "Now, spread those legs wide." Alyx complied and he reached between her butt cheeks and extracted the plug in one quick motion, depositing it in the trashcan. It thudded slightly as it hit the bottom of the can.

"Up you go." He grabbed her by her upper arms and helped her stand. "We'll play without it tonight and, as I said, you'll get the new one tomorrow."

Butterflies swarmed Alyx's stomach. Giant ones. But everything he told her had been true so far and she did trust him. He'd work his erotic magic and make the pain feel good.

The lesson began and Alyx quickly slipped into a sexual coma. Up and down. In and out. Restrained and freed. Mouths, tongues, legs spread. On her hands and knees. On her back. On her stomach. He was pure animal. And she fucking adored this beast.

Four orgasms and she was shot. And, oh yeah, she *loved* toys.

Daniel held her in the aftercare chair, covering her with the soft blanket and snuggled her under his chin until she dozed. She didn't have any idea how long she languished in his secure embrace, drunk on that scrumptious cocktail of oxytocin, dopamine and estrogen, maybe even a kick of testosterone thrown in.

Opening her eyes, her gaze fell on his gorgeous face. His eyes were closed, his long dark lashes nearly landing on his cheeks, his breathing steady and even. Was he asleep? Her eyes drifted over his naked shoulder and chest. She feathered her fingertips over his nipple, playing with the little hairs that circled it and smiled to herself. So handsome, so peaceful. Her heart sprinted.

He must have sensed that she'd come around. He spoke to her, his eyelids still shut, "You're back, little subbie. You okay?"

"Mmm, I'm good."

"Just good?" A mischievous grin quirked his lips, but he still hadn't opened his eyes.

Alyx giggled. "Well," she struggled for the right words.

"That was amazing. I can't even think of how to describe what that felt like. Nirvana, maybe." She laughed again, embarrassed at her assessment of the absolutely insane session they'd had in the rec room over the last couple of hours.

"I love the sound of your laugh." Daniel lifted his head off the chair and gazed down at her. "I'm glad you enjoyed yourself. I hit subspace myself, only we call it Domspace. The high a Dom gets from pleasing his sub." He ran his thumb across her chin and parted her lips, planting a chaste kiss on her mouth. "I love your lips," he whispered against them. Even that was enough to force her to squeeze her thighs together, stemming the rising heat between her legs.

How could she still want him after she'd just spent hours fucking him? Like being a drug addict, she seemed to worship him, nonstop.

This was so far out of control. Thankfully she'd be forced to walk away at the end of the week. She'd go cold turkey.

She savored the delectable tidbits of pineapple as he pushed them past her lips, feeding her. She swallowed the sweetness, moaning. Again, they slept together and he held her throughout the night. Yet something niggled at her, an inner voice telling her that even though this felt so right, something very wrong would soon ruin every last bit of joy.

Chapter 6

Wednesday

Dawn stretched across the sky in pink and gray hues as Daniel pulled Alyx into the curve of his body, his little sub soundly sleeping, his arm wrapped securely around her waist. He'd nearly lost his mind last night, he'd fucked her so hard. Even he was sore and he could only imagine how raw Alyx felt. And yet he was horned up for her already and he couldn't blame it on the normal morning woody. Never had he reacted to a woman with this intensity. Never. Ever. He thought about Lacey. What a total screw-up he was. He'd talked himself into thinking this would be meaningless sex and Lacey would never know, but now...

Jesus, he didn't know what he would do. His conscience plagued him.

Alyx shifted under his arm and a tiny giggle slipped from her lips. He wondered if she was dreaming, and if so, what fantasies inhabited her mind? He kissed her shoulder and she tittered again.

"Your chin is scratchy, mister," she said playfully.

"Sorry, little one." She pivoted in his arms and nuzzled her face against his chest, her breath warm on his skin. He ran his hand up and down her spine, landing on her butt cheek. He gave a squeeze. "You okay this morning? I might have been a little rough on you last night."

Her lazy eyes reached him and her head tilted back. "I guess I like it rough. You'll get no complaints from this little subbie."

"Glad to hear it." He leaned in and kissed her tenderly. "No sex this morning. We're taking a break."

"Seriously?" She wrapped her hand around his erection.

"Aren't you sore?" His eyebrows arched.

Her lips quirked down in a girlish pout. "I wouldn't want to take advantage of my tired little Dom."

Alyx wriggled out of his grasp and slung her legs over the side of the bed to get up. Daniel grabbed her upper arms and dragged her back, pinning her to the mattress. She shrieked in protest. "What did you say, little subbie?" He pressed his body into hers, his boner already at her slick core. Securing her wrists in one hand, he threw them above her head and held them there. "Perhaps I should spank you for disrespect." Her eyes twinkled.

"You wouldn't." Alyx giggled as she struggled to free herself.

"I am capable of many, many things." Daniel kissed her savagely and she stopped wriggling. Their breathing synchronized as he inhaled her like a starving man gobbling food. Her sultry eyes smoldered, her face flushed, her heart thudded like a tiny bird against his chest.

He took her slow, easy, and their shared orgasm came like a prayer, an incantation, the silent warm embrace of an angel.

They decided to skip the workout again this morning, agreeing they'd burned enough calories last night and considering they burned off some more before they got out of bed. However, Daniel didn't forget about the new, *and bigger*, butt plug he'd promised. Alyx had to admit its girth left her slightly aroused all day, not that she needed any enhancement to get her in the mood around Dr. Taylor.

The rest of the day rolled by like the sex that morning, slow and easy. They read, watched old movies on TV and napped most of it away until it was time to spruce up for the fundraiser. He gave her relief from the plug, but just for the evening. Well, she'd resorted to begging and he'd finally relented.

A few hours later, Alyx finished dressing in the green bedroom. Daniel, who got dressed quicker than she did, waited for her at the bottom of the stairs.

"Wow," he gushed as she descended the staircase. "You clean up real nice." He extended his hand toward her as she landed on the last step, effectively erasing their difference in height. His hands settled on her hips and he held her there. His eyes traveled over the pink cashmere hugging her curves. Although he really liked her naked, he had to admit she looked damn fine dressed to the nines.

"Are you implying that I was *dirty* before?" Her lip curled into a feigned pout that launched him into the sexual stratosphere. The mere curve of her lips could do that.

"I like you dirty," he said, gripping her hips tighter. "Especially when I'm the one to mess you up."

As he tugged her closer, she gave her adorable smile. "You're rather fetching yourself, Dr. Taylor. I'm a total sucker for a guy in a suit, never mind a tuxedo." She grasped the ends of his bow-tie and tugged slightly, then pulled one end up a little. "There," she said, smoothing both ends down. "Perfect." But then she draped her arms over his shoulders and stared into him, her voice barely audible. "Daniel. Are you sure this is a good idea?"

"Don't get me wrong." He slipped his arms around her waist. "These events can be horribly boring, so I suggest you drink until you drop. I certainly intend to."

With Mason already behind the wheel, Daniel opened the back door of the silver SUV and Alyx glided across the slick leather seat, her sleek legs pulling the black patent leather stilettos in behind her. She slid over, making room for him. Overwhelmed by her beauty, he couldn't believe she was the same woman he'd met in Jack's office only a few days ago. He'd thought her pretty then, but now, he decided she was easily the most beautiful woman he'd ever seen, the most stunning woman he'd ever made love to.

Shit. Had he actually just said that? Even to himself? This was about the fucking, and had nothing to do with that four-letter word: *love*.

Keep telling yourself that, doc, keep telling yourself. Before things go sideways.

Daniel flipped on the stereo from the back seat and her playlist flashed onto the screen. He pressed the top 25 list and Rihanna's voice floated on the airwaves, telling Eminem how much she loves the way it hurts, the way he lies. He heard the parts he wanted to, or perhaps the ones he didn't. He was in way, way over his head. The problem being, what was he going to do about it?

They entered the front drive of the The Pearl. Daniel escorted Alyx through the front door, his hand under her elbow. The posh restaurant had been taken over for the evening's event, which on an off-season Wednesday was probably a blessing for the high-priced venue. Daniel felt Alyx's uneasiness and wanted to put his arm around her trim waist and embrace her. Then again, not only were they out in public, his mother was lurking about. Best to keep his hands to himself.

Not less than thirty seconds after entering the dining room, he heard, "Daniel!" as his mother beelined to him in a flash. "I was so afraid you wouldn't make it." She circled him in a warm hug and kissed his cheek, then retreated and wiped her lipstick off his face with her thumb. He squirmed like a six-year-old.

"Hello, Mom. I'm glad I could make it." Nothing wrong with a tiny white lie, right? His mother immediately landed her eyes on Alyx. Daniel inhaled slowly. "Mom, meet Alyx Cameron. Alyx, meet my mother, Dr. Laura Taylor."

They exchanged pleasantries and Daniel added, "I'm working as a consultant with Ms. Cameron this week, she's here from out of town. We've been up late most nights trying to fine-tune the protocols for her new project."

"Really?" Daniel's mother said. "How interesting. What line of work are you in, Ms. Cameron?"

Alyx hesitated. "I'm so sorry if I sound rude, but I'm afraid it's not something I'm at liberty to discuss." A waiter came by and offered them white wine from a silver tray. One by one, they indulged.

"Top secret?" Daniel's mother said, taking a sip. "Perhaps a new drug that'll make our hearts beat twenty years beyond its expiration date?" She laughed. His mother obviously assumed Alyx worked for a pharmaceutical company, a perfectly logical conclusion and one Daniel could work with.

"Mom, Alyx and I have had a grueling few days working on her protocols and we'd love to forget about work until the torture begins anew."

Alyx coughed and sputtered. Daniel gently patted her bare back. He met her stare and struggled not to crack a grin. "You okay, Alyx?" She didn't answer him. She probably wanted to smack him.

"Well," his mother said, "I need to make the rounds." She stopped to chuckle at her own joke. "Oh, you know what I mean, not rounds… but *rounds*. I need to get a-round and greet everyone. I'll catch you two later. You're sitting at my table, of course. I didn't realize you were bringing a guest, darling, so I'll have the server set another place."

His mother scurried away in a flourish and Alyx faced Daniel. "Asshole. I can't believe you said what you did."

Daniel grinned impishly. "That would be, Sir Asshole, if you please." The expression on Alyx's face made him laugh out loud.

She shook her head. "I'm not sure I'm going to survive tonight, never mind the rest of the week."

"I'm not certain I can keep my hands off you the next few hours. I nearly yanked you into my arms twice already, and we've only been here like two minutes." Frank Sinatra crooned *Bewitched, Bothered and Bewildered* and Daniel wondered if the DJ could read his mind. A few couples straggled onto the dance floor.

"Perhaps we can get away with dancing. It would be like prom. I can try to cop a feel without the chaperones noticing. I do love a challenge."

"So do I. And by the way, I'm an FBI agent trained in three distinct fighting disciplines."

He smiled, definitely up to the challenge. "Drink up," he ordered as each chugged the last of their wine. He placed her glass on a nearby table, then settled his hand on the soft skin of her back and ushered her onto the dance floor. He circled one arm around her waist, then grasped her hand and tugged her into his body, but not close enough that she could sense his erection. Their eyes met, and his heart lurched at the wanting in her gaze. "You're a gorgeous woman, Alyx." She flushed crimson and cast her eyes downward. Jesus, he couldn't wait to get her home.

They ate their appetizer, a delightful concoction of grilled shrimp with mango salsa, and then filet mignon with a horse-radish sauce, new potatoes and green beans with hazelnuts. Vi stopped at their table and chatted aimlessly about her new grandchild. Speeches punctuated their dinner and Daniel grew impatient, checking his watch to see how soon he could orchestrate their escape.

His mother's acceptance speech was last on the agenda and Daniel sighed with frustration, he couldn't leave until his mother finished her remarks. They danced a final time so it didn't seem as if they were making a run for it as soon as the program ended. Daniel held Alyx a little too close, but he almost didn't care. He leaned into her ear. "I need to get you home. I intend for us to play on the bondage bed tonight. I can't wait to have you restrained and at my mercy while I do evil things to you."

Alyx inhaled sharply and her body tensed.

"Excited already, little subbie? I want my mouth on you, and especially on that sweet spot between your legs." He studied her face, but she refused to make eye contact, gazing over his shoulder; but the pulse in her neck pounded like a jackhammer.

"God, Daniel," she said a little too loudly. "Don't say shit like that to me and then expect me to act normal."

"Ah, but watching you get all excited is half the fun." Jesus, Jesus, he couldn't wait to get her home. She was right, he was getting himself so excited that he might find it difficult to walk out nonchalantly himself.

The song ended. He marched her back to the table to retrieve her handbag. They approached his mother to levy their congratulations again and say their goodbyes. The second she laid eyes on them her expression shifted. To Alyx, she said, "Are you all right, my dear? You look a bit flushed."

"Uh, it's a little warm in here. Probably all the dancing."

Alyx's eyes furtively glanced in Daniel's direction. His mother's gaze flitted back and forth between them, her eyebrows creasing.

"We need to get going, Mom. Alyx and I still have several hours of torturous work ahead of us tonight." Alyx flared her nostrils and Daniel swallowed a laugh.

"Understood," she said, "Your work must be exhausting, yet I imagine quite satisfying."

"You have no idea, Mom," Daniel added, desperately struggling to keep the smirk off his face.

"Thank you both for taking a few hours away from your work to make an old woman happy. Ms. Cameron, it was delightful to make your acquaintance." She extended her hand and Alyx shook it.

"A pleasure meeting you too, Dr. Taylor."

"Don't work my son too hard tonight."

It was all Daniel could do to keep from choking. One look at Alyx and he'd totally lose it.

"Good night, Mom," Daniel said, leaning in and giving her a peck on the cheek.

"Night, night, dear."

Mason pulled the car around to the front as soon as they exited the door. Alyx glared at Daniel. "You're an ass. What are you, like twelve? The whole night was laced with sexual innuendo. If your mother doesn't suspect that this was something other than a business relationship, then she's an idiot. And I doubt that, based on the fact that's she's an expert in human behavior." Alyx sighed loudly.

"I know. I plead carnal insanity. I was overcome by your feminine wiles." Daniel peered straight ahead as Alyx continued to glare. He held the door open for her as she settled her sexy pink cashmere-clad body into the seat. Sitting next to her, he couldn't contain himself any longer and pulled her onto his lap. He wrapped his arms around her and nuzzled her neck. "You smell delicious. You always do. Makes me want to taste every inch of you."

They stayed quiet for the remainder of the trip and an odd peacefulness washed over Daniel.

In the TV room, Daniel headed for the bar. "I'm having a scotch. Want one?"

Alyx sat on a barstool. "Yes, please." Daniel removed his tuxedo coat and hung it on the back of the other stool. He reached for his tie. She stopped him. "Here, let me do that." She tugged on the end of the bow and pulled the knot lose, then slid the silky black material out from beneath his collar and draped it across the back of her neck. Sliding her fingers inside his collar, she pushed the button out of the hole and freed his neck from the restraint. Two more buttons and she stopped. Daniel flaunted a naughty grin then grasped the ends of his bow-tie and retied it around Alyx's neck. He stepped back and appraised his handiwork.

"I like it. In fact, you'll only wear my bow-tie in the rec room tonight."

Alyx blinked her bright eyes, so demure. "Yes, Sir. Whatever you say, Sir."

Daniel leaned in and kissed her gently. Alyx wrapped her arms around his neck. She spread her knees and he moved in, clutching her to his chest. The kiss proved urgent, deep, and Daniel's insides surged with the thrill of what was to come. And oh, he would make her come, hard and often.

"Let's skip the drink," he muttered, "I don't think I can wait any longer to have you naked and spread-eagle on my bondage bed." Several moments skidded by. He tilted his head to one side. "And, my little pet, tonight's the night I claim your sweet ass."

Alyx lay unrestrained, face up on the bondage bed. She gritted her teeth at the raw carnal feelings burning inside her. A week ago, she would have vowed that anal sex would never be on her list of erotic activities and couldn't imagine there could be anything even remotely pleasurable about anything in her ass. The first time there's a finger in your ass, well, it feels like a finger in your ass, but at a certain point everything goes right. Now she had to admit that wearing the anal plug had awakened waves of unfamiliar, yet delectable, feelings.

Naked and erect, Daniel straddled her hips, resting his adorable bottom on her thighs. "We'll take this slow. Real slow. I'm going to blindfold you. It will help you focus." The deep timbre of his voice nearly made her come and he'd barely touched her. He secured the black silk sash over her eyes, tying it on the side. Massaging her breasts, he leaned in and sucked her nipples hard, then plundered her mouth, their tongues dancing a familiar tango.

He settled between her legs and ran his hands up her thighs to her bottom, kneading the flesh. A warm tingle erupted, her soft tissues already engorged. "Let's get you lubed up," Daniel whispered, "first here." His fingers pulled back her folds exposing her engorged clit. Just imagining his eyes gazing at her as his fingers probed sent her soaring. "Oh babe, don't you dare come yet. We're going to do this right and I promise the high will be incredible."

Alyx believed him. Every word. She'd learned that holding back her orgasm as long as possible made for an incredibly satisfying climax.

Daniel opened her legs wider and propped up her knees. He applied a generous amount of lubricant to her anus. "Don't think, Alyx. Just feel." Alyx obeyed.

One finger slid in gently. Unfamiliar nerves fired. Another

finger. He moved them in circular motion. Gently. Rhythmically. Her body ached for him and she moaned at the exquisite sensation. This went on for a long minute, maybe several, until she thought she'd explode.

"Oh no," Daniel urged. "Not yet, little pet."

"I don't think I can wait," Alyx muttered. "It's too hard."

"We're in protocol. I'd liked to be addressed properly, little subbie."

"Yes, Sir, I mean, no, Sir. I don't think I can hold on much longer. "

"Too much talking, hush."

Daniel flipped her onto her stomach with one quick move. An arm slid under her and she was on hands and knees. "Put your face on the pillow, hold onto the headboard and keep your adorable butt in the air," he whispered near her ear. She heard the tear of the condom wrapper. This was it. Here he comes. They both would.

More lube, more rubbing, circling her back entrance. Blind, she focused on his touch. No distractions. The tip of his cock hit her anus, unhurriedly, he pressed in. The fingers of his left hand were entwined with hers, his other guiding his dick inside. She bucked, not out of fear or resistance but because she wanted to wrap her arms around him. Not touching him was the worst torture. A second later, his shaft was in her anus. Her thighs, her stomach, her whole body tightened. Every muscle stiffened. "Relax, Alyx," he whispered in her ear. "This is going to feel incredible. Trust me."

He slid into her. In. Out. In. Out. Her vision went white under the blindfold. He freed his hand from hers and his fingers pinched her clit. "Come now," he said. She screamed, as he relentlessly thrust in and out of her, her mind in splinters and her vagina convulsing around his fingers. The familiar moan when Daniel climaxed made Alyx smile.

"Fuck," she yelled. "Fuck. Fuck. Fuck."

"Fuck is right," Daniel said. "You're mind-blowing, little subbie." He turned her over, removing the blindfold. He stripped off the condom and heaved it on the floor, using a wet nap from the bedside table to clean his hands. He pressed his chest against hers, his arms beside her shoulders, corded muscles bulging. Alyx focused on his gorgeous eyes, dark with passion. Arousal flared. Again.

"One more," he said. Daniel plunged his cock into her throbbing vagina. He thrust against her swollen sensitive tissues sending tremors vibrating through her. His steady rhythm took her past her climax and passion built as he brought her to another unbelievable orgasm. A screaming one. For both.

An eternity later she opened her eyes and blinked. She moaned. Shivered. Exhaustion swamped her. Her muscles limp. Daniel pushed away strands of damp hair from her face, then pulled her on top of him, wrapping her securely in an embrace. He chuckled. "So? What say you, little subbie?"

Alyx laughed. "I'll write that check for the hundred bucks first thing in the morning."

Thursday

Alyx had been twitchy all morning. Daniel saw her standing in front of the open refrigerator and came around behind her.

"Shit, Daniel! Don't sneak up on me like that!"

"I didn't sneak up on you, I simply walked over to see if I could help."

She was nervous, had to be, but wouldn't admit it to him. He asked her ten times to tell him how she felt about going to the club tonight, but she kept insisting it was no big deal. She was fine, fine, fine. Now that he thought about it, everything was always "fine" with her and it was starting to worry him. What was it about her that prevented her from expressing her feelings? Possibly having no parent around had made her too self-reliant. Although, he shouldn't talk, he wasn't exactly Mr. Let-Me-Express-My-Feelings-Freely, either.

Daniel had already decided to keep her out of the rec room today, figuring she'd have enough of the BDSM lifestyle after tonight's introduction to the club. Plus, he'd played pretty hard with her last night. The image of her sprawled across the bondage bed—so fucking gorgeous—might haunt him for all eternity. He'd stared at her for several minutes before touching. The blindfold had hidden not only her gaze, but also his indulgence in some serious eye worship. He prayed that image was seared into his retinas until he was an old man. And claiming her anal virginity had sent him on a high he might never come down from. Just thinking about how passionately they both came sent roiling ecstasy through him.

After the refrigerator incident, he decided Alyx needed a distraction and sent Mason out on special assignment. Mason returned around noon with the required item. Daniel grabbed it and headed for the deck, first peeking at his little subbie through the French doors. She lay stretched out on the double lounger with her e-reader, but he could tell, even with her sunglasses on, that her eyes were focused elsewhere. He guessed her mind was on Steve, her Dom for Saturday night, imagining him looming menacingly over her, and Daniel had to admit the image spiked even his anxiety level.

Pushing one door open a crack he yelled, "Close your eyes, Alyx, I have a surprise." She glanced his way, and he made sure to keep the offering behind his back as best he could. The sucker was six feet long.

Alyx flicked her sunglasses up and looked his way. "I mean it, Alyx. Close your eyes or I'll spank you right out here on the deck even if you are on your own time." He struggled not to smile and hoped she'd be happy with her surprise, and seriously distracted for a few hours.

"They're closed. Okay, Master?" She leaned her head back on the oversized chair and threw her forearm over her eyes.

A more carnal method of distraction came to mind—strapping her to the bondage bench and fucking her senseless. She did seem to like that—but he let that thought die a quick death. "Okay, I'm coming out. Keep your eyes closed until I tell you." He made his way across the decking, the slick polyurethane board between his hands, and stopped at the foot of her chair. "Open."

It took her a few seconds to focus, then her eyes widened and she sat up abruptly. "Oh. My. God. Where did you get that?"

"You need a distraction, the tension wafting off you is driving me crazy. I thought perhaps physical exertion of a different kind might help you relax."

Alyx jumped up and planted a giant kiss on his cheek. She pulled back and blurted, "God, I love you." Immediately her eyes impossibly widened, she pulled away and slapped her hand across her mouth. Awkward silence lingered. Alyx dropped her hand, "Oh, Daniel, I'm sorry. I-I didn't mean that. I-I meant I loved you for doing this, not, well—"

Daniel put a hand on her shoulder. "Relax, I know what you meant. Don't give it another thought." But his heart had nearly leapt out of his chest at her words. He'd been struggling with his intense feelings for her nearly since she arrived, and almost wished it were true. What would he do if she'd actually said those words for real? His pulse quickened at the thought of truly being in love with this woman, and to have that love returned. "I know you got cheated out of a surfing weekend with your friends. You had to be disappointed."

Alyx grabbed the board and laid it out on the decking. She stroked it as if it were a treasured pet. "Do you surf?"

"No. I dabbled a little as a kid, but I never really got the hang of it."

"It's already waxed? You are officially my favorite person. *Ever*. I'm going in right this second." She ran off into the surf like an energetic teenager. Daniel beamed. He'd achieved his objective.

He watched her surf wave after wave, uneasy a few times when it seemed like she was underwater too long. But each time she surfaced with a child-like grin. She stayed out there for two hours and Daniel began to worry that, after this much physical exertion, she'd be too exhausted to stay focused at the club tonight. Too late now, however. He'd just have to do his best to keep her on task.

Eventually she dragged herself onto the beach and headed his way. She rested the board against the railing and Daniel gave her a towel. Intending to wrap her in the cotton-soft fabric, she derailed him by throwing her arms around his neck and landing a giant wet kiss on his cheek, all signs of the earlier slip of her tongue gone.

"Thank you, thank you, thank you," she said near his ear, and gooseflesh traveled down his body. She pulled back and smiled at him. Mesmerized, he couldn't move. The water dancing on her dark eyelashes lent an encrusted diamond motif to her brilliant ice-blue eyes. Her skin glowed, her cheeks bright pink as if the ocean had repeatedly slapped her. And, he decided, she couldn't possibly be any more beautiful. Her panting breaths made her chest heave in and out; her perfect breasts were slick with the briny ocean water and barely covered by her tiny red bikini top. Her chocolatey wave of hair was tousled and she ran her fingers through it, which only highlighted her exquisitely toned body and hiked her perky breasts even higher.

He wrapped her in the warm towel and hugged her to his chest. "You're very welcome, little pet." The scent of the clean ocean mixed with her essence filled his head. He decided right then and there that he'd remember this moment of pure unadulterated joy for the rest of his life.

"You look like you had fun," he said.

"I did. And you were right. It was the perfect distraction."

"Good, I'm glad. Now why don't I run you a bath?" he suggested. "You need to relax. Come."

Tugging her inside, he led her up the stairs and into the green *boudoir's* bathroom. He squirted foaming bath gel into the tub and made the water hot. He desperately wanted to crawl in behind her and lather her beautiful body with suds and massage the knots out of her tight and probably tired muscles. But he refrained, and not without tremendous effort.

After a half-hour, he came to get her. Her eyes were closed and she appeared so incredibly peaceful, he wanted to leave her be. Sitting on the edge of the tub, he grazed her cheek with the back of his hand and her eyelids fluttered opened, her gaze meeting his. She looked so young and innocent, which threw him off kilter. His throat constricted at the thought of what the next few days would bring. Signs of danger flooded his head. Red flags flew. How had he not seen this coming? It started out as fun and games, but now he felt terror invading his every waking thought, not to mention his dreams.

"Feel better?" he crooned.

"Mmm," she muttered. "Much."

"Alyx, are you sure about this? In the beginning, I never thought you'd follow through and then, well, I kind of got caught up in the fun of training you, but now, well, I'm worried. This is dangerous. I think you should reconsider."

"Don't be ridiculous, Daniel," she said, bristling and sitting up straight. Bubbles lingered on her shoulders and breasts, then slid down her wet skin. It distracted him for a second. "I'm not giving in now, not after I've subjected myself to a week of torture under your iron hand."

Daniel's heart seized up. She hated him? She hated this whole experience with him?

"Oh, Daniel, don't look so crestfallen. I was joking." Her smile warmed him and he made himself breathe. "Really, it's been crazy, I'll admit that, but it's been awesome. Freaky and wonderful, actually." She kissed the back of his hand, her lips lingering on his skin too long. "You're too sweet, really."

"Okay, that's enough to ruin a Dom's reputation. Please, do not say that to anyone at the club. I'll never be able to show my face there again." Not that he really wanted to. After this whole thing was over he'd never go back.

"Don't worry, your secret is safe with me. I won't out you to your buddies."

"Come on. Out. The water is getting cold."

"Could you please get the bathroom cup, I need to rinse out the conditioner in my hair."

Daniel doused her hair with cups of warm water until the last remnants had washed away. She held his hand and he pulled her onto the fluffy white rug and swaddled her in a navy-blue bath sheet. He hugged her tightly to his chest. "Are you sure, Alyx? I could invent some excuse to get you out of this if you want me to."

"No. I have to see this through, it's the right thing to do," she continued softly, her voice like a cashmere sweater against his chest. "We have to think of all those women who at this very moment are being hurt, women who haven't seen their families in a long time, families who don't even know if they're still alive. Everything will be fine. One of us will get them back, and I really want that person to be me." She tilted her head up and planted a gentle kiss on his chin. "I'll be fine, don't worry."

She was right, of course. But he did worry, and he would continue to until this craziness came to an end and he had her back safely in his arms. *And,* there he was again, thinking about not saying goodbye to her after their time together ended.

Alyx rubbed her hair vigorously with a hand towel to remove the excess moisture. She still couldn't believe she'd dropped the L bomb on him and that he'd so graciously allowed her to escape total embarrassment. But she wondered at her words. Could she really be falling for him? Somehow, he made her feel— She wrinkled her brow, struggling to find the word. And then it came to her. *Free.* He'd freed her not only from her clothing, but from the fear of embarrassment, shame, the freedom to voice her release when an orgasm ripped through her. She'd never felt more alive. Never felt so vulnerable and yet, so damn safe.

"Here," Daniel said, startling her. He strolled into the green bedroom unannounced, like always, and handed her a shiny black shopping bag. "I had Jack send over something for you to wear tonight from the fetish shop at the club." Alyx threw the towel on the bedside chair and tugged the tie on Daniel's robe around her tighter, she wasn't sure why, it's not like Daniel wouldn't take if off her this very minute if he felt like it. It seemed like he always felt like seeing her naked. She accepted the bag with a sense of dread chilling her body. She'd seen this stuff online and it freaked her out, trashy clothing with cutouts in the most inappropriate places.

"I'm afraid to look," she said derisively.

"I think you'll find it acceptable," Daniel said, flashing her a devilish wink. "If not, well, too bad. I want. You do."

She placed the bag on the bed and tentatively unfolded the

silver tissue paper imprinted with images of handcuffs and floggers. "Cute," she commented, lifting the skimpy black item from the bag, a black bustier with red laces up the front. "I hope there's more." Reaching into the bag, she pulled out a matching mini skirt. She sighed. "Well, not much as it turns out." She rolled her eyes. The thought of wearing such skimpy clothing out in public unnerved her, however she didn't have much of a choice. Reaching inside the bag again, she rooted around. Empty. She flashed him an incredulous expression. "No underwear?"

"Nope. Consider yourself lucky, most subs are kept totally naked at the club. I'm letting you off easy." He headed for the door, then turned, his hand on the knob. "I'll leave you to get ready. We need to be at the club by eight."

Alyx blew out her hair so it fell in soft waves over her shoulders, figuring it would act like protection over the skimpy outfit. She applied more makeup than usual, shading her eyes with smoky dark shadow and some serious Cleopatra-style eyeliner. She kept her lips light, which hopefully would offset the dark eye makeup. Slipping on the black stilettos Daniel had bought her to wear to the fundraiser, she surveyed herself in the mirror. The reflection portrayed a woman she didn't know. Maybe good? She was playing a part and this was merely her costume. Pretending to be someone else might save her sanity.

Daniel knocked on her bedroom door and then entered, again without permission. His eyes lit up. "Wow," he blurted. "You look hot."

Alyx huffed. She didn't think she looked so horrible the other way. "Thanks." She could easily return the compliment. He wore dark jeans and a black leather blazer over a charcoal gray tailored shirt. She liked him in clothes, although she liked him more without. Jesus, she had to stop thinking like that.

Reaching into his jacket pocket, Daniel pulled out a folded

piece of paper. "You'll need to bring your medical form to show you're disease free. Put it in your purse. They'll ask for it." Alyx stowed the report as directed. "Ready?" He extended his hand.

"As I'll ever be." He held her hand firmly as he escorted her down the winding staircase and into the foyer.

"Mason will drive you. I'll leave first and he'll follow a few minutes behind. Zach, the security guard at the door, is expecting you. Do whatever he says. Jack will meet you inside and you'll go through the usual routine for interviewing a prospective member. I'll be at the bar and Jack will introduce us, then you let me take it from there. Understand?"

Alyx hesitated as she contemplated what tonight would bring. She wouldn't have to perform until Saturday, so tonight shouldn't be too terrible. "Yes, Sir," she finally said. "I've got this."

"Good girl." Daniel opened the front door and ushered her out to the SUV, Mason already at the wheel. He buckled her into her seatbelt, then gripped her chin. "You'll be okay, baby, just follow Jack's lead." He planted a quick kiss on her lips and withdrew.

Alyx grabbed his wrist. He turned and their eyes met. "Thanks, Daniel. I mean for coming with me tonight. Knowing you'll be there eases my anxiety."

He gave her a wink and squeezed her hand, then bent and put the back of her hand to his lips. He kissed it softly. "You're welcome." He shut the door and walked over to his car. He pulled out of the driveway and she watched the red taillights disappear. She tried to slow her breathing and gave herself a pep talk. *Get your shit together, Alyx. This is only the dress rehearsal. You can do this.*

Mason pulled into the long driveway of the St. Andrews Club. Daniel's car was parked in the side lot and Alyx relaxed somewhat, reminding herself that Daniel was inside and would keep an eye on her. Her heart was pounding more than she'd expected. She assumed this would be easier.

Opening the door, Mason extended his hand as support in maneuvering the steep step down. She didn't need to do a face plant in her ridiculously high-heeled shoes. "Good luck, Miss Cameron," Mason said kindly.

"Thank you, Mason." But she sincerely hoped luck wouldn't be required for tonight's activities.

Big brass hinges and wooden planking, complete with a large round doorknocker, made it seem like she'd arrived at the door of a medieval castle. She gave two raps with the knocker and the door opened. A huge man greeted her, dressed in a simple black suit, white shirt and no tie. He must've had a serious case of acne as a youth and he'd definitely had his nose broken once or twice. "Yes? May I help you?"

"I'm Alyx Cameron, I believe Jack is expecting me."

"Oh, of course, Miss Cameron, nice to meet you." His intimidating demeanor softened and he extended his hand toward her. "I'm Zach. Come in."

Zach closed the door behind her and she surveyed the magnificent anteroom. Black and white striped wallpaper decorated the walls and a large mahogany Queen Ann style desk sat in the center of the room. Shiny black ceramic tile covered the floor and recessed lighting cast a romantic glow over the room.

Taking a seat behind the desk, Zach pulled out some papers from a file cabinet to the right. "Do you have your medical form?" Alyx handed him the paper from her purse. "Excellent," he said. "You need to fill out the appropriate paperwork before I can admit you. Come sit and make sure you read it carefully. The last chick that didn't read the fine print got herself into some serious shit. There are punishments for breaking the rules and take my word for it, it's something you want to avoid, especially on your first visit." Zach handed her a three-page document.

Alyx sat in the black upholstered chair beside Zach's desk and began to read. Zach was right. If you interfered with a scene in progress they could discipline you right on the spot. The punishment was the Dom's choice and ranged from spanking, to flogging, to public display without clothing. Yikes! Alyx scribbled her name on the last page and handed the forms back to Zach. He picked up the wall phone behind him and dialed four numbers. "She's here, boss." He turned to Alyx. "Master Jack will be out to get you in a minute."

Master Jack? "Thanks," she sputtered. Where had her voice gone? Her hands were sweaty and her pulse raced. What had she gotten herself into? Playing with Daniel was one thing, but the thought about what she was about to walk into had her seriously doubting her whole involvement in this crazy assignment.

She reminded herself to keep the focus on the *why*, the chance to save those poor women from a hideous fate.

A door to the right opened and Jack strode into the room dressed in black leather pants and a black silk shirt. He was a handsome man, his full head of silver hair slicked back and a friendly smile revealing straight white teeth, although he vaguely resembled a gangster she'd once seen in a movie.

"Alyx," he exclaimed. "So good to see you." He walked directly to her, seized her hand and laced his fingers through hers. "Ready?"

He held her hand like he was her boyfriend, the same way Daniel did and she began to wonder if all Doms acted like this. "Yes."

"Good girl. We'll start in my office and I will explain how the club works, then I'll give you the fifty-cent tour and introduce you to some of our members."

"Yes, Sir. Time to get to work." She tried to sound enthusiastic. Jack opened the door and tugged her through the mass of twisting flesh on the dance floor. Heavy metal music played over the sound system, luckily not so loud that you couldn't hear yourself think. The smell of leather and human musk filled the air. Alyx almost felt like she'd landed in *Dante's Inferno*. Bodies clad in leather and latex, or nothing at all. Flesh pressed flesh in carnal gyrations. Studded collars attached to leashes around both men's and women's necks, and many had piercings in places that made her want to grimace. *Oh boy.* If she'd seen this stuff the first night she'd arrived she might've seriously considered rescinding her agreement to tackle this assignment.

Alyx glanced to the left and noticed that the place was gigantic, with a second floor guarded by a black wrought-iron railing and large lighted display windows on the far wall, but she couldn't see what was on display. Reaching the other side of the dance floor she spied a bar constructed entirely of glass that ran the length of the room. The motif—a riot of blue, chrome, steel and glass—actually reminded her of her upscale gym. The similarity of the two suddenly struck her: sweat, pain, physical exertion, moans and groans, even screams.

The satisfaction of pushing your body to insane limits.

Gazing at the large man behind the bar, she wondered if that was Steve, the Dom they'd arranged for her to scene with on Saturday. He was attractive and, big, definitely a body builder. His bright, animated eyes tracked her as he talked to someone. Alyx's heart rate increased as she approached the burly bartender. He waved at her. She guessed he'd been expecting her and that Jack would introduce them shortly. But then she realized he was talking to Daniel, who acted like he didn't know her.

Jack ushered Alyx into his office. She walked left and stood in front of one of the two cherry-red couches that faced each other, then placed her purse on the black rectangular coffee table.

"Sit," Jack said. It sounded like an order. "Let's talk." Alyx sat, keeping her knees clamped tightly together. Jack settled in next to her. "It's important for you to understand how the club works so you don't get yourself into a situation you hadn't anticipated. I'll begin by explaining the culture. Doms have all the control. You can expect to be touched without your permission, although no one may touch you intimately without permission. If you are in the company of a Dom for the purpose of scening with him, he has control over who and how you may be touched. Some Dom's enjoy having other men touch their subs sexually and, basically, you give over control of your body to him. You will negotiate this with him before you agree to scene with him. That means you will clearly state your limits and he will honor those. Daniel outlined your limits and explained the use of safe words, correct?"

She laced her fingers together to keep them still. "Yes, of course."

"Good. Now, don't be shocked if a Dom asks you to come home with him for the night or even for the weekend. It's common practice for submissives to go home with a Dom and then at the end of the night, or the weekend, the interaction is over and there will be someone new next time. Simply say you're not interested in going home with him and that should be the end of it. To ease your anxiety, please know that we have dungeon monitors who keep their eyes on all activities and who will intervene in the event that something doesn't look right. They're effectively our version of bouncers, and they wear black polo shirts with the club crest on the pocket. I'll point them out as we walk around. If you ever need help or have a question, ask them. They're all experienced Doms and well respected here and more than willing to help you.

"The last thing you need to remember is that protocol is always in effect at the club. Daniel explained protocol to you, right?"

"He did."

"Good, as a submissive at the club, if you are not in the company of a Dom, any Dom can ask for the inspection or slave position and you must comply. The surrender position shouldn't be necessary unless you royally screw up, which I don't anticipate happening.

"All right, I don't want to overwhelm you, I'll explain some of the other nuances of being a submissive as we take the tour. I'll introduce you to Steve, who'll be scening with you on Saturday. You'll also receive a pair of handcuffs that all new submissives in training wear. Daniel explained the coding system we use?"

Alyx answered, "Yes."

"And you've agreed to blue for bondage, green for sex, yellow for mild pain. Is that right?"

"Yes," she said, but her mouth had gone dry and she struggled to swallow.

"You all right?" Jack said. "Seem a little anxious."

"Don't they say butterflies before a performance is a good thing?"

Jack chuckled. "Be assured that everyone will be keeping an eye out for you. I pride myself on screening our members carefully and we rarely have someone act inappropriately. In the event we do, I throw them out and permanently revoke their membership. Doms pay a lot of money for the privilege of playing here and they pay their dues upfront. If I kick them out, they do not get a refund. That's pretty good incentive to make them play by the rules.

"All right, enough talk for now. I'll explain more as the need arises. For tonight, you will be my submissive until I release you to Daniel later in the evening. That means no one can touch you without my permission. I will allow some of the Doms I know well to touch you, so that you are believable, including the dungeon monitors because they are my most trusted practitioners and experts in training submissives. Also, for your safety I want them all to know who you are. Daniel explained that they will be the only ones allowed to scene with you for now. You can branch out on your own once you feel comfortable."

Jack extended his hand again and Alyx walked out the door under his watchful eye. The first stop was the bar. Jack introduced her to Steve who gave her a warm welcome, taking her small hand in his massive grip. Daniel, sipping a drink, sat close enough to hear their conversation.

"Glad to finally meet you, Alyx," Steve said.

"Likewise," she replied softly.

"Alyx," Jack said, giving her a stern glare. "Protocol dictates every Dom be addressed as Master. Please address Steve as Master Steve, or Sir."

Alyx felt her teeth clench at Jack's directive. That word still grated on her nerves. "Yes, Sir," she said, trying to sound compliant. "Sorry, Master Steve." In her peripheral vision, she swore the corner of Daniel's mouth quirked up, but she was afraid to make eye contact.

"Good girl," Jack said. "You will address me as Master Jack and each dungeon monitor I introduce you to will receive the same respect."

"Yes, Sir."

"A pair of subbie cuffs, please, Master Steve," Jack said. Steve reached under the bar and retrieved a pair of fleece-lined black leather handcuffs. Alyx quickly noted the clasps that would allow them to be buckled together.

"Charms?" Steve said.

"Blue, green and yellow," Jack answered.

Steve attached the appropriate charms to each cuff.

"Wrists, please." She stretched out her arms in Steve's direction and he swiftly secured her wrists inside the soft cuffs. "There you go, little one, officially submissive." He beamed and Alyx tried to embrace his friendly demeanor, while all she could think about was his enormous dick and whether she'd be having sex with him on Saturday. Oh, brother.

"Alyx," Steve said, "this is Master Daniel." Steve pointed toward Daniel who offered his hand in welcome.

"Hello, Alyx. Pleasure," Daniel said.

"That's why I'm here, Sir. *Mostly*."

"You're new, I take it?" Daniel said.

"Yes, Sir. I'm here for the introductory tour to see if the club meets my needs," Alyx said.

"You're very lovely, hope you find the club to your liking. I'd be pleased to buy you a drink when you're done with the tour." Daniel's genuinely warm expression eased her anxiety somewhat and she fought the urge to throw herself into his arms.

"Excellent idea," Jack said. "Master Steve, give Alyx a drink and I'll have the usual."

"Tell me, darling, what's your poison?" Steve said, flashing a wicked grin.

"Scotch, lots of ice and a splash of water, Sir."

"What a coincidence. The same poison Master Daniel drinks." Alyx struggled to avoid Daniel's gaze. Even though the three of them knew the game she was playing, she had to stay in character.

Jack led Alyx by the hand, walking deeper into the club, drinks in hand. Alyx recoiled at the number of naked women collared and leashed to their Doms and also a goodly number of men equally engaged with either male or female Doms/Dommes.

Around the dance floor, the majority of space was dedicated to intimate seating areas with black leather couches and chairs separated by large potted plants. Couples were actively engaged in sexual practices and even though the lighting was dim, no doubt existed as to what body parts touched and penetrated. Women and men alike shrieked upon climax, plus plenty of moans and whimpers also made Alyx uncomfortable. Other Doms provided aftercare, something Alyx now recognized and appreciated, as they wrapped their subs in soft blankets and fed them assorted juices and chocolate.

"Alyx, this is Master Sam, one of our dungeon monitors," Jack said, distracting Alyx from her observations. "Master Sam, meet Alyx, the prospective member I was telling you about."

Sam eyed Alyx carefully and her first thought was his size. Were all these guys wannabe World Wrestling Entertainment champs? She noted the black polo shirt with the club's crest on the pocket like Jack explained. "Pleasure, little pet," Sam said. And what was with all the cutesy names? Did they all use them: little one, pet, little subbie? Weird hearing stuff like that from guys she'd just met and it certainly would've earned a nasty remark if they pulled that crap anywhere else.

"Nice to meet you, Master Sam," Alyx choked out.

"I'm giving Alyx the tour," Jack said.

"Good," and then to Alyx, "maybe I'll catch you later," Sam said. His words sounded ominous. And what would he do with her once he caught her? She tried to smile convincingly as Jack escorted her farther into the pulsing underbelly of the club.

Master Mark, Master Jerry, Master Kevin and Mistresses Donna and Olivia came across their path, all dungeon monitors and all, intimidating. When had she become such a wimp? As an agent for the FBI she prided herself on being the intimidating one and this role reversal was serving to heighten her anxiety. She sighed, just get through it one night at a time and soon enough you'll be back to your old persona, she reminded herself.

Masters Mark and Jerry requested permission to touch Alyx and she struggled to stay in character and not deck them both. Master Kevin demanded the inspection position and slid his hands so far up her thigh she'd been prepared for a vaginal assault, but as she kept her eyes focused on the floor, she realized he was checking her anxiety level rather than copping a feel. Mistress Olivia ran a hand over her breast. Alyx had never even entertained the thought of being accosted by a woman at the club. Anything goes it seems.

Jack pointed to the second floor. "Upstairs are the private playrooms for those who don't care to play in public. Each has a particular piece of equipment and a bed with restraints. Doms reserve them for a set time. Steve will bring you to one of those when you arrive on Saturday so you can get acquainted and practice your scene. He'll let me know if you're ready to scene in public. Other than that, I think it goes without saying, but you're *not* to go up there with anyone else."

"No, Sir, won't be happening."

"Good."

Things were going reasonably well until they reached the back of the room. She'd wondered what was behind the lighted display windows and even with all her research and Daniel's coaching she wasn't prepared for it. All kinds of apparatus were being used, some equipment she recognized from Daniel's rec room, but also things like stocks where people were secured by their appendages and necks into demeaning positions while their naked bodies were flagellated by all manners of whips, canes, paddles, leather straps and floggers. One guy dripped candle wax on to the tender parts of his submissive's body while strapped to a bondage bench. Threesomes and foursomes abounded, varied combinations of men and women engaged in all manner of oral, anal and vaginal sex. On display for anyone to watch. This was what they called "scening," Jack explained. Doms signed up to use the space, then put on a "scene" with their sub, while others engaged in voyeurism. When done, they cleaned all the equipment before others took their turn. Alyx's thoughts cut to her scene with Master Steve on Saturday. If she passed his "test" would she then be required to perform in one of these display windows?

Just when she thought it couldn't get more brutal, Jack escorted her through a dark hallway and explained what the theme rooms were. One room mimicked an office, another like the inside of an Arabian tent, and yet another replicated a medical examining room. The hallway ended in a massive door similar to the gothic front entrance of the club and Jack explained that this was the dungeon. Alyx told herself the screams emanating from inside were "safe, sane and consensual." But the urge to dash in there and rescue someone overwhelmed her.

"You're pretty tense, little one," Jack said, giving her hand a squeeze. He hadn't let go of her since he'd escorted her away from the bar. "Perhaps we should avoid the dungeon at this point. Under no conditions should you let anyone bring you in there, understand?"

Alyx smiled weakly. "Sound advice, Sir."

"Good girl. Besides, it would be much, much harder to supervise you in there. I want someone to have eyes on you at all times."

"Safety first, Master Jack," Alyx said, hoping to lighten the tension that had put a crick in her neck.

"Exactly," Jack said.

Jack pulled her by the hand, leading her back to the main room. Another overly ripped dungeon monitor stopped Jack. "I need to speak with you, boss," he said but quickly shifted his gaze to Alyx. Jack introduced him as Master Colin.

"Hello, little one," Colin said. He tucked his hands into his armpits. "Permission to touch your sub, Master Jack?"

"Yes," Jack answered.

Colin placed his hand on Alyx's shoulder then ran it down her arm and around her waist. He pulled her closer to him and gazed deeply into her eyes. "She's very lovely," Colin said to Jack, but his eyes stayed on Alyx. "Such a sweet little thing, she'll be a welcome addition." Alyx tried not to squirm as Colin slid his other hand over her breast, lingering over her nipple, then gave it a little tug. Alyx let out a squeal and Colin smirked before releasing her.

"Yeah," Colin said. "She's gonna be all kinds of fun."

Alyx bit her tongue, afraid that she'd drawn blood, but managed to not say anything impertinent.

"What did you need?" Jack said, diverting Colin's focus.

"I think we've got a situation in the lower dungeon. It's one of our regular subs and I'm pretty sure she's faking it with Master Geoffrey. He's too inexperienced and, well, you know how Tracy can be."

"All right." Jack sighed. "Break the news to Master Geoffrey and hook him up with someone who won't make a fool out of him."

"You got it, boss."

Colin strolled off into the club's nether regions and Alyx drained the rest of her drink and exhaled relief.

"You did well," Jack said, smiling wide. "I'm sure this is difficult."

"Well, Sir, it's definitely going against my ingrained desire to clobber a guy. Not to mention my self-defense training. I seriously need to keep that trigger in check. Good thing I'm not carrying my service revolver."

Jack smirked and put his arm around Alyx's shoulders. He kissed the top of her head. "I know, little one. I know."

They ambled back toward the front of the room and Jack

identified what he called the submissives' pen, a roped off area where about twenty women sat together and chatted. Some sipped on a cocktail, all were outfitted in fetish gear and a few were manacled with chains hooked to the floor. Alyx recalled Daniel explaining that when a Dom wanted to leave his sub unattended for a few minutes he would chain her to the floor in the submissives' waiting area. Jack further explained that as an unattached sub, this is where you waited to be approached by a Dom.

"Let's head back to the bar. I think you could use a second drink." He hugged her and gave her a kiss on the cheek, then kissed her for real. This caught Alyx off-guard and she wanted to recoil from his attentions. Didn't he have a girlfriend? A submissive of his own? Lisa, she'd met her that other night. I guess sharing was acceptable in the land of *the lifestyle.* Everyone touched everyone and people openly took what they wanted, whenever they wanted to, and you just had to, *submit.* They obviously had a totally different attitude about sex and it didn't have anything to do with monogamy.

Jack picked up Alyx by her waist and perched her on a barstool. Steve sauntered over, leaving Daniel at the other end of the bar. "Another drink, little subbie?"

"Yes, please, Master Steve." Once she started "working" at the club she'd switch to club soda, but for tonight she needed a drink, or two.

"Why don't you head to the end of the bar? I believe Master Daniel has been waiting patiently for the privilege of your company." Steve said to Jack, "Will you hand over possession of the new trainee to Master Daniel?"

"I think that will be acceptable. We'll see you again this weekend, Alyx."

"Yes, Master Jack. Thank you for the tour and also the lesson."

"Good. I'm glad to officially welcome you to the St.

Andrews Club, Ms. Cameron. Now, when you arrive on Saturday you will report to Master Steve. He'll put you in your cuffs and inspect your attire for the evening. You must comply with everything he tells you or he will issue you a punishment. Are we clear?"

Alyx nodded.

"Let me hear you, pet," he said.

"Yes, Sir. Report to Master Steve upon arrival and do whatever he commands."

"He's in charge of the trainees and has total control. Anyone who wants to play with you will need his permission. This isn't only for you but the protocol for all new submissives who come here without a Dom of their own."

"Yes, Sir."

"I will also have my sub, Lisa, give you a quick tour. She'll show you the locker room, the first aid supplies, the restrooms and introduce you to the other trainees. They will be helpful, sort of a support system, and can field any questions from the female perspective."

"Great, Sir. Much appreciated."

Steve leaned his massive forearms on the bar and gave her a wink. "I'm looking forward to Saturday, little subbie. Come ready to play. I've got a great scene planned."

Alyx's stomach did a summersault and she struggled to stay in character. She wanted to say something, but couldn't think of a damned thing that didn't sound stupid or wouldn't be an outright lie. She smiled politely and slipped off the stool, anxious to make her way toward Daniel.

Jack put his hand on her ass, "Now, I believe Master Daniel is somewhat impatient to see how you're doing. Go." He rubbed her butt cheek like he owned it, then gave her a nudge in Daniel's direction. Steve placed her drink in front of Daniel, who patted the empty seat next to him. She sipped her cocktail, trying to steady her shaking hand.

"Breathe, little subbie," Daniel urged. He scrutinized her face. "How you holding up?"

"Honestly, Master Daniel," she began, trying not to smirk at the title, "It's all I can do to not smack someone right in the face."

"Why am I not surprised?" He squeezed her hand reassuringly and she relaxed at the warmth of his skin against hers. "Truthfully, I'm pretty much in the same place. If Jack or any of the other Masters puts another hand on you I just might punch someone myself."

His comment accelerated her heart rate and once again she struggled to make sense of her feelings for Daniel. Visiting the club had been somewhat of a wake-up call: she began to comprehend that a lot of what she'd presumed had been personal affection from Daniel was common in the Dom/sub relationship. She hadn't gleaned this from her prior research, she thought Doms were these alpha males who liked control and had no interest in actual feelings. But now she understood that they were incredibly affectionate, protective and even warm. The intimacy they offered wasn't only sexual, it was personal, unnervingly personal.

"Come," Daniel said. "Let's go sit in one of the secluded areas where I can play with you. You need to start getting acclimated to scening in public. You're going to get that lesson now." Before Alyx could answer, he placed her drink in her hand and tugged her behind him like the slave she'd agreed to become. He found an empty love seat and faced her. "Drink up, it'll give you courage."

She frowned. "Courage? For what?"

He put the edge of the glass to her lips. "Trust me." Alyx finished the icy cold scotch in a few quick gulps. "That's my girl." He downed the rest of his own drink, then placed the empty glasses on a side table. He sank into the soft cushions, pulling Alyx onto his lap. His erection pressed into her thigh and her breath hitched with a strange tingling excitement.

Time unraveled endlessly, turbulently, until once again Daniel feasted his eyes on Alyx, as Jack returned her to the bar. He'd followed Alyx and Jack around for a bit and witnessed at least three of the Masters, his former friends, manhandling Alyx as she made her way through the maze of heaving flesh. Having her back in his arms began to calm him and he desperately wished this night would end. Yet he had to make this convincing. He sorely wanted to fuck her right here on the loveseat, and he would have with a regular submissive in the old days. But somehow, scening in public, especially with Alyx, didn't hold the allure it used to. He wanted her alone, in private and to himself.

Daniel wrapped Alyx tightly in his arms. He buried his nose in her hair and inhaled her fragrant essence, then pushed her hair off her face and nibbled at her ear. Alyx giggled like she always did when he kissed anywhere near her neck. "I missed you." He sighed. "And seeing everyone touch you nearly killed me."

Alyx faced him, her normally light eyes darkened in the dimly lit room. "Sir, I didn't like those men touching me, not like I like it when you do."

"I like touching you, little subbie." Daniel eased a hand into her bodice and searched out a nipple. His tongue claimed her mouth as he gently twisted the erect nipple between his fingers. Alyx let a tiny squeak escape her. Deftly, he unlaced the bustier and opened it to reveal her breasts. Rolling her left nipple between his fingers, Alyx gasped and covered herself with her hands. Daniel grabbed both her wrists and pulled them to her lap. "Be still, little pet, submissives allow their Doms to expose them and play with them in public."

Using one hand, he buckled the cuffs on her wrists together. "Keep your hands here. Do not move them or I will be forced to spank you right here on the couch in front of everyone." He watched as Alyx surveyed the people seated nearby. Worry pinched her eyebrows. No way he'd actually spank her here, although he had no intention of letting her know that. He'd stop playing like this a year ago, having lost his taste for public sexual displays, but he had to keep up appearances for the sake of getting the job done. For Alyx.

With a hand on her chest, Daniel forced her to lay back, her head resting on the small couch's arm. He opened the bustier wider and grasped a breast in his hand and began to massage the warm flesh. "Close your eyes, little subbie," he ordered. "Just forget where you are and only feel my hands."

Daniel leaned over and kissed her full lips, gently letting his tongue dance with hers. His palm drifted across her flat stomach and he slid his fingers into the waistband of her skirt. Alyx squeezed her knees together in response to his probing fingers. Removing his hand, he pulled one knee up and pressed it into the back of the couch. "Put your other foot on the floor," he whispered. Alyx hesitated and he responded by placing it there himself.

Alyx opened her eyes and stared at him. "I don't want to do this here with people watching." Daniel knew this would be difficult, but he wanted her to do this with him before she was forced to play with Steve in public. On the other hand, he sorely wished he could talk her out of this whole ridiculous charade, although he considered that highly unlikely.

"You will do as you're told, little subbie," Daniel said, trying to sound intimidating. "I doubt that you're going to stay still, so I'm going to restrain you." With a swift motion, he had her wrists over her head and cuffs snapped to a ring hanging off the loveseat's arm.

Alyx gasped. "Geez, does everything around here have restraints on it?"

"You have no idea," Daniel said. "Now, quiet. You're in protocol and you will not speak unless I give you permission."

Alyx's gaze bit into him and he wanted to grab her and make a run for it, but he couldn't. He had to get the job done. They were nearly at the finish line and he couldn't fade now. Besides, having her here, nearly naked, had his blood rushing and his erection straining his pants. The sooner he got this job done the sooner he'd have her home where they could really let loose.

Daniel let his hand fall between her legs, hiking the hem of her skirt up. One hand stroked her inner thigh, stopping an inch short of the V between her legs. "Relax, little pet. Put your mind on a beach somewhere and let me take you where you need to be." He studied her face. "What is it, Alyx? You may speak."

"I don't want you to make me come in public. Please, Daniel, don't make me."

"It will be expected, Alyx. How do you plan to be convincing if you don't?"

"Well, Sir, I planned on faking it with Steve or any other Dom that I had to play with."

Daniel tried not to laugh. "Oh, baby, that's not going to fly here. Everyone will know." But then he blurted, "Alyx, please tell me you haven't been pulling that shit on me."

Alyx's eyes widened and Daniel became fearful of her answer. Could he have been so overconfident that he could have been duped? He knew when he made a woman come. He considered himself quite adept at his skill in that regard. But now?

"Well," she began, and his stomach clenched as he

prepared himself for truth. "That was my plan, but unfortunately your exceptional sexpertise derailed me." She smiled at him, a wry smile.

Relief flooded through him. "Sexpertise? Did you coin that phrase? I've never heard it before." Daniel placed his hand on the inside of her thigh and pressed it into the back of the couch, hiking her knee nearly to her waist.

"Uh… What was the question again, Sir?"

"Never mind, little subbie. That's enough jabbering with those sexy lips of yours. Keep quiet and close your eyes. The sooner we're done here the sooner I can get you home for some real fun."

He shifted sideways a little, slipping his other hand between her open legs and she stiffened and gasped. He could see she held her breath as his fingers drew little lines up and down her sensitive flesh. He spread her thighs open wider and plunged two fingers into the soft, wet folds between her legs. Her back arched in response to his touch.

"Always so wet, baby. I like that, Alyx. Very much." He thrust his fingers in and out in a punishing rhythm as her hips rose to meet his relentless probing. He moved a hand to her chest and one wide palm covered her breast as he pinched her nipple. His other hand continued to tease her. He kept his fingers inside her, pumping in and out, then working his fingers over her clit. He pressed deeply inside her, alternating with slipping between her folds and circling her clit. Her breathing increased and he felt her tissues become engorged.

Twisting his hand sideways to catch her clit between his thumb and fingers, he pinched it gently before each thrust. She gasped when he pushed three fingers inside her, ruthlessly stretching her open. He pulled out slowly, circling her entrance, in and out in a fast driving rhythm.

In response to the relentless plunging force of multiple fingers, her insides tightened. The pinnacle. "Come for me, baby," he whispered as his lips pressed against hers. He squeezed her clit a tad harder and her orgasm barreled through her. She shuddered and convulsed and her hips gave little jerks. Her insides spasmed around his fingers and he left them inside her until her breathing evened out.

Alyx slowly opened her eyes and his fingers settled on her chin, holding it firmly in place. He kissed her deeply. She moaned again into his mouth as they melded their lips in a wet embrace. "Nicely done, little subbie," he said, for her ears only.

She blinked her baby blues at him and then noticed they'd acquired an audience. Doms were observing and smiling. Alyx buried her head in Daniel's chest and groaned. "I can't believe I just did that."

Daniel rubbed her back as she nuzzled his chest. Her warm breath penetrated his shirt and the heat of her threatened to be his undoing. He released her manacled wrists from over her head and rested them on her stomach. He rubbed her arms vigorously, assuring that the blood flowed properly through her limbs. Unhooking her wrists from each other, he raised and nibbled her fingers, kissing each one separately before helping her to sit up. Lacing her top back to conceal her beautiful breasts, he tugged on the ends of the ribbons, tying them into a perfect bow. He cuffed his fingers around her wrist and helped her stand, pulling down the hem of her short skirt to make sure she was covered. He ran his fingertips across her lips tenderly then took another kiss. "I think you've had enough of the club. Let's go, little subbie, and now that I have you warmed up, I can't wait to get you home."

Alyx's eyes widened and he realized she was holding her breath again. "Breathe, little one," he urged. Daniel winked and pulling her into his body, gave her butt cheek a pinch. She squealed.

He led her by the hand and didn't stop to talk to anyone as they fled the St. Andrews Club.

Alyx remained quiet as the car headed homeward on Montauk Highway, her eyes searching the dark night through the passenger side window. Suddenly he worried that Alyx's time at the club had traumatized her. She'd come magnificently for him, but perhaps it had been too much for her and once again he fretted over her Saturday evening debut with Steve. Shit. If only he could turn back the clock to the night he met her. He should have refused them and convinced Agent Scarborough this was a terrible idea.

Maybe then, Daniel furrowed his brow. Maybe what?

Perhaps the FBI wouldn't have put Alyx in this position? Maybe she'd have worked with a different trainer? Maybe? Maybe nothing. Then he'd never have met her and that thought sent him into a tailspin.

"You okay?" Daniel finally said.

"I'm fine," she muttered. There. Her favorite word again. *Fine.* "I-I just never thought I'd ever do something like that. Maybe I'm becoming a slut?" She continued to gaze out the window. Daniel reached over and secured her hand in his. He squeezed it affectionately and she slipped her fingers through his and squeezed back. She turned to him, but he couldn't read her facial expression in the shadows.

"You're not a slut. Don't do this to yourself. Besides, plenty of people get off on having public sex. I wouldn't consider that something that classifies somebody as a slut."

She pressed her forehead against the window. "I guess," she mumbled.

"You were aroused," he said.

"I know," she confessed. "That's what upsets me."

The automatic garage door opener allowed them entrance and Daniel walked behind Alyx as they strode through the kitchen. Alyx stopped in front of the French doors that led to the back deck. Daniel focused on her reflection in the glass and came up behind her. He put his arms around her. Her breathing quickly aligned with his and it calmed him. He still had to get her into the rec room tonight. They only had two nights left and he intended to make the most of it. In forty-eight hours, she'd be gone from his life.

Or, hopefully not.

"Let's go, little subbie, you're not done yet. I went easy on you today because I knew you were anxious about going to the club. Tonight we'll play with hot wax, and if you're really bad I just might flog you *and* spank you. How much fun would that be?"

Alyx swiveled in his arms and wrapped herself around his body, hugging him close. "Hot wax? Is there no end to your talents, Dr. Taylor?"

"I'm a full-service Dominant, Miss Cameron. I aim to please, and there's nothing I won't give you if you want it." Even if she didn't realize she wanted it.

"And I'm yours, Master Daniel, for whatever pleases you." Daniel's eyebrows arched, nearly reaching his forehead. Alyx didn't drop her gaze.

"Boy, you've come a long way in a week. I had serious doubts that I'd ever get you to be this compliant."

"Well, I'll agree with that," she muttered before touching her pouty lips to his. She kissed him and then pulled back. "Do with me what you will, Sir, because the end is in sight. I'm sure a year from now I'll have convinced myself this was merely a figment of my overactive, erotic imagination. It never really happened."

"Oh, it happened all right, Miss Cameron. It happened and it was spectacular. And tonight shall be a night you'll never forget."

Alyx couldn't believe she wanted more. More sex. More pain. More Daniel. *More, more, more.* Not after this entire week of carnal indulgences and then having to perform with Daniel at the club? With some of her previous lovers she hadn't had this much sex in a month, never mind a week, but just hearing Daniel threaten that tonight would be unforgettable, had her pulse racing, her heart practically leaving her body.

"Okay, little subbie," releasing her from his tight embrace. He grabbed her by the shoulders and faced her away from him. "I want you in the rec room in ten minutes. No clothing, slave position in front of the St. Andrews Cross."

Alyx had no breath, no spit in her mouth, even as adrenaline ignited her blood.

Daniel prodded her behind. "Off you go."

Chapter 7

Friday

Melancholy swarmed Alyx as she watched Daniel sleeping, his face a picture of unadulterated male beauty. She chuckled quietly to herself. A poor choice of words, as technically there had been plenty of adultery. Well, not actually adultery, because neither of them had been cheating on anybody, but still...

The sadness came because she knew she had to return home today and regain her sanity before she went to work at the club. She needed not only to calm her emotions, she needed to rest her lady bits after last night's exertions. A smile grabbed her lips, recalling their session in the rec room, which had undoubtedly been the hottest night of sex she'd ever had and very likely the best damn time she'd *ever* have.

Daniel gave a little snort and moved off his side and stretched out on his back, his arms over his head. Alyx slung an arm over his broad chest and nuzzled her face into his neck. The masculine scent of him, mixed with the leftover cologne essence became a smell she'd never forget, a sweet elixir, a bewitching love potion. Maybe she'd steal one of his tee-shirts to keep as a memento of their time together. *Good God.* What was with her and tee-shirts? She'd kept one of Jason's around for nearly six months after their break up and she didn't even like Jason. She wondered if a name existed for such an obsession. And was it a sign of some terrible flaw in her personality.

Daniel would be upset with her for leaving early, but it was the right thing to do. She needed to detox from him as soon as possible, reminding herself that he didn't have feelings for her and what she'd thought might be affection was simply the way Doms were. Last night at the club had convinced her of that, the way Jack and all the Masters had treated her with such personal attention made her accept reality. No harm, no foul, she guessed. She'd had a wonderful week playing with Daniel and now the time had come for her to use what he'd taught her to catch those sadistic slavers and hopefully bring home the female prisoners. Alyx closed her eyes and let the essence of Daniel fill her head.

"Good morning, sunshine," his sultry voice crooned. He draped his arm over her naked shoulder and pulled her into him, her breasts pressed tightly into his chest. "Did you sleep well?"

"Yes," she said, while thinking: might as well get this over with as soon as possible. She added, "I need to go home today. I'll leave right after breakfast."

Daniel's face darkened. "What? Why? We have one more day."

"Well, Daniel, there are so many reasons. You've taught me all I need for the club and, well, I'm exhausted. I need to mentally prepare myself and honestly, after last night's festivities, I need to give my body a rest. I'm pretty sore and if I walk into the club like this I'll look like I have a stick up my ass, or, more appropriately, like I have a giant butt plug up my ass."

Daniel rubbed a thumb across her cheek then over her chin. His expression confused her. Was he in pain? "Baby, I don't want you to go yet. I want another day. One more day."

"Daniel, you're sweet, you really are, and honestly, a week ago I'd never have thought that word would describe you." She leaned in and gave him a quick kiss on his forehead. She threw the covers back and began to make her escape. His strong hand grabbed her upper arm and he flung her back forcefully on the mattress, covering her body with his. The weight of him, his warm skin pressed against hers, made the blood sing in her veins. He grabbed her wrists and threw them over her head, securing them both in one massive hand.

"Please, Alyx. Stay another day." His dark eyes smoldered with sensuality and Alyx felt her resolve lessen. But no, she couldn't let him dazzle her with his sexpertise. Not now, never again.

"I can't, Daniel. I need to go home." She squirmed under him, trying to gain her freedom. His erection pressed into her stomach and she sighed. Was he ever satiated? Well, she had to admit that she didn't think she could ever get enough of him either and that was why she needed to make her escape. "Please, let me up, Daniel," she tried to sound angry, but barely convinced herself. She tried to free her wrists but couldn't budge them. She pushed her chest into his, but couldn't move him off her.

"You're on my time, little subbie, and our arrangement doesn't end until tonight," he said in his authoritative Dom tone. But then he smiled.

"Nice try, buddy, but that shit isn't going to work anymore. We've done enough and there's no way you can stop me from going home. I'll remind you that I have my firearm with me, don't make me use it to make my getaway." Alyx chuckled.

"Now, let me go." She kissed him on the mouth and the intensity of his return kiss set her libido into the red zone.

Hmm… she thought, maybe one last time?

"I won't," he said stubbornly, tightening his grip on her wrists.

Alyx considered her next move. "Well, mister, if you ask me nicely, maybe I might just fuck *you* before I go."

Daniel touched his nose to hers. "I don't know, Agent Cameron, I'm used to being in charge and I'm not sure I'm capable of giving up the reins."

"Do you trust me, Sir?" she said, their eyes only inches apart.

Daniel frowned, apparently considering her question. "Yes."

"Then we're going to play a little game called Honor Bondage." She firmly wedged her thigh between his legs and curled her foot around his calf. Using her hips, she swiftly flipped him onto his back, pinning his arms to the pillow.

"You little devil," he said, playfully. "Pretty sneaky using your FBI combat skills on me. You're lucky I don't put you over my knee right this second and teach you a lesson about topping from the bottom."

"Oh, I thoroughly intend on being on top, Sir. Now, hold onto the spindles on the headboard and keep them there. This is a test of how much control you have, mister. I want you to stay still, you do not have permission to move. Is that clear?"

After a too-long pause, he mumbled, "Yes, ma'am."

Alyx curved his fingers around the headboard spindles, thrilled at the fact that his breathing was labored. She had this one opportunity to let him know what things would have been like if they hadn't played this ridiculous Dom/sub game for the past week.

She dragged her hands over his chest and settled them on his tight stomach. "Honor bondage dispenses with the need for physical restraints like cuffs, or ropes, in a scene, because you essentially must hold a fixed position through the force of your will. In essence you are bound by the Mistress's will. Do you understand?"

"Yes ma'am," Daniel said and she could see the laugh he was trying to suppress.

"Good," she said, unable to add on the word *boy*, that just sounded perverted. "Close your eyes and keep them closed. This is all about feeling, Daniel. Set your mind free and let me please you." Daniel closed his eyes and she slid her body down and knelt between his legs, then grabbed his ankles and spread them wide. That sexy salute of his warmed every bit of her body, mind, soul.

"Now it will be more difficult to keep your legs still because there's nothing to anchor them. If you can't stay still then I will be forced to restrain you." Daniel frowned briefly and Alyx understood Daniel would never allow her to tie him up and that was fine, she had no intention on following through on that threat anyway. Straddling his hips, she leaned in and placed her mouth on his nipple, running her hands across his chest. She sucked until his nipples hardened, good and firm.

Her kisses were everywhere and he yielded to the ministrations of her lips as they finally landed between his legs. She took him into her mouth and carefully teased him with her tongue. His hips began to writhe under her and she quickly set him free. She snapped, "Do. Not. Move. Mister." His eyes still closed tightly, her warm, wet lips slid over his shaft again. She sucked hard and he thrust himself deeply into her mouth. The strokes of her tongue grew more forceful and he writhed beneath her once more.

"Fuck," he yelled. "You're slaying me, woman."

Releasing him again, "Quiet," she barked. This time she sucked hard on the tip of his erection before she slid his hardness into her mouth. She shoved her hands underneath him and grabbed the cheeks of his ass and squeezed. The muscles hardened at her touch. Massaging his skin, she pressed him more deeply into her mouth until he hit the back of her throat.

"Jesus, Alyx, I can't take any more of this I need to be inside you." He swooped down on her and pulled her to his mouth, kissing her passionately. "You little vixen, how am I ever going to let you go?" In one quick motion, he picked her up and impaled her on his dick and the initial burst of soreness made all the breath whoosh out of her, as if she'd just taken a blow to the chest. It vanished instantly and their oneness filled her with a sense of wholeness, as if it would never be this way again. Their hands locked together as she pumped up and down on him, burying him inside her to the hilt. They exploded at the same time and it was difficult to tell who was louder.

Alyx collapsed on Daniel's chest, damp with sweat, as their breathing calmed and the syncopating rhythms of their hearts merged. Her arms circled his neck and she held him tightly to her chest.

She had to go.

Daniel paced. He ran his hands through his hair in frustration. Alyx promised she'd call as soon as she got back to her apartment. He'd offered to have Mason drive her home but she'd insisted on taking the Jitney. That was four hours ago, she should easily be home by now.

Letting her go was the most difficult thing Daniel had done in a long time. Nothing he said could convince her to stay tonight even though it would be a shorter trip to the club from his house. She insisted on going home, needing time to mentally prepare for her club debut. He worried, remembering how she'd struggled to understand what she'd witnessed at the St. Andrews Club last night. He brought her there because he didn't want her freaking out during the night when she'd have to perform. Jesus, he hated this whole situation. His attempt to talk her out of this insane assignment had been futile. She was committed to saving these women and nothing he said could change that.

Dialing her number again, it went directly to voicemail. He texted her. No response. *Fuck.* Where could she be? Perhaps there had been an accident. Images of a bus wreck had her lying in the middle of the Long Island Expressway. She'd call him if she were in trouble, right?

Another hour passed and he needed to do something. Dialing Rob Scarborough's number, his gruff voice answered. "Dr. Taylor?"

"Scarborough, have you heard from Alyx today?"

"No. Why? Is something wrong?"

"I don't know. She insisted on going back to her apartment today to mentally prepare herself for tomorrow night. She left right after breakfast and promised to call me as soon as she got home, but I haven't heard a word. I've called her and texted her at least a dozen times."

"Look, Daniel, I have two college-age kids and they always promise to call me when they get back to school to let me know they arrived safely. Honestly, I don't think they've ever remembered, not once. As soon as they're back at school I'm totally out of their minds. The first few times I panicked, but now, I stopped asking. If something terrible happened, unfortunately, I'd find out soon enough."

"Alyx isn't some irresponsible college kid who got distracted by returning to the company of her friends. I'm worried, Rob. Really worried."

"Let me try her, she won't ignore my call. I'll tell her to put you out of your misery and ring you."

"Thanks, Rob, I appreciate it." Agent Scarborough hung up. Daniel waited, staring at the clock on the digital readout on the microwave—4:12. He sat on the kitchen stool and thrummed his fingers on the cool granite countertop. Lydia came into the kitchen carrying plastic grocery bags.

"Good afternoon, Dr. Taylor." She placed her merchandise on the counter and started unpacking the items from farm stand.

"Lydia," he said, more curtly than intended.

"Is something wrong, Sir?" she said with concern.

"I'm not sure." His phone rang and he jumped, checking the readout. Scarborough. His pulse raced. "Rob!"

"Daniel, Alyx didn't answer my call either, so I had Matt call her and his went right to voicemail also."

"What could have happened? The slavers couldn't have targeted her yet, could they?"

"No, no way. Don't know what it could be. Maybe she fell asleep and her phone is off. It's probably nothing, but Matt volunteered to go over and check on her. He lives in Brooklyn so I probably won't hear anything for an hour or so. Hang tight and I'll get back to you as soon as I find out what's going on."

Daniel decided he couldn't stand one more minute of this. "Lydia, tell Mason to text me Alyx's address, I know it's on 20th between 8th and 9th but I don't recall the building and apartment number." He jumped up, grabbed his car keys and headed for the garage.

"Yes, Sir," she said to his back.

Gravel spit into the air as he sped out of his driveway. He shoved his phone into the dock. Alyx's playlist popped up and he hit the play button. He didn't recognize the song until he heard the reprise, "*This girl is on fire.*" Alicia Keys—*Girl on Fire.*

His Mercedes could fly if he commanded. The speedometer hit ninety-five once he entered the expressway. If he got pulled over by a cop he'd play his emergency doctor card. The MD on his license plate had gotten him out of a ticket before.

Turning onto 20th street, his heart stopped. An ambulance and more cop cars than he could count filled the cramped roadway. He left his car in the middle of the street and bolted toward her building. The yellow crime tape stretched across the entranceway made his stomach lurch. A uniformed NYPD officer put out his hands and stopped Daniel from crossing to the front steps of her complex. "Sir, this is a crime scene. You cannot enter."

Daniel nearly punched him in the face, but decided the better course of action would be to be honest. He reached for his wallet and flashed his ID. "I'm here to see Alyx Cameron, is she injured?" Agent Scarborough exited from a dark sedan with red lights flashing on the dashboard. "Rob," he yelled. "What the hell?"

Agent Scarborough glanced his way. "I just got here and don't have all the details. Come with me." He brandished his ID and the officer lifted the yellow tape, allowing them both to pass underneath.

"Is she okay?" he asked Agent Scarborough. "Jesus."

Agent Scarborough didn't answer him and Daniel ran up the stairs to the fourth floor behind him. The door to her apartment was wide-open and a mob of uniformed and plain-clothes cops milled around. Scarborough flashed his ID again and entered. Daniel held his breath in anticipation of some-thing terrible. If she was dead, or seriously hurt, he'd put his hands around the throat of the sick fuck that did it, and squeeze.

Alyx sat on her living room couch next to a man of about thirty. He had his hand on her back and rubbed gently. Her head hung in her hands, tufts of her hair tangled in her tight grip. She wore a white fleece bathrobe and her feet were bare. He couldn't see her face.

"Alyx," he exclaimed.

Slowly, she raised her head, her steel-blue eyes drained, so cold. A red welt crossed her right cheek and her bottom lip—the one he loved to nibble on—was bloodied. His gut wrenched, but quickly turned to relief. She was alive.

On his knees before her, he took her chin in his hand and moved it from side to side, checking for marks. "What happened?"

She didn't answer him, just stared. Daniel looked to the kind-faced man beside her.

"I'm Matt," he said. "You must be Daniel."

"Yes," Daniel said. "Can you explain why this is a crime scene?"

"Jason, Alyx's ex-boyfriend, decided to pay her an unwelcome visit."

Alyx's bloody lip turned his stomach oily and he worried at her lack of emotion. Perhaps she was in shock. She buried her face in her hands again. Matt's voice continued.

"He was here when she got home and apparently long enough to get that hook drilled into her bedroom ceiling. He had her suspended. When I arrived, I found him standing in front of her with his gun."

"Matt," Alyx cried, dropping her hands from her face. "He doesn't need to know all the gory details"

"Yes, he does. In case you haven't noticed, the guy cares about what happens to you."

Alyx sighed and threw herself against the back of the couch, crossing her arms over her chest.

"I pulled my service revolver, but wasn't sure what to do. If his gun went off…" Now Matt closed his eyes and pressed his lips together. "He was yelling at her loud enough that he didn't hear me approach. I got him in a headlock and wrestled him to the ground. He was pretty drunk so I had him handcuffed in less than thirty seconds."

"Where is he?" barked Daniel. He'd kill the scumbag with his bare hands.

"They hauled his ass to his precinct. IA was quick to show up. Too quick. Apparently, they already had him on their radar. There've been a ton of complaints and he's pretty close to getting booted off the force anyway. This will seal the deal."

Daniel hesitated then ambled into Alyx's bedroom. The pale blue walls and comforter decorated with indigo pillows reminded him of the shades of blues her eyes could morph into. Agent Scarborough and two other men assessed the scene as the CSI photographer captured the required images.

Scarborough pointed to the far wall. The building was obviously old, with thick wooden beams running across the white stucco ceiling. A large eyehook had been screwed into one of the beams in the ceiling and a chain with metal shackles hung menacingly in the air. He pictured Alyx suspended from the ceiling at the mercy of that fuckwad. His gut wrenched. *Jesus.*

Daniel sucked in a deep breath and exhaled slowly, running his hand through his hair. Returning to Alyx's side, he sat and grabbed her hand, sliding the sleeve up. Nasty abrasions circled her wrist. He checked the other one, the same thing only bloody. He looked to Matt. "Okay if I tend to her injuries?"

"Yeah, we have all the evidence we need."

"Alyx, do you have a first aid kit?" Daniel said.

"Yes," her voice barely audible. "Under the sink in the bathroom."

Daniel retrieved the kit and laid it on the kitchen counter. He returned to Alyx's side and pulled her from the couch. He led her to the sink, then grabbed her by the waist and gently placed her on the counter. Removing his sport coat, he draped it over a kitchen chair and rolled up the sleeves of his tailored white shirt.

He repeated the motion with her bathrobe's sleeves then set about cleaning the wounds and applying an antibacterial cream, finishing with gauze bandages. Gently wiping the blood from her cut lip, he placed a dab of cream there also. Ice, he needed ice. Opening the freezer, he retrieved a package of cut corn, wrapped it in a kitchen towel and placed it along the side of her face. "Hold this," he ordered. He slid her off the counter and carried her back to the living room, taking a seat in the overstuffed chair, not unlike the one he used for aftercare in his rec room. Settling her on his lap, he pressed her head onto his shoulder and held the ice pack in place himself.

Time seemed to stand still as Daniel watched the melee of police personnel going about their business. Eventually the throng of officers began to disperse. Scarborough came over and sat alongside Matt.

"Obviously, this changes the plans for tomorrow," Daniel stated.

"I agree," Agent Scarborough answered, "there's no way I'm sending her undercover after this clusterfuck."

Alyx sat up as if someone had zapped her with a cattle prod. "What?" she yelled. "I'm fine. There's no way I'm *not* finishing this assignment, not after doing all the prep work with this guy." She pointed her thumb at Daniel.

This guy? Daniel nearly exploded with rage. He tried to check his anger at her easy dismissal of their time together. Regardless of her insult, he totally agreed with Rob on this point. "No way," he snapped. "You're in no condition to submit to the demands of the club. Not like this."

Alyx glared at him. "Not your call."

"Yes, it is. You've been attacked and shackled to your

bedroom ceiling. You've been both physically and mentally traumatized. Rushing into this assignment now will wind up getting those innocent women killed."

She jumped off his lap and faced him, hands on her hips. "Daniel, in case you've forgotten, you're not in charge of me anymore. Not that you ever really were. We were playing a game. You're not my Dom and I'm not your submissive"

Daniel swallowed back the fury rising inside. Back again at the first night they met. He'd started to believe that perhaps something more was going on between them. But now, what a fool he'd been.

Rob Scarborough sighed. "Alyx, like it or not, it is *my* call. After an incident like this, Bureau policy dictates that we secure your service revolver and you sit at a desk until further notice. I shouldn't have to explain this to you."

Alyx pointed her finger at him this time. "Really, Rob? This is personal, not job related. And if Matt hadn't stumbled in here you wouldn't even know about it. I would have gotten out of this mess on my own somehow."

Nobody responded.

"And," Alyx went on, "this assignment is so far off the grid that I think Bureau *rules* are pretty much out the window right about now. Why don't you call Merryl and ask her? Actually, let me talk to her." Her eyes didn't leave Rob's face, her body rigid, her jaw tight.

Rob hesitated, then pulled his phone from his pocket. "Not your place. I'll run it by Merryl and we'll see." Rob walked into the kitchen and began a heated discussion with his boss. Lots of fast whispers, only every several words could be deciphered, if that.

Alyx barged in after him. "Give me the phone," she demanded, then grabbed it from him. "Merryl, this is Alyx. I can't back away from this assignment now. I've invested too much and worked too hard. I'll never forgive the Bureau or myself if another one of these women dies. I'm committed to finding them. I can handle myself just fine." Alyx had already decided that even if Merryl denied her request she'd find a way to continue with her mission to track down this evil ring of human traffickers.

"I don't know, Alyx," Merryl said. "I don't need one of my best agents losing her shit in the field."

"Listen to me, Merryl. I won't let you down. I can do this."

After an agonizingly long silence, "All right. Put Rob back on the phone."

Rob had been lurking in the background and when Alyx pointed the phone is his direction he yanked it out of her hand. Alyx left him alone and headed back to the living room.

"All right," Rob said, exiting the kitchen. "You're good to go, but you better be sure that you have your shit together or so many heads will roll in our office it'll look like something out of a goddamned horror flick."

The ride back to Daniel's house was shrouded in silence. Etta James sang softly on the car stereo as Daniel tried to tamp down his anger. Was he the only one who could see the word disaster written all over this situation? The FBI had soundly outvoted him, and he had to admit that Alyx was right about one thing, he had no control over what she did or didn't do. At least he'd won a small victory in taking her back to his house for the night. The way he figured it, he had about eighteen hours to talk her out of this craziness. That's if she'd even talk to him. He couldn't figure her out. When he'd first arrived at her apartment she appeared the helpless victim and had let him tend to her. All he'd wanted was to hold her until she cried, letting out the fear and sadness engulfing her.

Etta stopped crooning and the only sound in the car came from the pinging of the directional signal as he entered his driveway. He pulled into the garage, switched off the ignition and sat in morose silence. The urge to grab Alyx and shake some sense into her overwhelmed him. Instead, he exited the car, retrieved her overnight bag from the trunk and walked over and opened her door.

"Thank you," she said, following him into the kitchen, the buzz of the garage door grating on his overwrought nerves. She kept walking, up the stairs, then slammed her bedroom door. His back ached, like he'd been leaning over an operating table all day. He threw his keys into the basket on the counter and wandered into the TV room, heaving himself onto the couch. He closed his eyes not knowing what to do next.

After about thirty minutes the soft sound of footsteps on the kitchen floor roused him. It was late and he realized neither of them had probably eaten anything since early in the day. Entering the kitchen, he found her standing at the break- fast bar, her hands clutching the counter as if she needed it for support. Silently, he opened the fridge and found cold chicken, coleslaw and fruit salad. Lydia left something for him most nights because she never knew what time he'd be home from the hospital.

"We should eat something." He removed bowls from the refrigerator and selected plates and silverware from the cabinetry.

"I'm not hungry," Alyx said.

"I didn't ask you if you were hungry. You'll eat something. That's an order."

"We're back to that again? You're not in charge of me."

Daniel sighed. "You know, Alyx, I have no clue what's going on with you. When I first got to your apartment you seemed like you wanted me to take care of you, to comfort you, but then you turned into super-agent or something."

He set out the food and scooped the salad and fruit onto her plate along with a chicken breast and placed it on the counter. She stood there like a zombie, saying nothing.

"Sit down," he ordered. "Do I have to cut this up and force feed you? Because I will."

She glared at him and the anger in his gut swelled into his throat again. Finally, she said, "Fine, I'll eat. I wouldn't want you to get the urge to spank me or anything." A light bulb lit up in his brain. Maybe that's exactly what she needed. Why couldn't she admit she was in trouble?

"Good girl," he said settling into a seat next to her. This gave new meaning to the expression "cold shoulder." He doled out his own food, pouring them each a glass of Pinot Grigio. "Alyx, this whole situation has to be upsetting you. He had you shackled, essentially a prisoner. That's not something anyone shrugs off this lightly. I want you to tell me what you're feeling."

"I don't feel anything. He was an awful man and he got what he deserved." She speared a piece of honeydew melon and put it into her mouth, then sipped at her wine.

"That's not normal. You should be feeling something. You just won't admit it to me and maybe you won't admit it to yourself."

Alyx studied her food and cut a piece off the chicken on her plate. She brought it to her lips and hesitated, then popped it into her mouth, but didn't respond.

"Let me ask you something." Daniel examined her beautiful profile. "Look at me," he commanded. Her sad eyes wrenched his gut, her expression stoic. "You act all fearless most of the time and it pisses me off."

She seemed to consider his statement for a minute. "Too bad."

"I think you were afraid today. Very afraid."

"I wasn't. I'm never afraid."

"I don't believe that, Alyx, not for a single second."

"Too bad," she said again.

"How about as a little girl. Tell me one time when you were afraid."

"I wasn't. Ever."

Just as he suspected, she was out of touch with her feelings. What had caused her to bottle up her emotions? If she didn't learn to release them they'd eat her from the inside out. The stress would eventually kill her. He'd certainly seen the effects of too much stress on the human body.

They finished their dinner and Daniel cleared the dishes, stacked them in the sink and stowed the leftovers.

"Come with me," he said, taking Alyx by the elbow and guiding her out of the kitchen.

"Where?" She yanked her arm back but he held on tightly.

Hmm, he thought, Superwoman one minute and errant child the next. Something was going on with her and since she either couldn't or wouldn't tell him what it was, then he intended to either fuck it, or spank it out of her.

Alyx couldn't understand why she felt compelled to treat Daniel so badly. He'd been nothing but nice to her, concerned for her health and well-being. She had been glad to see him when he appeared unexpectedly at her apartment. His gentleness as he cared for her injuries, made her feel loved. *Shit, Alyx.* Stay away from the L word, she chastised herself. This wasn't love, this was simply an assignment.

Daniel pushed on her elbow, guiding her up the stairs. She needed to go to bed, get some sleep, or she'd be a total fuck-up at the club tomorrow. Admittedly, she didn't relish the thought of playing the scene that Jack had arranged for her. Everyone agreed Daniel couldn't appear to be her Dom even though they'd left together the other night. It had to seem like she was new, unattached, in order to make her a candidate for the slaver's auction. She'd be playing with Steve and both Jack and Daniel reassured her that he was a well-respected, competent and caring Dom. First, he'd bring her to a private room so they could "get acquainted" and practice the scene. Her heart pounded just thinking about being intimate with the burly bartender. He was nice enough when she met him at the bar the other night, and she knew he wouldn't hurt her.

Well, not much anyway. They did have to make it convincing.

"Alyx," Daniel said, interrupting her thoughts. "You're wound tighter than a drum. Tension is oozing off you." They'd arrived in his bedroom without her realizing it. He came up behind her and grabbed her shoulders and started to work out the knots in her neck that had suddenly become painful.

"I'm fine, you don't have to worry about me. I'm good under pressure. I'll do fine tomorrow at the club, you won't be embarrassed."

Daniel made her face him. He chucked her chin up and forced her eyes to meet his. "You're really starting to piss me off, Alyx. Why can't you admit that you're in over your head? Shit."

Alyx stared into his dark eyes, but she couldn't understand why he was so angry. This had nothing to do with him anymore. His job was done and she could take it from here.

"Lose the clothes," he commanded.

Her eyes blazed with fury. "No." Who did he think he was? They were done with this whole Dom/sub charade. He couldn't make her do anything. Even if she secretly wanted to.

"I'm going to get you to feel something one way or another, Alyx. For one more night I intend to be your Dom and I'm going to give you what you need, not what you want. Because for some reason you are ignoring your feelings and it's unhealthy. Now, I'm not going to say it again. Take off your clothes. Or I'll do it myself."

Alyx couldn't move and fear gripped her, although she'd never, ever, admit it to him. She'd never admit it to any man. Maybe sex would make her feel better. She did crave the way he made love to her. His rough, bossy bedroom persona excited her and she had already been saddened over the fact their relationship had come to an end, even if it was only make-believe. After tonight she could go back to being the strong independent woman she'd been before. Fine, she'd play the game one more night.

"Go ahead, have your way with me. I don't care either way."

Alyx couldn't believe she'd said that. She really did want him to make love to her, but she'd never give him the satisfaction of letting him know. How many times had she been disappointed in love? Well, five boyfriends, plus her father, that would make exactly six times. Six for six. A perfect record.

Getting in Alyx's face, he jabbed her in the sternum with two hard fingers. "I want you back in protocol. And I want you to show some respect. This petulant child act is inappropriate and stops right this second." Daniel withdrew his fingers instantly and stepped back. This was killing him. What if this backfired and she cracked? He wanted to fold her into his embrace and just love her. Hold her until she regained her sanity and could think clearly. But no, he would be doing her no service by being soft. He needed his mega-Dom persona to get her through this.

He tightened his lips, then blew them back out, rubbing the anger off his face with his hands. He knew better than to deal with a sub when he was angry. *Control, man.*

He fully expected her to lash out at him, but instead her eyes were focused on the floor. "Yes, Sir." He opened his mouth to speak, then stared down at his hands.

"Good girl," he said reflexively. He discarded his jacket and shirt and threw them on the bedside chair. Alyx yanked off her tee-shirt in full tantrum mode, like the first time he'd met her. Back to square one.

He could watch her strip all day and he felt himself harden. He hoped he was making the right decision because he was sure she was expecting something else from him. Well, perhaps he would fulfill her wishes afterward, but first he intended to give her what she needed, not what she thought she wanted.

Daniel unbuttoned his jeans, but left them on. Alyx stood before him in her underwear and he wanted to dip his hands into her bra, then take those luscious breasts into his mouth and suck ravenously on her sweet nipples. But, he reminded himself she needed something else from him. *Focus, man.*

He pulled back the covers on the bed and sat on the edge. "Lose the underwear. All of it."

She hesitated briefly and then complied. "Come here," he commanded, extending his hand. Slowly, she inched her way toward him, then stopped, her knees pressed against his. Her breasts were even with his mouth and he fought the urge to bite her nipple. Instead, he grabbed her arm and threw her, stomach-down, over his thighs.

"Wait," she screamed. "What the fuck do you think you're doing, asshole?"

"Protocol, Alyx. We'll do this all night until you behave appropriately." His left hand pressed on her back and he scissored his legs around hers. She squirmed and bucked on his lap and he held her firmly, her strength no match for his.

"I don't deserve a punishment. Let me up." She pounded her fists into his leg and growled.

"This isn't punishment, Alyx, this is about you feeling something. Your emotions are buried so deep they'll kill you if you don't let them out."

"Fine I'll take whatever you want to dole out. I'm tougher than you, I'll outlast you."

He smiled. *Oh really, little missy, we'll see about that.*

"One," she yelled. "Go ahead you wimp, I can count higher than your little pea brain. ONE."

"No, little subbie, since this isn't punishment, there will be no counting. I will continue until I decide to stop."

That shut her up.

He trailed his fingers over her bare bottom, massaging her firm, silken skin, bringing the blood to the surface. Her body was rigid, her muscles like steel. But he was up to the challenge and wouldn't quit until she yielded her emotions to him. "Flatten your hands on the floor to brace yourself. We're going to be a while." His hand stroked her bottom again. He smacked her and the sharp intake of breath told him he had her attention. The next set of swats came in rapid succession. He hit one cheek, then the other, waiting for the stinging to die down before giving another. She struggled again, trying to escape the impact of his hand. He paused and lightly massaged the pink skin on her adorable little ass.

"Tell me, Alyx, how did you feel when you realized Jason was in your apartment?" He rubbed her butt cheeks slowly, the skin hot on his palm. "Out with it," he commanded and then smacked her.

"Nothing," she screamed. "I felt nothing."

His hand slapped her ass five times in a row. "I don't believe you. Liar. Tell me the truth. How did you feel when Jason suspended you from the ceiling?"

Alyx kicked and thrashed, and pounded on his legs with her fists. "I didn't care. I knew I could wait him out and when I got free I'd probably shoot the bastard."

Daniel's hand froze. She was close. He had to get her there. Another five swats, and she stopped beating on him and dropped her head, her hands flush against the parquet floor.

"You intended to kill him? Are you a murderer?" Daniel knew he was pushing the envelope and hoped he hadn't gone too far.

"No," she cried, "I wanted him dead. But I wouldn't have killed him, I would have called for backup once I had him at the other end of my gun."

"Tell me how you felt, Alyx. How did you feel when he attacked you?" He smacked her again, harder then he'd ever smacked anyone. "Start talking."

"Fine," she sobbed. "I was mad. Fucking furious. But when he overpowered me and strung me up like an animal I was terrified. I never let anyone get the upper hand on me, never. My father would be furious if he knew some guy had gotten over on me like that." Her cries had reached hysteria and her body suddenly went limp, unable to fight him any longer. Sobs wracked her and he waited as the tension seeped out of her. He stroked her bottom lovingly, caressing the heated skin to soothe the pain.

"You were afraid, Alyx," he said softly. "There's no shame in fear. Now, we'll talk about where you learned this."

He pulled her flaccid body into his arms and settled her against his chest, leaning his back into the pillows propped against the headboard. Tears choked her, but he hoped her worries had started to dissipate. Pressing her head onto his shoulder, he wrapped her in his arms and held her until she calmed. He chucked her chin up so he could see her face and stroked away the streaming tears from her cheeks with his thumb, then offered her a tissue to wipe her nose. He hoped this ordeal had left her empty of the pain she'd been holding onto, leaving her clean and whole again.

"You made me cry on purpose," she declared, snuggling

against his chest again.

"I know," he confessed. He leaned his chin on her head and caressed her arm.

"You spanked me so I would cry?"

"Yes. That was the point. Spankings can be used as punishment or for erotic foreplay. But, sometimes, physical pain can be used to help people release bottled up emotional pain. Now, let's talk about how you learned that fear was an unacceptable emotion."

"I don't know. I was pretty fearless as a kid. At three, my parents found me twenty feet off the ground in the giant oak tree in front of our house. My father told me at least a hundred times that my mother nearly had a stroke when she found me. My dad, on the other hand, was so proud of me. He told me all his life that a Cameron doesn't show fear, ever."

"And you believed him?"

"He was my dad. I was a young girl. Whatever he said was gospel."

"Look, Alyx, if he started telling you that at such a young age it could be considered a form of brainwashing. Even though you've felt fear, and briefly acknowledged it, you buried it someplace where you thought you wouldn't ever have to deal with it."

"I guess, sort of makes sense."

"But, it's dangerous to live like that. Fear is important for our survival. It prevents us from taking unnecessary risks. It keeps us safe. Do you understand that fear is a good thing?"

"I guess," she said again, and he heard the smile in her voice.

He pulled her up to face him and kissed the remnants of tears from her eyelashes. "Good girl. Now tell me how you feel about tomorrow."

This time he saw it in full living HD color. Her eyes a deep, dark blue. Terror. And that made him very, very glad.

Chapter 8

Saturday

Alyx and Daniel slept late, like teenagers-with-nothing-to-do-late, and decided to forgo working out again this morning. Both agreed they usually took weekends off anyway. Alyx threw on one of Daniel's tailored white shirts, as she hadn't brought clothes to hang around in. What a fuckety-fuck-fucking night. She hadn't seen it coming, either. After the spanking ordeal, which she hadn't enjoyed at all, it had been nothing like the other times, they'd had mind-bending, toe-curling sex. If she were totally honest with herself, they'd actually made love. Although she'd thoroughly enjoyed the crazy, raw sex they'd had over the past week, it had always been just another screw, and that had been fine. But last night was different and now a wondrous energy throbbed in her veins. Like a huge raincloud had passed over her, washing her clean, and she felt ready—both physically and emotionally—to do what was needed at the club in order to free the imprisoned women.

"Can't believe it's nearly noon," Daniel said, interrupting

her inner monologue. He dragged on a pair of tan linen pants, no underwear, and slipped a navy-blue tee over his head. "I don't think I've ever slept till noon." He came over and put his arms around Alyx and pulled her into his chest. "You okay? Last night was pretty intense for me, it had to take a toll on you."

"I'm fine."

"Now, see, there you go. *Again*. Your tedious response. Tell me how you really feel."

Alyx wrapped her arms around Daniel's waist. "Well, I'm good, really good. Like my body feels after a great workout. Only I guess you could call this an emotional exercise."

"Much better," he said. "That's my girl. Now let's go and eat. I'm starving."

Alyx smelled some sweetly delicious concoction as she entered the kitchen. Lydia had taken the liberty of making homemade waffles. Although she liked to cook, Alyx couldn't remember ever having waffles from scratch. Since her mother left when she was so young and her father wasn't exactly a chef, they'd relied mostly on frozen and microwave stuff. Their housekeeper, Greta, made an effort, but her culinary skills left a lot to be desired.

Daniel ushered Alyx outside to sit at the table. The noon sun proved still warm for September and she mused over the fact that winter wasn't far away. She added her favorite creamer to the steaming mug of coffee and sipped, burning her tongue a little. Daniel reached into his pocket and placed something wrapped in pink tissue paper on her plate. "What's that?" she said.

"It's your graduation present." He took his seat next to her at the table.

Alyx picked up the lightweight package and slowly opened the tissue. Out fell her hair clip from their initial and confrontational meeting. She laughed. "I never thought I'd see this again after that night."

"Me either. I still can't believe you showed up and you actually stayed. I planned to keep it as a testament to my intimidation factor." He grinned. "Apparently, I've lost my edge."

"Apparently."

Daniel buried his beautiful face behind the New York Times. Alyx selected the sports section and leaned back in her chair. "The Giants play at four on Sunday."

Daniel peered at her around the paper. "You're a Giants fan?"

"Of course."

"I had no idea. You have impeccable tastes."

Lydia came outside and placed a stack of warm waffles in between their plates along with a pitcher of hot maple syrup. "This is wonderful, thank you so much, Lydia," Alyx said. Lydia beamed at the praise, but suddenly her gaze drifted behind Alyx and her lips curled downward, her eyes wide.

"Daniel," someone shrieked. Daniel promptly dropped the paper from in front of his face and glanced up. A tall, leggy blonde wearing a tight, white, off-the-shoulder blouse atop black jeans stood in the doorway. Her appearance oozed money. Alyx couldn't see her eyes because they were hidden behind dark oversized sunglasses. A large black Chanel bag hung on her right shoulder while her left hand sat primly on her hip.

"Lacey," Daniel said, getting to his feet. "I thought you weren't due back for another week."

Lacey didn't move and fixed her eyes on Alyx. "Apparently," she said. "Who is your friend? And why is she wearing one of your shirts?"

Daniel stepped closer to Lacey, but she recoiled from him

like he had some serious disease. "It's not what you think, Lacey."

"Oh really, Daniel? You're a mind reader now. Do tell. What the hell am I thinking?"

"This is Alyx Cameron, and I'm sort of babysitting her for a friend."

Babysitting? Alyx thought. Yet she decided to keep her mouth shut and let this play out. In a few hours, she'd be out of here and this would be nothing but a bad memory.

"Babysitting, my ass," Lacey shrieked. "You've had this little tramp in that rec room of yours. And after you promised me you'd left all that sick shit behind you."

Daniel kept his voice calm. "I don't want to talk about this now, Lacey. And you're being rude to my guest."

"You think this is rude?" she snapped. "Just wait. I came by to tell you we're expected at my parent's house for dinner tomorrow to iron out plans for the engagement party."

Alyx's eyes immediately fixed on Lacey's ring finger. How come he'd never mentioned he had a girlfriend, no wait—a fiancée? A giant diamond solitaire glinted in the sunlight. No denying it now. Daniel had asked her to marry him and the thought sent a wave of nausea through her stomach worse than food poisoning. *God, what a fucking week.* Alyx felt like she'd been through literal Hell.

Lacey whirled on her four-inch heels and stormed out. Daniel still held the newspaper in his fisted hand and he threw it to the floor. "Damn," he said and then followed after Lacey.

Alyx tried to regain her emotional equilibrium. Her eyes sought out Lydia, who hadn't moved a muscle. "Well, that was awkward."

Lydia blew out a long breath. "I'll say, and then some."

"I didn't know Dr. Taylor had a fiancée, Lydia. He never mentioned it."

"Well, I'll mention a few things. She's a gold digger if you ask me. Her father got caught in that big Ponzi scheme and lost his shirt. The word around town is he's broke. And besides, she's always ordering Dr. Taylor around and making him do things he doesn't want to do."

Alyx found that odd. She would have assumed Daniel to be the "boss" in any relationship he was in. "She's very beautiful. I'll give her that."

"Skin-deep beauty isn't worth much if you ask me," Lydia offered. "Excuse me, Ms. Cameron, but I think I'll head back to the kitchen, I've already said more than is appropriate. Please forgive me for interfering."

As she hastened her exit, Alyx couldn't decide what to do. The amazing waffles were getting cold. She should pack up and leave. But she needed a ride. Matt would bring her car out later, but for now she was stranded. She had no desire to talk about this with Daniel. He didn't owe her anything. His problem would be with Lacey and he'd have to figure that out on his own. But she decided the waffles smelled too good to ignore and she needed to put something in her stomach. Rob Scarborough wouldn't be here for a few more hours. She buttered her waffles and smothered them in the warm syrup and tried to eat quickly, the lump in her throat making it difficult to swallow. After a week of convincing herself this had merely been a silly game, she'd finally considered the possibility that she felt something solid for him, and that perhaps he felt the same.

How could he have cheated on his fiancée like that? Suddenly, she saw Daniel in a whole new light. How had she been so wrong? Never would she have pegged him as a two-faced cheating bastard.

When she finished eating, Daniel still hadn't returned and she escaped to her room. According to the rules she could do as she pleased between noon and four so she could ignore him. And besides, this whole ridiculous charade was over anyway.

She grabbed a random section of the newspaper and bolted up the stairs, locking the door behind her.

The sound of tires pealing out of the driveway caught her attention. She ran to the window to see a white Porsche Carrera roaring away, gravel and dust spewing behind it. Daniel stood in the driveway and raked his fingers through his hair, then bent over, landing his hands on his knees, as if he'd just completed an arduous run. Slowly rising, he clasped his hands behind his head and pressed his elbows against his ears. He winced, then dropped his arms to his sides. He lumbered toward the house. Alyx quickly scooted across the room and jumped back onto the bed.

Then came a loud knock. "Alyx, open the door," Daniel yelled. He knocked again, more pounding. She didn't move. "Alyx, I know you're in there."

"This is my time. Mine! I want to be left alone. Go away!"

"Alyx," Daniel lowered his voice, making it sound ominous. "Jesus fucking Christ, Alyx, open this fucking door or I'll break the goddamn thing down myself."

"That'll be the last mistake you make."

The sound of the door splintering under the force of Daniel's body made her shriek. The door gave way and he entered.

"Shit." He rubbed his shoulder. "That hurt. It looks easier on television." A flicker of a smile crossed his lips.

Alyx was afraid to laugh, she couldn't gauge his anger. Their eyes locked together.

"I'm sorry," he said, walking toward the bed. "I should have told you, I was trying to. Waiting for the perfect moment." He sat on the edge of the bed and faced her. Alyx moved back and leaned against the silky, green European pillow shams decorating the headboard and drew her knees into her chest. Daniel on a bed was dangerous and she didn't trust herself to stay away from him. Now that she knew he had a girlfriend, everything was different. Well, not even a girlfriend, a friggin' fiancée.

"Babysitting me? Really Daniel? What woman would be stupid enough to accept that lame excuse? Not to mention you made me feel like a twelve-year-old. Which, by the way, according the penal code, would make you a pedophile."

Daniel yanked on his hair again. "I know, that was a stupid, stupid thing to say. I panicked and I didn't want to tell her why you were really here."

"Somehow, I don't think the truth would make this much better in Lacey's eyes."

"I will say this. Lacey is more concerned about taking my name and moving in here as my wife than she is about our relationship."

"That's fucked up, Daniel. You're marrying someone who is more concerned with your status than with you?"

Daniel inched closer to Alyx. He reached over and removed her hands from her knees, lacing his fingers through hers. "Look, this week didn't go the way I thought it would. Not at all. I—"

Alyx decided she didn't want to hear what might come out of his mouth next. "Daniel, the week is over and you've been great, really, you have. I was nervous but you were a pro and now we're done and I'll be out of your hair in a few hours."

"What if I don't want you out of my hair?" His smoldering dark eyes set her blood rushing into all the wrong places. If she didn't get him out of this room in the next thirty seconds she'd be sorry. Hell, they'd both be.

She thought carefully about what she needed to say. "You're not thinking clearly. I don't want to be in a relationship with you. You're too controlling and we come from totally different worlds. We have nothing in common."

She pulled free from his grasp and jumped off the bed. "Now, please leave me alone so I can get ready. Rob will be here soon and I haven't showered yet." Alyx marched into the bathroom and shut and locked the door. She leaned her back against it and buried her face in her hands. As much as she wanted his arms around her, she knew she had no business wishing for something like that. He had a fiancée who he'd patch things up with and she'd get to work and accomplish the task she'd set out to. Then she'd go back to her apartment and put her life back in order. Perhaps she'd go on a vacation first. The Bureau damn well better give her some time off after such a grueling assignment. Plus, after the horrible scene with Jason, she wasn't so sure she'd ever be comfortable in that apartment again anyway. Maybe she should move, ask for a transfer to another state. Start over?

Right now, however, she needed to get into the zone, prepare for the club. She cranked up the hot water in the shower.

Alyx managed to avoid Daniel all afternoon. She'd heard his car pull out of the driveway shortly after she'd escaped to the bathroom. A shopping bag waited outside her door, something to wear at the club tonight. A short, inappropriately short, mini-dress made of black latex, and sans underwear as per club rules. The low-cut bodice squished her boobs so tightly, if she hiccupped her nipples would pop out. She'd used the curling iron on her hair until it fell around her shoulders in a waterfall of chestnut ringlets. Her makeup was heavier than normal and would appear garish in the daylight, but she had to admit, for a harlot, she looked pretty good. But then the reality of what lay ahead hit her and she inhaled deeply, hoping against hope for some semblance of calm. She'd have to perform sexual acts with Steve and perhaps one other Dom tonight and she needed to gear herself up for it.

Rob arrived a little late and blamed it on the traffic.

"Great," Alyx muttered. "I'll be late on the first night and they'll probably trap me in the middle of a circle-jerk."

Rob smirked. "Now, that would be unfortunate."

Alyx rolled her eyes at him.

Daniel hadn't returned and so she said her goodbyes to Lydia and Mason, thanking them for their exceptional hospitality. Lydia surprised her by pulling her into a motherly hug and then drew back, holding onto her upper arms. "I'm sad to see you leave, Ms. Cameron. I like who Dr. Taylor is when you're around. We'll miss you. I think Dr. Taylor will too."

Alyx beamed at Lydia's kind words, then followed Rob out.

"Ready?" he said as they buckled their seatbelts.

"As I'll ever be."

"Good girl," he said, but Alyx heard Daniel's voice. Her stomach sank, her mind spinning.

"What did you just say?"

"I said, 'good.'"

"No, no, no. You said 'good girl.' Seriously? You're one of them? A Dom?" It felt like she'd stumbled upon a coven of vampires. Were these Doms everywhere?

Heading east on Montauk Highway, Rob smiled, a little too smugly. "How do you think I know Jack? We were in the Marines together, but I really know him because we played at the same club when we were both stationed in Tampa."

"Are you kidding me, you're really a Dom? Shit. Do you have a submissive chained at home?"

"I do have a submissive and actually you've met her. She's an ADA in Manhattan. But I don't have her chained at home. It's not like that. Didn't Daniel explain the relationship to you?"

Alyx couldn't find any words to express what she felt. Geez, how could she not have seen this coming? She reflected back to the night she met Daniel. Jack and Rob had sat there implacably while she and Daniel role-played Dom and submissive. How could she have been so blind?

Rob changed the subject. "Matt's bringing your car out tonight. It will be parked in the lot at the club, he'll leave the keys at the front desk."

"Finally, some good news."

"We've rented you a small cottage two blocks from Gull Road. The directions and the keys will be in the visor above the driver's seat. We'll have surveillance on you in two shifts. Matt's taking the first shift. Paul will be the follow-up. You have Paul's number, right?"

"Yes, we worked that investment fraud scheme together."

"Good. Matt's got your tracking device, he'll get it to you before you leave."

"Got it," Alyx said, peering out the side window at the moonless night. She shivered.

"You all right?" Rob said with concern.

"Yeah. The anticipation is the worst part."

"I hear you."

Zach welcomed her back with his big puppy-dog smile, one that softened his scary, pockmarked face. "Sign in, please," he instructed, pointing to the clipboard atop his desk. "You look mighty fine this evening, Miss Cameron."

"Thank you, Sir."

"I'm not a Dom, Miss Cameron, you needn't address me as such."

"I didn't realize."

"Nah, not my thing. I only work here part time. I work security at a bank during the day."

"Oh, I see." She wondered what Zach thought about the goings-on inside, but decided against engaging him in additional conversation. She'd cut it close and being late would get her in trouble with Master Steve, and it didn't seem to matter whether she was a fake submissive or not. She fully expected that Steve would have no problem treating her like a real submissive and probably thoroughly enjoy swatting her ass with his giant, meaty paw.

"Have fun," Zach shouted to her back as she ventured toward the inner sanctum of carnal pain. She tried to slow her breathing. Unsuccessfully.

Heading toward the bar, Steve was talking to Colin, Colin's hand wrapped around a bottle of beer. Steve's eyes brightened as she approached.

"Good evening, Master Steve," she said, hoping her voice sounded more confident than she felt. "And you too, Master Colin."

"Good evening, little subbie," Steve said. "You cut it a bit close, don't you think? I don't tolerate lateness."

"Sorry, Sir. It won't happen again."

Colin cracked a sly grin. "Glad to see you came back for more, pet."

Oh, God. How would she ever get through this night?

Steve extended his hand. "I'll lock up your purse behind the bar. Lisa will show you the locker room and get you a lock. In the future, you can keep your personal stuff there."

Alyx handed over her purse and Steve came out from behind the bar. "Give me your wrists, little one." She offered them willingly. Steve grimaced. "What's going on here? Did Daniel do this to you?"

Alyx assessed the abrasions on her wrists. The thought that Steve assumed Daniel had hurt her punched a hole in her chest. "No! Daniel would *never* hurt me." She thrust her hands behind her back.

Steve's concerned expression unsettled her. She didn't even know this guy. He said, "Are you gonna tell me what happened?"

"I'd rather not, it wasn't Daniel. It's nothing for you to worry about."

"Alyx, trust is paramount in the lifestyle. I need to know if you're in trouble or I won't be comfortable working with you." He placed his large hands on her shoulders, his eyes probing hers.

"Okay, okay. I had a run-in with an old boyfriend, but I handled it. He's in jail."

His coal-black eyes unsettled her. "It's taken care of then?"

"Yes. Promise. I'm fine."

It didn't seem like he believed her, even as he added, "All right. Wrists please." Slipping on the soft leather handcuffs with the appropriate charms, he pivoted her away from him, securing her hands behind her with a quick snap. She gasped. Was he starting already? What about the tour with Lisa? Her heart jumped into her throat.

He gripped both her shoulders so she had to turn and face him. Putting a finger under her chin, he forced her eyes upward. He studied her from head to toe with those black laser-focus eyes. She stared into his massive chest that strained the limits of his black polo. Everything about him seemed tight, his muscles, his posture, glossy dark hair tied in a small ponytail.

"Breathe, darling," he whispered near her ear. "It's not going to be as bad as you're imagining."

"Yes, Sir," she managed to utter. Although somehow, she didn't believe him.

"I like what you're wearing." He slid his big hand under the hem of her short skirt and let his fingers travel up the side of her thigh, nearly to her hip. Her jaw clenched in anticipation of his probing fingers finding their way between her legs. "Good girl, no underwear. For now, you may leave everything on. I may remove your clothing once you're a bit more relaxed."

God. She didn't want to be walking around the club half naked. Or fully nude either. Now that she thought about it, she wore only one piece of clothing, which severely limited the options. But she couldn't say no. He was the boss of her for the foreseeable future and… *Oh Lord,* she must not get distracted. *Concentrate.* She could do this.

"Breathe, little subbie," Steve chided her. Again. "I don't need you passing out on me before we even start." He gazed intently at her and ran the back of his hand over her cheek. "I'll treat you well, you'll leave here a smiling woman. I promise."

"Yes, Sir," she managed.

Jack came out of his office and walked toward her, then Alyx noticed Rob at his side and Lisa trailing behind him. Thankfully, *Lisa.* A momentary escape.

"Welcome back, little one," Jack said, placing his hand on the side of her arm.

"Thank you, Sir."

"Master Steve, how are things progressing?"

"She's doing fine. Arrived in the nick of time. Almost earned a punishment in the first minute."

"Now that would have been most unfortunate, Master Steve." Jack smirked and she thought Rob might be enjoying this a tad too much.

"For her," Steve added. "I would have thoroughly enjoyed it." He flashed Alyx a wicked smile and her belly clenched in that weird-good way. This couldn't be turning her on. Just couldn't.

Steve faced Jack again. "Colin has agreed to provide an assist when I bring Alyx upstairs to get acquainted and practice our scene."

Alyx inhaled sharply, her eyes wide and she knew everyone heard her.

"Two of you?" she rasped. "Sirs."

They ignored her, talking as if she weren't standing right in the middle of three, no, *four* scary Doms, counting Rob's affiliation with the lifestyle.

Steve continued, "He'll evaluate the scene to make sure it's convincing and to test how she performs in front of others."

"Good. That's wise," Jack said. "If she's not ready to scene in public then I want her kept on the side. She can serve drinks like Darrin and Carol until you think she's ready." Alyx tried to regulate her breathing for about the tenth time since she'd arrived. In and out, she coached herself, slowly, oh-so-slowly. "Lisa, please familiarize Alyx with the facility and introduce her to as many subs as you can. Then park her in the submissives' pen."

"Yes, Master."

Steve reached behind Alyx and unhooked her wrists. He rubbed her arms up and down briskly, bringing the blood to the surface and her skin instantly warmed and tingled. Oh, boy. She was working herself into a frenzy at the thought of being intimate with Steve while Colin observed. Two men. Ugh, she'd never done anything like that before and she wondered what Daniel would think. She had to stop thinking about him. Their time together had ended. He was probably having make-up sex with Lacey at this very moment. Hell, they were probably both laughing at her.

"You all right, little subbie?" Steve said. He still held her upper arms firmly. Alyx gazed into his dark eyes. Unexpectedly, they seemed warm, not what she'd been expecting at all.

"Yes, Sir."

"Give me a color."

She had the sudden urge to say red, or maybe yellow and make a run for it. "Green, Sir. Definitely green."

Steve smiled warmly. "Good girl." He released her upper arms and positioned her toward the dance floor. "Now, go with Lisa and I'll come for you in about a half-hour and we'll get started."

Colin reached over and rubbed her ass with his hand. It felt like a hot iron. He leaned in, close to her ear. "Don't worry, little pet. We'll take excellent care of you. That's what we do." He pinched her butt and a tiny yelp escaped her. "Damn, she's gonna be a whole lot of fun," he said to the tiny posse of enormous Doms.

"That she is," Steve said.

Lisa led her deeper into the mass of twirling naked and half-naked bodies and Alyx's pulse slowed, free of the testosterone flood that had stolen her breath.

"They're pretty intense," Lisa said. "You'll get used to it."

"I don't have any other choice."

"Come on, we'll start at the back. There's a huge powder room near the emergency exit. It's where we hide out for a minute if we need to. Then I'll show you where you can stow your stuff and I'll introduce you to some of the girls. They're great. Except for Stacy, she's a real bitch and don't trust anything she says."

Lisa opened the gold-painted door and they entered a large room covered in the same black-and-white striped wallpaper as the foyer. The onyx marble sinks with gilded faucets were sunk into a pink sandstone vanity. In the ornately framed mirror, the reflections of three women stared back at them. Lisa introduced her to Lily, Meghan, and Abigail, each adorned with the requisite subbie handcuffs. They seemed nice enough, like normal people, and Alyx thought about Rob's admission that his submissive was an assistant in the Manhattan DA's office.

She was beginning to see this whole lifestyle thing in a new light.

The three girls left and Alyx and Lisa stood alone in front of the mirrored wall above the gleaming ebony sinks. They checked their hair and makeup, when unexpectedly the door flew open and two huge men in dark suits grabbed them, placing a cloth with a sickening sweet scent over their mouths and noses.

Alyx gagged. She stomped her heel into the guy's foot but it felt like concrete. She kicked him hard and struggled to swivel her body into position to get a shot at the brute, but he had her securely trapped in a bear hug. Stars erupted in her eyes as her knees gave way and she collapsed into a cloud of swirling darkness.

Her last thought. Daniel. His warning blared in her dizziness. He'd been right. Something terrible. Wrong.

Daniel paced. He'd been doing a lot of pacing since he met the formerly fearless Alyx Cameron. Jack had told him to stay away from the club tonight, that he would be a distraction for Alyx. He'd agreed, but not for the reason Jack mentioned, but because the idea of another man touching her had his guts tied into a Gordian knot. Steve would be good to her, he knew that, and hopefully this whole ridiculous charade would be over soon and he could go back to his life with the just the normal craziness at the hospital. Lacey would forgive him. He'd already promised her he'd dismantle the rec room before she moved in. Now, she insisted she wanted it gone by the end of the week. Okay, he'd humor her. After spending time in there with Alyx he'd decided he'd never entertain another woman in there again anyway. Memories of her sprawled across the bondage bed, her wrists and ankles shackled to the corners gave him an instant hard-on. Not good. He loved Lacey, right? Alyx had been a momentary distraction and once the rec room was gone he could banish her ghost from these walls.

Yet the thought of going back to his previous life left him with a twitchy pain in his chest. He'd probably have a myocardial infarction and be the laughingstock of the entire medical community. He pictured the front page of the local newspaper: *Prominent Long Island Heart Surgeon Drops Dead of Heart Attack.*

She'd left two hours ago. He wished he'd seen how hot she looked in the fetish wear he'd bought her. Probably better that he hadn't, he didn't need any more images of her hotness branded into his cerebral cortex.

The TV stared back at Daniel, some mindless sportscaster rattling off meaningless statistics. He tried to focus, but after about ten minutes, *Fuck Jack*, he thought. He couldn't sit here waiting to see how it went. One drink at the club, he told himself, to reassure himself she was okay.

Daniel parked in the lot of the St. Andrews club and had a long talk with himself. This was probably a bad idea. He should wait in the car until she came out. At least he was in the vicinity in case she needed him. Nobody expected the slavers to show up on the first night, so his anxiety was mostly over Steve scening with Alyx in public. Well, the private scening didn't thrill him all that much either. Steve promised that he wouldn't have intercourse with her, but if they both decided they wanted it, he couldn't stop them. Hell, Alyx might really like Steve. *Shit.* He was a cop. Perhaps Daniel had intentionally blocked that tidbit of information out of his muddled brain.

Jesus, his head hurt. He needed for this shit to be over. For real.

Daniel sprang from the car, slammed the door shut, and headed for the front door. Sitting and doing nothing was definitely not his style. Zach gave him the customary "Bro Welcome" and he entered the teeming mass of overcharged human flesh grinding and writhing on the dance floor.

As expected, Steve wasn't at the bar, and Daniel clenched

his teeth at the notion of what Steve was doing to Alyx upstairs. Jillian was tending bar and Daniel sat on a stool waiting for her to take his order.

Jack rushed toward his office, Agent Scarborough, Steve and Colin right behind him. Daniel's heart pounded, something had to be wrong. He followed them into Jack's office. Scarborough yelled into his phone. "Fuck, Matt, how could it have happened this fast? And nobody saw a fucking thing other than that van high-tailing it out of the parking lot?" Matt said something, but Daniel couldn't hear.

"Who was on the back exits?" A silence as Matt answered. "What do you mean no one?"

"Okay, okay, I get it. Fuck, Matt. Nothing's in place. We didn't even plant her tracking device."

Agent Scarborough shook his head and ran a hand through his hair, giving it a painful tug. "All right. Set up roadblocks over a five-mile perimeter and check every vehicle, even the trunks. They'll probably do a heat run, so even if we get a bead on them they're probably not heading directly for their home base. Alert everyone. Don't fuck this up, Matt." Scarborough pinched the bridge of his nose and struggled for a breath. "If we lose her, this could go to hell real fast." He paused to listen to Matt's comment before saying in a gritty whisper, "We can't lose her, Matt. I'll never be able to live with myself." He pushed the call release button and his shoulders slumped. He threw his phone on Jack's desk. "What a clusterfuck."

Agent Scarborough turned. Daniel stood in the doorway. "Oh geez. Daniel." Rob dragged his hands down his face. "Perhaps you should sit down."

"I don't need to sit down. Just tell me."

"Maybe *I* need to sit down." Jack fell into the chair behind his desk. "It seems that Lisa was walking Alyx around the club, introducing her to people and showing her where the submissives sit to wait on their Doms. They hit the ladies room in the back and that's the last we saw of them. The guys had to already be inside, because the emergency doors are all locked from the outside."

Jesus. The slavers had not only taken Alyx, but Jack's sub, too? Both *brunettes.* Daniel addressed Steve. "You never got her upstairs?"

"No," Steve said, his voice barely perceptible. "I told her to wait for me in the pen, but when I went to find her she wasn't there. We asked around and Lily said Alyx was with Lisa in the ladies' room. When we couldn't find them we checked the surveillance tapes outside all the exits and that's when we saw it. Two guys grabbed them and threw them in a van." Steve let out a massive sigh and dug his hands into the pockets of his black leather pants. "I'm sorry, buddy. I can't believe I lost her in the first fucking hour."

"I can't believe this," Daniel shouted. "But wait, you said the guys were already inside? How could that be?"

"Our guess is they're new members, signed up to scout out the women," Jack said.

"Well, then you have their identities in your membership rolls, right?" Daniel held onto a glimmer of hope that they could find a lead quickly.

Rob said, "It's not likely they used their real identities, but we've secured the records and I have someone researching it now. It will take some time. Time I'm afraid we don't have."

Daniel didn't know what to do with himself. He needed to do something. Anything.

"We've set up a perimeter search in a five-mile radius and we're checking video footage in the area. Maybe we'll get a hit on the vehicle leaving here," Agent Scarborough offered.

He'd worried all along that this might go badly for Alyx. He'd tried so hard to talk her out of this insane assignment but she wouldn't listen to him. Daniel struggled to make sense of his feelings and finally deciphered what it was: despair.

They'd never find her. The slavers had her, they'd sell her to some despicable sadist and she'd die at the end of a whip. His last meal gurgled in his stomach. He had to literally will himself not to throw up.

His eyes fell to Agent Scarborough. "So, you fucked this up? You weren't prepared for the possibility that she'd get picked up so fast?" Daniel fumed. "Son of a bitch."

"I never anticipated this, not in a million years," Scarborough muttered. "I wasn't even sure she'd get picked up. It was a long shot from the beginning. Our intel says they usually scout them out for a few days before they decide if they fit the profile. And they usually grab them on their way home, not in the club. This was a pretty ballsy move. They must be getting close to the auction and needed merchandise in a hurry." He exhaled heavily. "I figure they must have sized her up Thursday night."

The stab of blame nearly dropped Daniel to his knees, his lungs seized in his chest. If he hadn't insisted on bringing her to the club early this wouldn't have happened. Shit, this was all his fault. "Jesus," he exclaimed again. "And I was the one who forced her to come Thursday. If I hadn't—"

"Don't." Agent Scarborough put his hand up. "Don't do this to yourself. The what ifs are a one-way trip to nowhere. Better we come up with a plan."

The four men stared at Daniel. His anger suddenly exploded and he kicked over the chair in front of Jack's desk. He growled in anguish. Glaring at Scarborough, he asked, "So what are we going to do? I can't just sit here waiting."

"There's nothing you can do. Leave it to the professionals."

Daniel reached across the overturned chair and leveled a punch to Scarborough's jaw. The FBI chief fell across the desk and knocked Jack off the chair. The two men slumped to the floor. "You're not professionals. You're idiots." Steve and Colin grabbed Daniel by the arms and restrained him before he could further the assault.

"Get him out of here before he hurts himself," Scarborough yelled, getting to his feet. He reached down and offered a hand to Jack.

"Daniel, go home," Jack added. "We have to leave this to the FBI."

"Yeah, right," Daniel said, shrugging off the two burly Doms holding him back.

Colin and Steve escorted Daniel out to the parking lot through Jack's private exit. "Come on, buddy. Calm down, they'll find her," Steve said.

"Don't tell me to calm down," Daniel screamed. "They're a bunch of incompetent assholes."

Steve didn't respond and Daniel slowly made his way to his car. He faced the driver's side door and leaned into it, resting his arms on the roof and his head on his forearms. He couldn't go home.

Daniel pulled into the long familiar driveway. The home of his youth. It was late, but he didn't care. Lights remained on upstairs and he rang the doorbell. He had a key but didn't want to frighten his mother by just walking in. Tears welled in his eyes. Footsteps padded down the stairs and his mother's soft brown eyes peeked through the side window.

"Daniel!" She threw the door open wide. "What are you doing here at this time?" One look at his face and she said, "Oh, darling. What's wrong?"

For some reason, he couldn't move and she tugged on his sleeve and pulled him inside. She led him by the hand into the living room and pushed him onto the over-stuffed white sofa, then sat beside him. "Tell me. What is it? Lacey?"

"Mom, I—I don't know where to begin. It's Alyx. She's been kidnapped." His mother gasped and put her hand over her mouth. "You don't know the whole story about how I met her. I need to tell you." She settled both her hands on top of his, so lovingly as Daniel proceeded to explain how he'd come to meet the very special, Special Agent Alyx Cameron.

After he finished his sordid tale his mother asked, "They have no idea where she is? No tracking device, nothing?"

"No. Honestly, it happened so fast. They hadn't antici-pated her getting taken inside the club. The plan for tracking and surveillance was for when she left the club and at the place they arranged for her to live while undercover. And if I hadn't insisted on taking her to the club on Thursday this never would have happened. Jesus, Mom, it's all my fault." Daniel dropped his head in his hands and sobbed.

"Oh, sweetheart." His mother wrapped her arms around his broad shoulders and he let his head fall onto her shoulder. "I've never seen you cry, darling. Not since you were a baby." She held him tightly for a few minutes longer and then released him. "Daniel, beating yourself up about this won't help. In my experience, regret and guilt are never productive. They only hold you back from taking action."

"I know. That's what Agent Scarborough said."

"They'll figure it out. What is the plan?"

"I don't know. I was so disgusted with the whole situation I left them to do whatever FBI shit they do." He dug his elbows into his thighs and pressed his lips into his clasped hands. He paused for a minute, gathering his apology. "Mom, I'm sorry about revealing my involvement in the BDSM stuff. It's not something I ever wanted to share with you."

"Daniel, *please*. I've been a psychiatrist for over thirty years. Believe me, I've heard it all. You'd be surprised that the behaviors some label aberrant actually fall within normal psychological parameters. Men will be men. Women will be women. We're all just human."

They sat together in silence for a moment and then his mother held his chin in her hands and forced him to meet her gaze. "You care for her." It was a statement, not a question. "I could tell the other night. I've never seen you enjoy the company of a woman so much. She made you laugh. You don't laugh enough, Daniel. You never did. You were always such a serious child, so rigid, so solitary. It was like you were alone even when you were in a crowd."

Daniel peered into his mother's loving face, the tears wet on his cheeks. "I think I've lost my one real chance at happiness, Mom. I screwed up. I should have stopped her. Made her listen to reason."

"What about Lacey?"

"She showed up unexpectedly and Alyx was still at my house. Needless to say, she was furious, and rightly so. I never meant to hurt her. When I offered to do this with Alyx I didn't think of it as cheating, and I thought Alyx would be gone and what Lacey didn't know wouldn't matter. I know that's unacceptable and an insult to both Lacey and Alyx. On the other hand, if I hadn't agreed to this ridiculous proposal I'd never have met Alyx and known what it felt like to be this crazy in love. I do love her, Mom. I never felt this way about Lacey."

"Daniel," his mother said, her voice stern, her gaze leveled at him. "You'll work things out. Honestly, I was never convinced that Lacey was for you." She squeezed his hands affectionately.

"What if they don't find her in time? The thought of what they might be doing to her is ripping my guts out. If they kill her I'll go insane. Why didn't I stop her? I'll never forgive myself."

Placing her warm hands on either side of his head, she

looked at him lovingly. "You know full well that you couldn't keep Alyx from doing what she wanted. Don't beat yourself up over your inability to keep her safe. Now, let's think logically. She's a trained professional. She's strong and smart. Have faith in her to find her way back to you."

Guilt about bringing her to the club early was compounded by the fact that he might've seriously compromised the fearless Alyx Cameron by forcing her to admit she could be afraid. Maybe he'd made her an emotional cripple, having left her former fearlessness in his bedroom. Now she might be too afraid to fight her way back, to battle her way out of this dangerous and horrible plight. "Honestly, Mom, I don't even know if she feels the same way about me."

"Trust me, darling, she does, even if she hasn't admitted it to herself yet."

Alyx's head bumped against the metal sidewall of the van as it traveled along the unpaved road. A sickening sweet smell filled her nostrils and a wave of nausea roiled her stomach. Her head pounded, and the metallic tang of blood stung the inside of her lips. That bastard had squeezed her mouth so tight she'd split her bottom lip open—again. She reached for her face but her hand was tethered to the floor. *Damn.* Again. This was about the tenth time she'd been shackled this week, although this time wasn't a game. She'd wind up dead. Seriously. Dead. Her heart thudded loudly in her chest as the realization she'd been kidnapped settled in her psyche. She struggled to sit up but her ankles were also chained. The night was dark and the van seemed to be heading down an isolated road, no streetlights whatsoever, and there wasn't even moonlight.

Someone wailed. She moved her hand across the floor a

few inches and felt an arm. Lisa. They'd been in the bathroom when two men put a cloth over their mouths and she'd lost consciousness. She'd been off her guard, too worried over scening with Steve and never expecting the slavers to show up in the first fifteen minutes of her undercover assignment. No one had figured it'd happen this fast and definitely not inside the club. Nothing was in place. They'd barely set up perimeter surveillance. Hadn't planted her tracking device. What a mess. She had to think. But no time. Lisa whimpered again. Alyx leaned over as close as possible, keeping her voice low. "Lisa, Lisa, wake up, girl."

Lisa moaned louder. "Fuck."

"S…shush, Lisa, listen to me. The slavers have us in the back of a van and we have to work on a plan for escape."

"What the—? How the hell? Don't you FBI guys know what the fuck you're doing?"

"Yeah, well, I'd like to tell you not to worry but I'd be lying. I'm afraid we're on our own."

"I think I just got religion," she said, followed by a little sob.

"I'll figure out how to get us out of here. You're going to have to trust me. If I tell you to do something, do it without question."

"I may be a submissive but don't expect me to say 'yes, ma'am' or any of that shit. So, you got a plan?"

Alyx was impressed with Lisa's feistiness. If she'd been the sniveling, shy type, it would have made this situation all the worse. "No. No plan. This is going to have to be a figure-it-out-as-you-go thing."

"Great. That gives me tremendous confidence, thanks a million."

"My guess is that whatever we do, it will have to be fast and bold. They'll probably have us secured pretty quickly and once that happens it might be impossible to get free. Follow my lead. By the way, are you injured? You might need to run, and I mean move your ass."

"I think I'm fine, a bit of a headache from whatever crap they used to knock us out."

"Yeah, tell me about it."

The van came to an abrupt stop and Alyx held her breath. She thought back to Daniel's spanking intervention last night. The asshole. Well, he'd be pleased to know that she was fucking terrified and if she ever saw the bastard again, she'd have no problem telling him so. And that would drive her to get herself and Lisa out of this situation in one piece. She'd be elated to tell him exactly *how* terrified she was. Hell, she might spank *him*.

The side door of the van slid open and two men clambered in.

"Pretend you're still unconscious," Alyx whispered to Lisa. Alyx realized she and Lisa still wore the handcuffs all submissives wear while playing at the club. It identified their status as well as the behaviors they were willing to engage in by the different colored charms they wore. Alyx's soul pulsed with hope, the cuffs were lined with fleece and made of leather, *not* metal. If their captors forgot, and didn't replace them with something sturdier, she could most definitely get out of them.

The two men unhooked them from the chains and dragged them out, throwing them over their shoulders. Alyx stayed limp, surveying her surroundings, her chest inflated with a sudden optimism. She knew exactly where they were. The old Grumman site, where they used to manufacture fighter jets and space modules. If she could only find a way to contact the right someone.

Standing in front of a massive metal wall, one of the men punched a code into the doorframe's panel. The wall grinded noisily and a section of it moved up to allow them entry. Carried to the back of the giant airplane hangar and through a smaller door to a makeshift office, the men slid them to the ground, then reached overhead to grab the chains hanging from the ceiling. Attaching their handcuffs to the shackles they hoisted them up. Her captor gave the chain a yank and pulled Alyx onto her tiptoes, then anchored it against the hook on the wall behind her.

"Go let Stan know the final two pieces of merchandise just arrived," he ordered his companion.

"Can't we have some fun first?" the other man replied.

"No. Last time you damaged the merchandise so badly we had to hold her back for the next auction until she healed. Stan nearly had my head, you cost him some serious coin that time. Besides, they're unconscious."

"Makes no difference to me."

"Yeah, well I like my women a little more responsive than that. Now go and get Stan."

The slaver exited through another door and Alyx and Lisa were alone with their captor. Alyx felt her cheeks pinched between his thick fingers. "Wake up, bitch." She kept her eyes closed, but then he slapped her across the face and her eyes popped open. "That's better, doll-face." His feral gaze fell on her breasts before running salaciously over her body. "You are one mighty fine piece of ass."

A few seconds later the door opened again and the other slaver returned with a tall, overweight companion. Sweat hung on his upper lip, his hair arranged in a greasy comb-over. He wore a silky black shirt and cheap black pants. What a goddamned cliché, right out of central casting.

"You were only supposed to bring the one on the left, who's the other bitch?"

"They were together and I figured what the hell, two for the price of one. She's a brunette."

Stan came close to Lisa, who'd roused after hearing the

slap. He grabbed her chin, turning her head from side to side. "Name?"

"Lisa." Alyx was proud of Lisa; her voice came across strong and showed no sign of fear. Hopefully she could keep it together and Alyx could rely on her to help with their escape.

"Fuck," Stan yelled. "Do you know who this is?" His face blazed anger. "She's the club owner's sub. Are you out of your fucking minds? We don't take anyone that has someone who'll come after them. Her guy is going to be all over this. You've put the whole operation in jeopardy."

Stan began to pace, his fists balled at his sides, curses still flying out of his mouth. "We've got to get rid of her. Do whatever you want with her, then dump her body, use the boat we have docked at the Aquebogue Marina. I want her gone before sunrise." Stan walked over to Alyx and stood so close she could smell the garlic on his breath.

Stan seemed to have regained some of his composure. He leveled a smirk at her. "She's a beauty, she'll fetch a good price," he said to his companions. "I'm tempted to keep her for myself."

His hand reached out and stroked Alyx's breast through the thin latex of her impossibly tiny dress. "Bring them both to the demo room, we'll have some fun with them and then you get rid of yours. I'm taking this one. I'll meet you there in thirty minutes." Stan pinched her nipple through the dress and she clenched her jaw to suppress a yelp at the surge of pain shooting through her breast. He left through the door he'd entered. The other slavers unhooked them from the overhead chains and clicked their wrist restraints together, then led them by the handcuffs through the same exit Stan had used. Alyx struggled to stay upright in her black patent-leather stilettos; she didn't need to injure herself by falling flat on her face. They coaxed them through another vast empty hangar and entered a square room that must have served as an office when this was still a functioning research facility for the Grumman Corporation.

Alyx surveyed the contents of the room and her throat hitched. Daniel's warnings came back to her. An empty dog kennel sat in the corner of the room. Plus spanking horses, restraining benches and St. Andrew's crosses, enough for at least twenty women to be strapped into compliance. Shackles on chains hung from the ceiling, attached to an intricate roller system so they could be moved around the room as if on a sick-twisted merry-go-round. The walls had racks of whips and canes, nothing as mundane as a deerskin flogger for these sadists.

"This is where our buyers get to sample the goods before purchasing. You're the last ones we get to play with before the auction." His sleazy grin roiled her stomach. How to escape? How! Daniel had made it clear the longer they remained in the slavers' hands the worse it would be.

A voice came across an intercom system. "Cage them and come to the office to help me finish the paperwork, then we'll play."

The slaver depressed the lever on the wall speaker. "Yes, boss. Be right there."

Lisa's captor dragged her by the handcuffs to the open door of the cage, then shoved her onto her knees and kicked her into the kennel. Alyx was forced inside with Lisa. The door closed and they snapped the lock shut with a click and left the room.

"Lisa, we have to move fast. Unhook my cuffs," Alyx ordered. She wriggled into position and pushed her clasped wrists into Lisa's hands. No locks on these playtime cuffs, thankfully. Not much room to maneuver inside the cramped cage either, but they managed to get their wrists unhooked relatively quickly.

"How are we going to get out of this cage? It's got a metal padlock," Lisa said.

"Watch," Alyx offered. She leaned over her chest and bit at the material of her dress until she reached the underwire, inching it out. She bent the wire into a ninety-degree angle, then slipped the "handle" of the make-shift wrench into the keyhole. She pressed down with her thumb, feeling for the opening that would release the locking mechanism. Most likely the key would turn to the right, so she moved the pick into the top part of the lock and wiggled it around, pushing it right. Ten seconds passed. Damn. She wriggled the wire with too much force and it felt like it bent in the wrong direction. It wouldn't catch.

Twenty seconds. *Damn. C'mon.*

Finally, the lock gave. *Thank you, God.*

"Shit. That was impressive," Lisa exclaimed. "Did they teach you that in FBI school?"

"Not exactly."

Alyx exited first and put a hand out to help Lisa to her feet. "Let's go, move it. Do you know where we are?"

"Yeah, it's the old Grumman Plant in Calverton. I used to come here with an ex-boyfriend when they had the skydiving place."

"Exactly. Now this is likely our only chance to make a break for it." Alyx slipped out of her black stilettos and held them in her hands. "We won't be able to run in these things."

"Right," Lisa agreed, removing her silver fuck-me heels.

Alyx grabbed Lisa by the shoulders. "If we run into trouble I'll try to hold them off, but you have to run for your life—literally. Stay off the road, run through the woods until you get to a house. First call 911, then Jack, if you can. He can reach my boss."

"Got it. Totally, let's go."

They sprinted for the door and found it unlocked. There

was a God, there was. The hangar they'd passed through proved deserted and they bolted toward the exit. Freedom. She hit the button that controlled the massive metal door and the loud noise made her cringe, but they had no other recourse. Sliding underneath they made a run for it. Right into two burly men whooshing around the corner.

"Faster," Alyx yelled, spurring Lisa into action. Lisa ran in the opposite direction and disappeared into darkness. Racing for her life. Luckily the outside wasn't lit up like it would have been if it hadn't been abandoned. Alyx quickly dropped her shoes and leveled the first guy with a kick to the side of his knees. He hit the cement roadway in a heap. The second one got a knee in the groin. She poked two fingers into his eyeballs. He grunted and fell to the ground, writhing in pain. Alyx headed in Lisa's direction when Stan and his two goons bolted out the door and grabbed her. Someone had her hair in a death grip and her head jerked back viciously. She pivoted and leveled a right hook to his nose. Blood gushed down his face. Snap of bone. Not his. Hers. Pain seared through her arm in a raging torrent of heat.

"You little bitch." Stan backhanded her in the face and she plummeted, her head hitting the cement with a sickening thud. Stars erupted in front of her eyes and she struggled not to vomit onto his cheap shoes. Blood seeped from her lip again and she wiped it away with the back of her undamaged hand. Stan dragged her to her feet by her hair, pulling both arms taut behind her back. The searing agony in her wrist threatened to steal her consciousness.

"You'll pay for this, sweetheart," he vowed. Then to his cronies he barked, "Go after the other one and don't come back without her."

Stan dragged Alyx back into the hangar and into the demo room and shackled her into the chains hanging from the ceiling. Her heart sank and the ache in her arm made her gasp. Everything Daniel warned her about was about to happen and she steeled herself for lethal pain and agony.

Daniel leaned over the bar in the den of his empty house and hung his head in his hands. He tugged at the roots in despair. Grumbling, he poured himself a scotch. Visions of Alyx being raped by her tormentors threatened to snatch his soul. Not being able to do anything to save her sent his blood pressure through the roof. His heart pounded as white-hot anger seared his veins. He sat heavily on the couch and switched on the TV. Staring at the coffee table, he envisioned Alyx on her hands and knees, her cute little ass in the air. A huge knot formed in his chest, his breath difficult to regulate. Panic gripped him.

The clock on the DVR displayed 2:53. They could do a lot of damage to her in eight hours. His fist pounded the cushion and he spilled some of his scotch. He threw his head back against the couch and closed his eyes and plunged into the dark daydream he'd indulged in over the past week. He tried to talk himself back to sanity, but he feared it impossible. He'd never forgive himself for letting her do this. Hell, he'd never forgive himself for getting involved in this pernicious mess in the first place. He tried to concentrate on slowing his breathing. Futile. He exhaled, a hard gust, then slugged the rest of his scotch and headed to the bar for a refill. He tightened his fingers around the curves of the tumbler, hesitated. His jaw tensed, then he hurled the glass at the wall, watching it burst into sparklers, heard the tremendous clatter, smelled the cloud of scotch. Rage assaulted his five senses. His soul deflated.

In the distance, a phone ringing. Where had he left it? He hurried for his jacket, which hung on the back of one of the kitchen stools. Jack's ID flashed on the screen.

"Jack, tell me you have her."

"Not entirely, but we have a line on them. We're on our way now."

"How? Where?"

"They took them to the abandoned Grumman Facility, in Calverton, you know where that is?"

"Of course."

"Alyx was able to free Lisa and herself and fought off a couple of thugs so Lisa could make a run for it. State police have Lisa and she's unharmed."

"But Alyx is still in there with them?" His heart sank. He needed to get her out of there, have her safely in his arms.

"Yes, Suffolk County PD and the state police are surrounding the place now, but Rob said not to breach the property until the FBI gets there. We don't need anyone bungling this any more than we already have. We're about ten minutes out."

"On my way," Daniel said.

"Daniel, we'll probably get there before you. I'll keep in touch, you might want to meet us at the hospital if necessary."

Good idea, thought Daniel, if Alyx was hurt he wanted to be there to take care of her. "All right, let me know the second you find her."

"I will. Drive carefully, I'm sure you've knocked one or two back by now, and we don't need you to make this mess any more tragic than it already is."

"Okay, but please, Jack, call me as soon as you know something, even if it's bad. Not knowing is killing me."

"You have my word." The line went silent, dead.

Shackled in the Demo Room, Alyx tried to gather her wits. Odd, this was the same position she'd found herself in when Jason attacked her in her apartment. She had hoped to get the upper hand on him before Matt came to her rescue and she fully intended to do the same to this scumbag. Stan placed her feet into the black stilettos.

"I like you in your whore shoes," he said, rising to stand in front of her.

Alyx couldn't believe her luck. Was he actually arming her with a lethal weapon?

Circling around her, Stan regarded her as if she were prey. She tried to focus on her attack plan. It was just the two of them and she was sure she had better combat skills than this overweight sleaze ball. She needed to bide her time, pick the precise moment to strike. He'd be distracted by thoughts of playing with her and he also had no idea she was a highly-trained professional, two points for her side.

His slimy hand eased down the short zipper of her dress. She held her breath. Daniel's voice echoed in her brain, "Breathe, little subbie." She exhaled slowly and closed her eyes. *Focus, girl.*

His cold paws slid inside her dress and around her stomach, then toward her crotch. If he touched her there, she'd scream. Struggling to keep it together, she waited. She needed him in front of her. He grabbed her ass, sliding his hands over the back of her bare thighs. Revulsion rose in her throat. He pulled her hair, tilting her head back, and his teeth nipped at her earlobe. She bit her swollen lip to keep from crying out.

"Ready for some fun, little subbie?" he said into her ear.

The sound of Daniel's words crossing his lips sounded sacrilegious and her stomach heaved. She swallowed back the bile rising in her throat. "Do you enjoy the cane, little pet? I think we'll start with that."

Stan came around in front of her and grabbed the neckline of her low-cut dress. He tore at it, ripping the shoulder seams and the sad excuse for a dress fluttered to the floor. No underwear. Naked. He'd pay for this.

He was too close to her. She needed some space between them in order to get a good shot. He pinched her nipples hard and twisted them. She bit her lips to keep the scream buried, but he leaned in, sucking the flesh of her right breast into his mouth. He chomped down, hard and Alyx couldn't hold back the shriek. The sadistic smile on his face made her blood boil. She'd kill the fucker.

Behind her again, she felt the tip of the cane tracing lines across her back. She could do this. She steeled herself for the first blow. Daniel had taught her to lean into the pain. If she did, it wouldn't hurt so badly. Shit. Daniel's words came back to haunt her. He was right, she had no idea what she was getting herself into when she'd agreed to do this.

The snap of the wood against her back felt like acid on her skin. She couldn't keep herself from crying out as the lashes continued against her back, her ass and her thighs. She focused on her breathing and tried to send herself to a happy place. To stave off the blistering pain that threatened to shred not only her flesh, but her sanity. Can't pass out. Mustn't.

Finally, the rod hit the floor with a sickening thud and his face was in front of her. Sweat beaded on his forehead and his upper lip again. He licked his lips and released the buckle on his belt, then slid down his zipper.

Now or never. No way was she letting him get his disgusting dick anywhere near her. With the last bit of strength she could gather, she grasped the chain above her head firmly with her one good hand and drew her knees up. She unleashed a ferocious scream, and kicked him squarely in the face with the stiletto heels. One pierced an eyeball and blood gushed out thick and red. He flew backward and the back of his head smashed into the metal stanchion on one of the restraining benches. Alyx heard the crack of bone for a second time and this time it wasn't hers. His one good eye rolled back in his head and his body twitched violently a few times, then stilled.

Searing pain ran through her arms. Sobs wracked her body and hot wet tears streamed down her face. That moment, that half-second before her mind went completely dark, she muttered, "Daniel, where are you?"

Daniel had arrived at the intersection of county route 105 when his phone rang. He hit the hands-free button, "Speak."

Jack's voice came across the speaker. "Daniel, we've got her. They're transporting her to Peconic Medical Center."

"She's alive?" Daniel said, horrified at Jack's answer. Although somehow, if she hadn't survived, he didn't think Jack would tell him over the phone, he'd wait and tell him in person, right?

"Pretty beat up, a big bump on her head, and the EMTs think she has a broken wrist. They didn't say anything about rape and I didn't ask. She's not very coherent."

"I'm only five minutes from the hospital, I'll meet you there."

"Right, we're only a few minutes away ourselves. Oh, and Daniel, she did it. We found nearly seventy women. They were being held in dog cages."

Daniel swallowed hard. "Jesus Christ."

"Yeah, that's what I said."

Daniel pulled into the emergency room parking lot and mad-dashed for the automatic double doors. He had privileges here and fully intended to throw his weight around. The place buzzed with activity, unusual for this time of night. Especially with no full moon. Apparently, they'd already been informed of the incoming injured. The chief trauma nurse barked orders for additional personnel and demanded patients with minor complaints vacate the beds. Pure mayhem.

Grabbing a set of scrubs from the supply closet, he apprised the staff of what he expected when his patient arrived. The first in the parade of ambulances appeared. But no Alyx. He waited, anticipation overwhelming him. How badly was she hurt? How traumatized would she be? His gut wrenched at what she could have suffered at the hands of the slavers.

Jack's voice called out to him and he darted toward the emergency room doors. Scarborough trotted behind him, along with Matt. Daniel sprinted down the ramp toward them. He glared at Rob Scarborough. How could he have screwed this up so badly? But he'd take that up with him at a later date. First, he had to know how Alyx was.

Daniel squinted, squeezed his fists. "Tell me, Jack, what happened?"

"Alyx fought them off so Lisa could get away. She called me. They knew they were at the old Grumman place."

"What about Alyx?"

Rob Scarborough interjected, "We found her suspended from the ceiling in their version of a playroom for customers to sample the clientele. We're guessing she kicked the guy with her stilettos. He lost an eyeball and hit his head on the metal footing of a restraining bench."

"Dead in less than a minute, I figure," Matt added. "Fitting end, if you ask me. Although, I might have liked to torture the bastard myself a bit before I killed him."

Daniel seconded that thought.

Scarborough continued, "We found her unconscious, hanging from the ceiling, no clothing. He'd caned her, but we think that's as far as he got."

Daniel closed his eyes and tugged on his hair, pulling it painfully for the second time tonight. "Shit. Caned?"

Jack put his hand on Daniel's back and gave a rub. "Yeah, sorry, bud."

Another ambulance screeched closer and Daniel followed it with his eyes as it rolled into the lot. "This is her," Matt said, heading toward the flashing vehicle.

Chapter 9

Sunday

Darkness engulfed her. Or were her eyes still closed? She couldn't be sure. Every bone in her body ached. Her muscles felt like she'd spent hours being tortured by terrorists in some godforsaken foreign land. A punishing rhythm pounded in her head. Her lips stuck together. Maybe she was dead. Although, how could death be this painful?

Her mouth, so dry, she couldn't get enough saliva together to swallow. Staring at the ceiling she tried to piece together her surroundings and figure out where she was. Beeping noises echoed in the small space. Dizziness swarmed her. Was that her own moans, or—Jesus, her neck hurt. Neon green numbers ran across a monitor. She squinted, trying to focus on the readout.

"Hey, baby," she heard a man say. Haltingly, she turned her head in his direction. Vertigo rattled her stomach. She heaved. He rolled her quickly onto her side and pushed a plastic bowl under her chin. She gagged and spit into the bowl. She retched, over and over, but only bile came up.

He held her nape in his firm grip until the horrible nausea passed and she regained control. Gently rolling her onto her back, he placed the bowl on the bedside table and wiped her chin with a tissue.

"Fuck," she said. The room illuminated. Painful light. She closed her eyes.

"You know, after 'fine' I think that other f-word's your favorite. It's the first thing you say when you wake up in the morning."

Alyx opened her eyes and feasted them on Daniel's handsome face. She muttered, "It is *not*, get the fuck out." He smiled his beautiful smile and she felt a little better. She'd never seen him in his doctor's uniform before.

He peeled open her eyelids and flashed more light into her eyes. She tried to squeeze them closed. "The IV will help with the nausea, you're on some heavy pain meds. They're probably wreaking havoc on your stomach."

"I hope it's not codeine, codeine makes me crazy."

"Great, you're crazy enough, we don't need to add any boosters to that shit."

Alyx chuckled. Her ribs protested. "Ow. Don't make me laugh, it hurts too much." She attempted to lift her head but Daniel pushed her back onto the pillow.

"Easy, you've taken a pretty good beating. Let your body rest for a while."

Daniel felt her forehead, just like her father used to do when he thought she was coming down with something, which seemed odd, her temp was probably blinking on the monitor. "Well," she said, "that bastard must be hurting pretty badly himself. I gave as good as I got. I just wish we'd found the women."

"That's right. You don't know?"

Her puzzled expression answered his question.

"They found nearly seventy women in one of the hangars. Kept in dog kennels."

"You're kidding me? That's great, that's *everything*. At least this entire week wasn't a waste of time." Alyx mind-walked through her time with Daniel, deciphering her feelings. It hadn't been a waste. It'd been crazy, wild, and fun, well until she'd found out he had a fiancée. But she needed to forget about her week with Daniel. Move on.

"The story is all over the news, luckily they've kept your name out of it. So far." Daniel grabbed the TV remote from the bedside strap and switched to channel 12. The anchor reported the story in images: the hangar where countless women wrapped in blankets were carried to safety by a battalion of FBI agents and police officers. The reporter stated that the FBI raid had rescued sixty-nine women who'd nearly been sold into slavery, and over twenty employees of the 6X Enterprise were under arrest.

"What shape were the women in?" Alyx inquired.

"I can't say they were in great shape, most of them had been regularly abused. However, since the slavers wanted them in good condition to be sold, they'd been left alone in the past week. We only have about half of them here, the others were sent to Brookhaven Hospital."

A sense of pride overwhelmed her, endorphins flooded her brain. These women would have a chance to reunite with their families and eventually get their lives back. She averted her eyes from the images and asked Daniel to switch off the TV. "I'm so tired."

Daniel placed a spoon at her parched lips. "Here, open." The ice chips melted in her mouth, the cool liquid soothing her swollen flesh.

"How bad are my injuries?" she said, trying to move all her limbs for reassurance. "Anything permanent?"

"No, you'll mend with a little rest and rehab. Your wrist is broken. The swelling wasn't too bad so we casted it. You've got a serious concussion, which is adding to your nausea. Some minor cuts and bruises. The welts on your back should heal without leaving any permanent scaring provided we keep tending them." Daniel hesitated a moment, "I take it there was no rape, am I right?"

"No rape."

"Good, because if we had to do a rape kit—" His eyes widened in silent alarm. "We both know whose semen will show up."

"Yeah, that would've been awkward," Alyx said, heaving a sigh. "What time is it?"

"Nearly eight, at night. You've been out for almost thirteen hours."

"Seriously? It's Sunday night?"

"Yes." Daniel stroked Alyx's cheek with the back of his knuckles. "You scared the living shit of out me, Alyx. This is the second time."

"Sorry. But just so we're even, after that intervention you staged the other night to get me in touch with my feelings, well, you'll be pleased to know it worked. I was pretty much terrified the whole time." Alyx flashed him a nasty look and Daniel grimaced.

"I did worry maybe that hadn't been such a great idea and your former fearless self would have been better equipped to handle your situation."

"For a minute there, it seemed like all those horrible things you warned me about were coming true."

"Thankfully not all of them." Daniel rubbed her hand tenderly. "I'm livid that you were caned. Goddamnit, if you hadn't killed the guy, I would have."

Alyx gasped. "I killed him?"

"Yes. Those stilettos are multi-purpose it seems. Who knew? They brought his body here."

"Shit." Alyx inspected the cast on her arm. "My right hand? That's gonna suck." Annoyance fueled her simmering mood. It would be extraordinarily difficult to execute her daily tasks one-handed. She brushed her thumb over Daniel's knuckles, startling when she felt the abrasions.

"What happened?"

Daniel hesitated before answering. "Which time?"

"What do you mean, which time?"

Daniel smirked. "I punched your boss at the club when he told me he lost you and then when I examined you I saw the bite mark on your breast and... well, I lost it. I punched a wall."

"You punched Rob?"

"Yep. Right in the face. He went down like a ton of bricks." Daniel grinned, apparently proud of himself.

"Geez," Alyx said. Scowling, "Not too bright for a surgeon. You could have damaged your hand."

"Stupid me. It was worth it the first time, but the second time it garnered too much attention from the staff."

A nurse walked into the room and Alyx tried to extricate her hand from Daniel's grasp. She didn't think doctors usually held their patients' hands quite the way Daniel did now. He tightened his grip, keeping her hand prisoner inside his.

"Dr. Taylor, I didn't realize you were still here," the nurse said before turning to Alyx. "Glad to see you're awake, Agent Cameron. How are you feeling?"

"Like I've been run over by a freight train, thank you." Alyx tried to smile, but her swollen bottom lip nixed that.

The nurse checked her IV bag, then disconnected her from the beeping monitor. She fluffed her pillows and smoothed out the bed covers, her smile comforting. "As soon as Dr. Taylor rewrites your orders I'll get you something to eat and drink. Is there anything you need right now?"

"I really need to pee. Can you help me to the bathroom?"

"Of course," the kindly nurse said.

"I'll take her," Daniel said. Alyx clenched her jaw. This familiarity needed to end. Their ridiculous relationship would be something she'd never forget, but now they were nothing but... what exactly? She'd vowed to Daniel she would consider him a friend after this whole craziness had finished. Now she couldn't envision that happening. Lacey wouldn't want Daniel anywhere near her, and if she were Daniel's fiancée she'd feel exactly the same.

The nurse cast a furtive look at their clasped hands, seeming perplexed. She said, "I can handle this, doctor."

"I said, I'll do it," Daniel insisted, his tone filled with ice. But before the ridiculousness could escalate into a three-way argument, a figure appeared in the doorway, immediately silencing them. Daniel's face darkened. "Lacey, what are you doing here?" He dropped Alyx's hand. The nurse performed a vanishing act.

"You didn't show for dinner at my parents' house." Lacey glared at Alyx, then turned toward Daniel.

He said, "How did you know where to find me?"

"I tracked your cell phone."

"What the hell? That's way out of line, Lacey. You have no business keeping tabs on me like that."

"I thought you might be with your little tramp, but when I realized you were at the hospital I figured I'd jumped to the wrong conclusion. Apparently not." Her constant glare gave Alyx a chill.

"Watch your mouth, Lacey, you have no idea what you're talking about." Daniel pivoted toward Alyx. "I'm sorry." He rubbed his hands down his face but it couldn't erase the anger lines seared into his forehead.

Just like last time, Alyx had no desire to get in between the two of them and so she kept her mouth shut.

"I'll be right back," he said to Alyx. He walked toward Lacey, grabbed her by her upper arm and dragged her out into the hallway. Alyx could hear their angry exchange but couldn't quite make out the words. She closed her eyes and wished she could disappear like the nurse did. Her eyes filled with water. When had everything gotten so messed up?

Her stomach clenched, not from nausea, but from the total revulsion over the drastic life changes in less than ten days. She needed to escape. From her apartment, her job. But mostly, from Daniel.

He wouldn't return tonight. She could feel it. The bastard had made his choice. Now Alyx had to make hers.

Monday

The morning found Alyx greatly improved and she'd even managed to eat some cereal. She needed to call Matt, but had no idea what happened to her cell phone and wasn't sure she could recall his number. He could flash his FBI credentials at her apartment complex and bring a few things so she could make a break for it.

She was done with Daniel, he was back with Lacey and Alyx needed to get her life back.

Alyx slowly made her way to the bathroom mirror. Her reflection startled her. The bruises on her face, her fat lip. She'd seen this face before, too many times, on the victims of abuse. The bags under her eyes and the gray tinted complexion had replaced the healthy glow she'd achieved while sunning herself at the Hampton Shores beach.

She managed to brush her teeth left handed, but barely.

Padding her way back to the bed, she slipped under the covers and reached for the bedside telephone, dialing 411. A nurse entered with a vase of long-stemmed roses—a deep, deep crimson—wrapped in cellophane.

Alyx promptly hung up the phone. "You must have the wrong room."

"Nope. These are addressed to you. They arrived last night but, unfortunately, were sitting at the fourth-floor nurses' station. I'm so sorry." The nurse put the vase on the bedside table then handed the card to Alyx, her name clearly printed on the envelope along with the wrong room number. "How are you feeling this morning? Can I get you anything?" The nurse's warm fingers instinctively wrapped around Alyx's good wrist and her eyes fell to her watch. "You seem much better." Her caring smile appeared so genuine, and Alyx briefly considered how dedicated the good nurses were to their charges.

"I kept my breakfast down, that's a start." Alyx attempted to return the nurse's smile, yet her lips felt like they'd break into tiny raw cracks if she continued. Actually, weird, her entire body felt like her skin was too small for her.

"Excellent," the nurse said, "Dr. Taylor usually makes rounds early on Monday before he heads into his practice in the city."

"Oh," Alyx said. She'd fully intended to be gone before he got here. In fact, she thought she'd never see him again.

Focusing on the envelope, the nurse gave a mischievous grin. "Boyfriend?"

"Ah, no." Alyx couldn't imagine who'd sent them. Her pulse accelerated and she was glad the nurse had finished checking it. *It couldn't be.* She dared not hope.

Slipping a finger through the flap she opened it and removed the card.

. . .

I love you, Alyx
   I'm bringing you home to take care of you.
   I won't take no for an answer.

Always,
   Daniel

Alyx looked up. The nurse had vanished.

Before she could catch her breath and absorb the words written on the card, Daniel strode into the room like he owned the place. Her heart-rate spiked. Damn him, but gosh, he looked fine, like he'd stepped onto a Parisian runway for men's fashion week. He wore a fitted black suit that easily cost several grand. His crisp white shirt featured French cuffs, and gleaming silver cufflinks emblazoned with the letters DT peeked out from his sleeves. A red-and-white striped silk tie and matching pocket scarf completed the effect with stunning flair. Glistening gel kept his hair in place and the stubble she'd gotten so used to seeing, and feeling, had been shaved clean.

"I see you got my message," he said, beaming.

"Daniel," Alyx began. "What is going on?"

"I'm not buying any of that bullshit about how we were both pretending, acting. I wasn't, and I don't believe for one minute that you were either. I told Lacey the truth last night, that I was in love with you."

"But, but, Daniel…"

"I. Love. You. Irrevocably and unequivocally. You're stuck with me. Stop arguing."

"Look, we can talk in a few days. I need to go home and figure things out."

"Absolutely not. You can't take care of yourself and you'll do as you're told."

"You're not in charge of me anymore, Daniel. Don't pull that Dom crap on me."

"First of all, I'm insulted by that and secondly this is *Doc* crap, not Dom crap."

"Well, then I'm signing myself out against doctor's orders. I need to go home and try and regain some semblance of sanity."

Daniel walked over and faced her. "Do you love me, Alyx?"

Silence. More silence. "Maybe," she murmured, dropping her head, focusing on her fidgeting fingers that still held his note.

Daniel gently placed his knuckle under her chin and forced it up. "I can wait."

Alyx struggled to make sense of what he said. He couldn't really mean that. "Daniel, I'm flattered. And to be perfectly honest, I *think* I do love you. But I'll never be someone's wife or mother. I don't want that life. Doctor's wife. Raising spoiled children. Tennis at the club, lunching with the ladies."

"Stop," he ordered. "You can be whoever you want to be. If you love me, that's all I could ever ask of you and I'll take whatever you have to give."

Alyx couldn't believe this conversation. Truthfully, she'd never felt so strongly about anyone the way she did Daniel. She realized she'd never been in love before and wasn't even looking for it.

But now, here he was, professing his love for her and her heart suddenly broke free from its shackles.

They stared into each other. The eyes truly were windows. Emotions welled up.

"Besides," Daniel added. "I'm terrible at this relationship stuff, and my guess is you suck at it, too. So, we're perfect for each other. Let's figure it out as we go along."

Epilogue

The Caribbean sunshine warmed Alyx's skin but the heat from Daniel's hands scorched her as he rubbed coconut oil over her back. His thumbs dug into her shoulder blades as he merged his sunscreen duties with a mini-massage. She purred. Would she ever not react this way to his touch? She hoped not. Three months had passed, her injuries healed, albeit slowly, and she hadn't exactly been the model patient. The first day back at Daniel's seaside abode she'd been noncompliant and Lydia had ratted her out: forgetting to take her medication—complaining it made her head fuzzy, sleeping all day, not showering, and barely eating. Daniel had resorted to taking off an entire week to personally attend her, religiously applying the healing salve to her back and practically force-feeding her food and painkillers. He finally convinced her that she should channel her stubbornness into healing not burying her head in the pillow. She knew he was right. What had happened to her formerly fearless self? Eventually it retuned, after long walks and the security of Daniel's affection for her. The giant diamond solitaire on her finger a testament of his love.

Daniel had whisked her away on a private jet for a well-deserved vacation. Unconventional, the honeymoon *before* the wedding. But then they were writing their own rules, forging their own way. In everything. He laced up the back of her red bikini and slapped her ass, making her yelp. "There," he announced. "Sufficiently lubricated."

"You're hilarious," Alyx said, rising and repositioning herself on the magenta canvas lounger. "You want me to do you?"

Daniel widened his eyes. "Are you hitting on me, Ms. Cameron?"

"Sue me," she said. They both laughed.

"Well, we're going to have some playtime tonight. I brought lots of toys. Good thing we were on a private jet because I'd never have made it past security with that shit." His questioning expression and devilish smile sizzled her blood.

The noon sun announced the official onset of cocktail time and Daniel suggested a drink. Three rum punches later, Daniel said, "I think we should eat something."

"So sensible, Dr. Taylor. That's why I need you to take care of me." Her phone rang and she rummaged through her tote to retrieve it. "Hey, Rob, what's up?"

"Sorry to bother you on vacation, but I just received the okay for a new task force on human trafficking. I need somebody to head it. You interested?"

Alyx hesitated. She glanced at Daniel. They'd already agreed that after the wedding next month he'd pull out of his Hampton Shores office and limit himself to the Manhattan office. The beachside mansion would serve as their getaway spot. Their new apartment on Park Avenue was being furnished while they were away and she was ready to return to work. But she hadn't anticipated anything like this. The idea of having the chance to track down and incarcerate more of these evil people ignited her passion for the job again. During their recent months together Alyx had discovered how much she and Daniel had in common. Both stubborn, of course, kinky in the bedroom, but also committed to the mission of saving lives, each in their own way. "I think I am," she said to Rob.

"You had me worried for a moment. You took too long to answer."

"Sorry, vacation brain, and I'm three rum punches in." Alyx laughed.

"Maybe I should call back tomorrow morning when you're sober," Rob said.

"No! I'm in. Definitely. Thanks for the offer."

"Great, I'll let Merryl know. See you in a few weeks."

Alyx stowed her phone in her beach bag. Daniel peered at her, a little too seriously. She related her conversation with Rob and Daniel exclaimed, "That's incredible. I'm so happy for you. I'm glad to see the Bureau appreciated your hard work."

"Yeah, me too. I'm really excited about this."

"You should be." He took both of her hands in his, thumbing the sparkling rock on her finger. "I think we've got this new life worked out. Do you?"

"I do," Alyx said.

"And that will be the happiest day of my life, Special Agent Cameron. The day you say that at the altar."

He stood, taking her with him and secured her hand tightly in his. "Let's eat. I'm starved."

The End

Kendra Greenwood

Kendra Greenwood has always been a storyteller. She often told stories to her kids at bedtime in lieu of reading to them. A serious daydreamer, she used to think it the complete opposite of her education and work in the sciences, but now realizes scientists are the ultimate daydreamers. Fantasy has always been an escape for Kendra. Weaving a thrilling romantic tale around her favorite TV and film characters, her favorite way to fall asleep at night. Eventually she wrote them down and found a place to share her stories.

Kendra grew up on the beaches of Long Island's bucolic east end, but recently relocated to Virginia. When she's not writing you can find her in the kitchen whipping up something scrumptious or in the studio fusing glass into decorative dishes.

Follow her on:
Twitter @k51greenwood
Facebook Kendra Greenwood
Email kendra51greenwood@gmail.com

Don't miss these exciting titles by Kendra Greenwood and Blushing Books!

Steel and Desire Series
UnSub
UnBound
Unguarded

Unsaddened

Blushing Books

Blushing Books is the oldest eBook publisher on the web. We've been running websites that publish steamy romance and erotica since 1999, and we have been selling eBooks since 2003. We have free and promotional offerings that change weekly, so please do visit us at http://www.blushingbooks.com/free.

Blushing Books Newsletter

Please join the Blushing Books newsletter
to receive updates & special promotional offers.
You can also join by using your mobile phone:
Just text **BLUSHING** to 22828.

Every month, one new sign up via text messaging will receive
a $25.00 Amazon gift card, so sign up today!